Dead Eyes

Devon De'Ath

DEDICATION

In loving memory of Jim Overstreet :

The nicest guy at college, who passed away

in the midst of many who treasured his gentle kindness.

CONTENTS

1

Madness and Matricide

Tensed, rough male fingers dug into clumps of wet sand on a horseshoe-shaped beach. Ice cold saltwater spluttered from the scarred, weathered mouth of a gasping, bedraggled soul. Gulls whirled about the gunmetal firmament. Its oppressive hue mirrored in an angry sea which trampled the exhausted, prone hulk of an early forties man with foaming white horses. Wave upon wave rolled over him, funnelled through the inlet by surrounding pincers of rock, dunes and grass-capped headland. He pressed harder against the claggy surface to lift his upper body on shaking arms. Another coughing expulsion of chilled saline fluid heaved into a fight for air. He raised a bean-shaped head, bald on top with a thin, light brown stubbly beard clinging on for dear life to his pointed chin. His blurred vision cleared. Wooden beach huts and the gleaming white brilliance of the Edgcumbe Hotel beyond the car park of Summerleaze Beach shifted into sharper focus. Passing early morning sheets of drizzle swept across his saturated torso, adding insult to injury. A collie dog barked and barrelled towards him, tail seesawing like an antique water pump handle, driving it forward. It snuffled the drowned rat's ruddy complexion with a wet nose, then licked his face. A teenage girl with frizzy ginger hair hurried to retrieve the animal. Her strides lessened in breadth upon taking in the now kneeling man as he shivered at the collie's oral ministrations. She pushed the wild mop away from her eyes, ruffled by a Cornish, early autumn breeze.

"Are you okay, Mister?" She squatted to pull the dog clear. It whined and resisted, so she smoothed down his fur to induce calm. "Easy, Bailey."

The sodden man gazed into her freckled face with reddened eyes. "Please help me." He twisted to stare across the angry water. "My mother is still out there. Our inflatable boat folded."

The teenager gripped her chest. "That's awful." She released the dog and backed away for a moment. The seriousness of this situation shook her startled body into action. She wheeled about and ran for a circular roofed, two storey cream stone building adjoining the car park. Red, white and blue cross flags of the RNLI fluttered from ivory poles on either side of the structure. The girl hammered on the front door and shouted.

On the beach, the man sat dazed. The last hurrah of crashing waves still teased his hunched over form. He watched a dark blue roller door rise on the building his Good Samaritan ran to. Time stretched into infinity and he zoned out. The wail of approaching ambulance sirens shattered his groggy stupor. At the same moment, the powerful whir of a 50hp Mariner engine to the left, pulled his head around. A five metre, bright orange D class inflatable roared into the surf, crewed by three members of Bude Lifeboat Station. Signature orange waterproofs, red life jackets and white helmets sporting 'RNLI' in red lettering bobbed in the craft, their wearers' faces set grim to scan the water ahead as they rocketed away from shore.

"Take it easy, Fella." A stocky, rough-shaven paramedic helped the shivering figure into the back of his ambulance, a blanket wrapped around the balding man's shoulders.

Outside the vehicle's rear doors, a white haired, male RNLI station operator leaned through. "Can you tell me your mother's name and age?"

The patient hugged his opposite shoulders beneath the blanket. "Enid. She's sixty-eight."

"The girl who found you said your inflatable folded. Were you swept out to sea?"

A furious, dripping nod answered the question. "I brought Mum down last night. We camped by the roadside." He coughed. "My late father proposed to her in a boat out here, many years ago. She gets melancholy around their anniversary. I thought it would be nice to recreate the scene. You know: connect with the past. At first the long drive seemed worth it. But now…"

"Where did you come from?"

A plump, female paramedic with a flicking blonde ponytail lifted an oxygen mask towards his face. She frowned at the well-meaning interrogator, visibly moved by her patient's sweet tale regarding his mother.

The RNLI operator stepped back. "Okay. Enough questions for now. I'll radio the info through. Take care."

The other paramedic secured the doors, then moved to the driver's seat.

Bailey the collie barked while the ambulance rolled away from the beach car park. His owner coiled one end of the dog lead around her wrist. "He'll be all right, boy." She looked up at the station operator. "Won't he?"

"I'd have thought so. It's his mother I'm worried about." He plucked one bushy, silver eyebrow between precise fingers. "Well done today, Katie. I'll mention this to your parents when I see them next."

"I hope they find Enid alive and well, Mr Linnet."

Linnet winced. He squinted at the angry sea. "Me too, Sweetheart. Me too."

* * *

'Ashburnham' comprised a red brick, double-fronted, detached Victorian villa with twin lower bays and an arched window above an impressive white stone porch of small, Doric columns. The dwelling's remote, wood enshrouded setting made it appear like a house that once wandered off from a childhood school outing by accident and got separated from all the other houses in its class. A mischievous home that played hide and seek in the woods with its peers and still waited for one of them to come find it. Unlikely, with nothing but heath and wooded hills for two miles, even in the heart of Middle England. Shabby windows - several missing panes of glass - formed a logical progression from the patchwork of vanished roof tiles above. The worst offenders were boarded up, and the council (if they noticed the residence at all) considered it derelict and uninhabited. A gravel path led between clumps of tall grass to end at a spreading array of trees. Each new sapling springing up brought the stranglehold of nature closer to forever swallowing Ashburnham. Abundant ivy, wrapping around the superstructure, suggested Gaia's digestive process had already begun.

A shabby maroon 1999 model Rover 200, 3 door hatchback, bounced on lumpy tufts of grass that once formed a track to the metalled road. This vanishing trail lay far out of sight or earshot, through swathes of dense, dark coniferous forest. Clouds of blue oil smoke wafted from the car's rattling exhaust pipe. Its rusty tubing hung together with copious sealant and worn cable ties, clinging to life like a condemned man watching the clock until death pops in for tea. This sad vehicle with dented, mismatched body panels looked every one of its twenty years. It sounded them, too.

A burly, balding, six-foot-four man sporting a shallow, near invisible brown beard climbed out and banged the driver's door shut. It clicked without fully closing, only to receive a swift kick like a mistreated, disobedient animal. The car rocked on creaking suspension springs. All about the clearing, neither bird nor animal disturbed the sinister peace of that oppressive scene. The man sauntered around the side of the property, unopened post in Manila business envelopes tucked beneath one arm. Only special company entered Ashburnham through the front door. Mother hammered that home to him from childhood, despite using it herself. Brown, swaying bracken fronds dampened the base of his jeans, as the figure rounded one corner to a rear kitchen entrance. Gaps in the mortar years overdue for re-pointing, cried out like the distended mouths of tortured souls from some dark abyss. The man watched a beige, thick-legged garden spider dart out and sun itself on a split, frost damaged brick. The observer's steely grey eyes stared with unblinking intensity to accompany a constant frown, as though always deep in thought. Heaven help the mind-reader able to plumb the depths of that depraved mentality. His build and facial expression suggested someone you'd cross the street not to antagonise. Nightclub bouncers might call him, 'Sir,' despite a rough and shoddy appearance devoid of self-care or any attempt at personal grooming. Memories resurfaced of placing such a spider on his big sister's head one summer, in the far from halcyon days of his childhood. Her screams seemed to bend the trees with relentless ferocity. That cold-hearted, spiteful bitch had it coming. Yet it was he who suffered worst once Mother found out. Or to be specific: once Sally tattled on him to report the offence committed by her despised male sibling.

He left the arachnid to its optimistic sun bathing during early October in an English woodland glade.

At the kitchen door, he rummaged in a faded suede jacket for a ring of tarnished brass keys. He flicked three aside and inserted the fourth into a heavy mortise lock in the solid wooden portal. Without hesitation, he turned the handle and put his shoulder into the door panel. Swollen at the bottom and dropping off its hinges, figures of lesser frame might give up on this resistant access point as a lost cause. A scraping squeal to set teeth on edge followed a shudder from the weathered barrier. The man cast a glance over his shoulder. Close to the kitchen, a tidy rosebush stood in stark contrast to its surroundings. Despite being a living, organic feature, it looked artificial amidst any other obvious signs of human intervention or care. The man's grey eyes twinkled. He shook his head and disappeared inside the crumbling structure.

Ashburnham had always been off-grid from a utilities perspective. When it was built, electricity wasn't a consideration. Now its solitary occupant charged a bank of batteries from a collection of self-installed solar panels. These dotted prime spots around the superstructure's exterior, wherever gaps in the forest canopy allowed sunlight access. A quieter improvement on the generator that had gone before. The owner's mother raised him with an old-school mindset. He did everything by hand. Clothes and dishes were washed by hand. Heating and cooking took place via a range fuelled by wood, of which the surrounding environment offered an abundant supply. A natural spring fed water tanks and a nearby pond. Waste water filtered away through a reed bed. All of this kept tradespeople and visitors away. The fewer folk who realised anyone lived here, the better.

A lazy blowfly buzzed in circuits around the man's head as he sat down at a worn, rectangular pine kitchen table. He unfolded a charged laptop computer and pressed the power button. Its 'Windows' logo and the PC's sleek, high-tech appearance conflicted with a domestic interior subject to few alterations since the Victorians first built Ashburnham. A pay-as-you-go mobile Internet dongle slipped into one side of the computer, pressed by rough, workmanlike hands. Out here, signals were patchy. But the villa's elevated position - albeit masked from view by woodland - meant rudimentary surfing was possible, if pedestrian. Chunky fingers hammered away at a search engine. The follow-on click loaded an on-line news page for the *'Bude & Stratton Post.'* He hadn't checked in the fortnight since his trip down to Cornwall, but an article from an earlier issue caught his eye: *'68-year-old woman lost at sea during anniversary memorial gone wrong.'* The reader's empty grimace crinkled around the edges. He picked up the post collected from an urban PO Box and opened one of the business envelopes with a dirty butter knife. An elegant cursive font on a page header read: *'Peverill, Thwaite and Thomas - Solicitors.'* He scanned the document title: *'Estate Transfer of Property Deeds.'* Those crinkled mouth corners rose further. He sat back and allowed his eyes to wander around the room's high-ceilinged decorative moulding. *It's mine now.* That idle stare studied the laptop screen again. *They got one thing right in their article: Mum drowned. But she didn't drown at sea.* His torso slackened against the rickety wooden chair, whose joints wobbled from years of use and little attention. The final events in his difficult mother's unorthodox life lit up like a cinema projection on the interior of his closing eyelids.

* * *

TWO WEEKS EARLIER.

"Banjo? Banjo! I want my hair washed." The label: *'Mad, red-haired witch,'* summed up Enid to a tee. Crimson of face from over-familiarity with the gin bottle, her head resembled some gruesome strawberry tucked into a bed of copper wool loft insulation. Said mop appeared back-combed and electrified to match bulging white and black eyes ringed with ill-applied mascara. To the casual observer, she'd been the victim of a prank involving ink applied to a kaleidoscope lens used on both eyes. Fingers clutched at all times into her palms like frozen talons. If children stumbled upon Ashburnham for Trick or Treat (and none ever did, way out there), they'd run screaming in terror at the sight of her. Big-boned, brazen and boisterous, folk often wondered what possessed any man to hook up with this lumbering daughter of hell. Enid's late husband, Derek, only married her after she fell pregnant with their daughter, Sally. Now her second child, a son she called 'Banjo' remained the only soul to dwell with her and care for the harridan's wayward existence.

Stomping feet, like those of a sulking child, hammered on the staircase treads. Enid watched him ascend the entire run, her hawk-like fingers clasped around the upper newel. Her face shone with the gloating power of a totalitarian tyrant. Yet in the 'banana republic' that was the isolated, run down ruin of Ashburnham, only one citizen remained to do her bidding. Only one subject would heed Enid's edicts.

A lumbering, bald-topped man reached her side. "I washed your hair yesterday, Mum."

Enid bristled. "Don't you address your mother like that. If you don't behave yourself, I'll leave Ashburnham to a charity. Then where will you be after I'm gone? Do you think you'd survive in the outside world? Think how they'd treat you."

Banjo gritted his teeth. Two loud snorts of air puffed from flaring nostrils. His reddened face paled as he shut his eyes. "I'm sorry."

Enid glared. "Don't think I can't punish you. There'll be no tea, if you're not careful."

"For God's sake, I'm forty-two. A man. Fuck it, I'm a middle-aged man."

Enid swiped jagged talons across his right cheek, leaving red trails from their traverse. "Don't you swear at me, boy. If you're such a man, why don't you behave like one instead of acting such a big child?" Her eyes fogged. "Sally never swore." Enid's voice softened

chin to secure it in the hole. He twisted the cold tap closed and opened the hot to full blast.

"Banjo! What are you doing?" Enid attempted to stand, but her son's strong, left hand pressed hard. He shoved the back of her head, nose down, into scalding, rising water.

Banjo altered the spray to angle into her eyes. Odd splashes of the gushing hot torrent stung his hands and lower arms, yet any pain inflicted paled compared to rising euphoria within.

"How dare you try to drown me, *Sally*." Banjo growled in a guttural tone of warped arousal; the accusation addressed to his departed sister.

Enid coughed and gagged, gasping for air. She cut an intimidating figure, but her strength proved no match for the gloating passion of her beefcake son.

Banjo pressed harder. He holstered the spray between his mother's struggling head and the enamel basin edge, then turned off the taps as water cascaded over the lip to drench cracked bathroom floor tiles. Their dampened, alternating pattern of black and white glimmered in the light from that incandescent bulb.

Enid's arms flailed, a picture of slowing windmill sails in a slackening breeze. The flurry of bubbling, gurgling noises from a head which now resembled a boiled lobster, ceased. Her form went limp. Any resistance against Banjo's left hand halted in an instant.

The act of piercing compacted soil beneath the lush,

unkempt sward behind Ashburnham's rear kitchen took considerable effort. Banjo snapped one spade before he'd even dug a third of the pit. A hole he envisioned would conceal his dead mother's corpse from prying eyes or passing hungry animals. An old stone outbuilding, its roof sagging under the weight of near luminous moss, contained rusty implements collected over the life of the house. Banjo located another suitable tool. His fingers became tangled in thick, dusty spider webs stretching from the structure's wall to the replacement spade. A hoe and rake rested close by. The light feel of the spade's handle hinted at an internal feast partaken of by wood-consuming bugs. He took the rest of the job at a gentler pace, ears alert for the first creak or snap that would spell doom for this second essential item.

Afternoon light filtered between the treetops as he dragged Enid's body, feet first, wrapped in a white sheet from the kitchen. It parted the verdant grass of what had once been a back garden, before nature reclaimed her territory. Banjo had applied the sheet in the ground floor hallway. He'd enjoyed his journey down that dark, grand staircase, still dragging Enid feet first. Her head walloped every tread, rolling lifeless eyes up to expose their whites as her tongue lolled from one corner of an over-sized mouth. Banjo remembered other bone crunching impacts on this staircase. Horrible sounds. But that was long ago and compartmentalised somewhere inside his unreliable memory, which spat assorted images out with unassailable emotional force at random intervals.

Banjo rolled the contents of his sheet over the edge of the pit. No sense wasting a functional piece of fabric. It had served the purpose of keeping casual eyes from making a gruesome discovery spelling trouble. The body dropped into the hole with a too-soft, muffled thud which failed to satisfy. Banjo lifted the spade from where it stood erect in a pile of earth, then jammed the blade back in and unzipped his fly. "This will teach you, *Sally*. You evil cow." Again the statement addressed his absent sister.

A trickle of urine splattered bloated, pale facial skin below in Enid's last resting place. Banjo secured his trousers. "I hope you enjoy your drink, Sis."

The following afternoon, Banjo's maroon Rover bunny-hopped across the usual uneven tufts of grass, back to the house. He opened the boot and retrieved a new rosebush, purchased from a garden centre a short drive away. *Mum should have flowers. Dead people always have flowers.* The voice in his head spoke with different tones today. A quasi-sexual psychological release from dispatching his overbearing parent the day before, gave way to a gentler monologue. It reminded him of a child. One that no longer confused the woman buried behind the kitchen with his sibling.

After he'd planted the rose bush atop Enid's unmarked grave, more familiar, calculating mental whispers caused him to freeze. *What if the authorities look for Mum? They'll need to know how she died and see evidence.* He paced back and forth, flattening a rut into overgrown lushness beyond the kitchen window. Enid always told her children the story of how their father, Derek, proposed to her on a tiny boat off the Cornish coast. She'd become so excited, they almost capsized. Banjo twitched and jerked. The twanging thrummed in his throat again. *People get swept out to sea all the time and are never found. My story should sound believable. I need to be discovered while in trouble.* He stomped around to the front of the house, tugged open his car passenger door, then rifled through the glove box for a pocket road atlas of Great Britain. His shaking fingers thumbed to the page for Cornwall. "Bude. That's the place." He flicked from page to page. Empty eyes calculated his best route down to the West Country.

Cold shock stung with pins and needles as Banjo launched himself into the sea. It was a chilly morning on the Cornish coast. From his concealed position between rocks skirting one side of Summerleaze Beach, he'd clocked the teenage dog walker. A few good strokes should be enough to bring him around towards the sand in time for her arrival. Now he just needed to appear pathetic and concerned for his mother's welfare.

* * *

ASHBURNHAM - JUNE 1988.

"I'm sure it was a pike, Little Brother."

Pale of complexion and morbid of expression, Sally's upturned eyes were shadowed like a drug user making no effort to disguise their habit. Yet no pharmacological substances altered her personality or appetites. Straggly light-brown hair, parted in the middle, reached the base of her neck. Any soul might enter this world without a joyful bone in their body. Still, such disposition couldn't compete with the empty heart and psychotic spirit of this dreary-faced fourteen-year-old zombie. Or that's how her brother characterised her, despite an inability to articulate his sentiments. The vocabulary of a backward eleven-year-old failed to equip him with sufficient wordy weapons. Instead, he trudged along through their untidy back garden, kicking tiny stones towards his sister's ankles.

"Don't call me 'Little Brother,' Sal."

Sally turned. "Why not? It's what you are: my little brother."

"But it's not my name." The boy stamped his foot.

Sally wagged a slender index finger in the air. "Temper, temper. You're as unpredictable as our mother, sometimes."

A vengeful grin spread across the younger sibling's face. "I'll tell her you said that."

Sally adjusted one shoulder of her plain white summer dress. "And you think she'll believe you?"

"A pound note says she will."

Sally shook her head. "Don't be stupid, *Little Brother*." She accentuated the label he hated. "Besides, pound notes ceased being legal tender in March. Where *have* you been living?"

The boy scowled. "The same place as you. Out here in the middle of nowhere."

"Do you want to see this giant fish, or what?"

"Okay." He drew a circle in the grass with his foot.

Sally stepped forward and grabbed his hand. "I found it skulking beneath that overhanging tree. The water is deep enough on this side of the pond for a creature that size to submerge itself way out of sight."

"Like the Loch Ness Monster?"

Sally laughed. "Not in our woodland pond, Little Brother."

"I know that. I mean, it needs deep water like the Loch Ness Monster. You're such a bitch."

Sally let go. "I'm telling Mum you said that. The difference is, she *will* believe me."

A flash of fear danced behind the boy's eyes. He gulped. "Can I see the pike now?"

Sally edged around the tree. In front, the dark, weed-choked waters of a massive pond the size of a small fishing lake lay still, dead and glassy. "Don't get too close. You know you can't swim."

The boy crouched beside the water's edge. His fearful reflection made him retract in shock.

Sally giggled. "That's not the pike, it's your own face, silly."

Her brother scowled and leaned back over the surface. Sally's countenance rose triumphantly behind him, gazing into the liquid abyss.

Dirty, smelly water forced its way up the eleven-year-old's nose and flooded his ears in the pond's murky depths. He thrashed towards the surface, but made no headway in reaching that circle of light which represented salvation.

A resounding shock wave of something plunging into the water jostled his panicked form. One muscular arm reached around his chest, its power halting his frantic attempts to resist. When his face broke the surface, he found himself staring into the gentle eyes of his father. The slender, fit man kicked to keep them both afloat. At the water's edge, Sally wrung her hands and grizzled while their mother gazed into the pond with her intense, black-ringed eyes.

Sally reached out for father and son.

Enid grabbed her daughter's arm. "Careful, child. You'll end up in that stinking water again yourself."

Derek helped their son onto the bank, only for Enid to yank his left earlobe. She fumed. "What do you think you're playing at? You might have drowned. You almost killed your sister."

The boy winced as though his ear were about to detach.

Derek touched Enid's arm to release her furious pinch. "Be gentle, Love. He didn't do it on purpose. It was an accident."

Sally watched her brother glare in fury and shout.

"*She* did it." He jabbed an accusatory finger at her. "Sally pushed me in, then stepped on my head to keep me underwater."

Sally's jaw dropped. For some reason her clothes were also wet through. She caught Enid's furrowing eyebrows. "Mum, it's not true."

Enid placed both hands on her hips. She shot vacillating glances first to one child and then the other. Summary judgement followed in the form of a resounding slap across the boy's face, which knocked him to the ground.

"Enid. Stop it." Derek's voice rang heavy with desperation.

"He needs a short, sharp shock to break him out of his lying ways." She grabbed her son by a tuft of his fine, brown hair, then marched back towards the house. In the ensuing struggle and with Derek protesting all the way, a clump of the silken strands came away in her hand.

Sally covered her mouth as her brother tapped the bald spot, burst into tears and ran for the kitchen.

Later that night, a gentle door knock from soft knuckles was followed by a fleet form slipping into the boy's bedroom. Sally plonked down on the far end of her brother's mattress.

"I didn't push you into that pond, and I didn't step on your head. You know that."

The boy lay awake, eyes staring at the ceiling while he ignored her protestations. "Do I?"

Sally fidgeted. "At least Mum and Dad will pay for swimming lessons now. Something good came of it."

The boy rolled over to face the window. "You're an evil, disgusting witch, Sally. Go away and leave me alone."

Sally lingered a moment longer until a sharp foot kicked her from beneath the bedclothes. Without

Coralie adjusted a tight bun of greying dark hair. "A lady dragged her husband inside, five minutes after we opened. When I heard her shriek from the pavement, I thought there'd been an accident or robbery."

Gillian gasped. "Shriek?"

Andrew took up the retelling. "Yep. She charged in here, gabbing a mile a minute about how she'd been looking for an amber bracelet. The woman even had a perfect picture in her mind of what it should look like. She didn't want a clunky collection of large stones. Your Sterling Silver, Celtic design looping around a single honey amber stone, matched her vision." He cleared his throat and shot her a cheeky wink. "I've never been one to subscribe to the *'if you build it, they will come'* mantra, but in this case I don't know what else to say."

Gillian giggled. Her peachy shoulders jostled beneath the cascading bronze hair. "I'm a heavenly inspired jewellery designer. What else?"

Coralie flushed, then poked her in the ribs. "What else, indeed? We gave her one of your business cards with the website address."

Gillian wrinkled her nose. "You two are the best. Now I'd better knuckle down to it. I've still six hours work to complete on my headdress for the wedding tomorrow."

Andrew stepped back to examine their new painting again, unsure if it hung true. "I hope your gentleman appreciates the effort you've gone to. We're surprised you're not procuring a house in these parts."

Gillian shrugged. "Brent works long hours in the

city. He'll keep the studio flat up there for a time, but stay with me each Friday night through Monday morning. That's assuming you're okay with his part-time occupancy once we're hitched?"

Coralie brushed her arm before joining her husband's picture assessment. "Do what you like, Sweetheart. There's no change in the rent."

Gillian sighed and pushed open a '*Staff Only*' door to reach the back staircase. A rear exterior entrance to the building offered access for out of hours use. She called over her shoulder. "Like I said: you two are the best."

Living in a garret as a hand-to-mouth craftswoman felt bohemian and exciting when Gillian first left home. As someone who didn't put on airs, those unfamiliar with her family history would never guess she hailed from a wealthy background. That fact made her present lifestyle more thrilling than ever. Although, she sometimes wondered how she'd cope with tougher times and less pleasant landlords. Two white painted dormer windows jutted out of the red tiled roof above the Broad Street junction. To her left, across the rooftops, Gillian revelled in glimpses of the crenellated tower capping St. John's Church. Its banded, multi-hued stonework echoed the ecclesiastical equivalent of a giant Neapolitan ice cream. Tomorrow she'd walk down its aisle on her proud father's arm.

Gillian poured herself an orange juice, then settled at her craft bench facing out across the street. Positioned on a work stand, a beaded faux pearl and crystal bridal headdress glittered in the warm sunlight. Loops of fine golden leaves presented a flowing style. Combined with the spherical pearls, this adornment for her striking hair spoke of an autumn berry bush captured in time to celebrate the season of her nuptials. Gillian slipped a pair of thick-lensed work glasses on and lost herself in the job of completing this crowning, matrimonial glory.

It was late afternoon when the exterior rear door intercom buzzed from down in the back yard. Gillian pulled off her jeweller's eyewear to squint at the clock.

"Crumbs. Is that the time? Mum and Dad will be here in a couple of hours." She slipped down off a raised stool and moved to answer the intercom. "Hello?"

"Gillian? It's me, your eager Maid of Honour." A teasing female voice crackled through the speaker.

"Never heard of her," Gillian shouted into the device.

A pause. "Ha-Ha. Are you going to let me in, or what?"

Gillian poked her tongue through her teeth before pressing the door release button with one slender index finger. She caught the rear entrance bang shut far below, before the communication session timed out.

A minute later, a sharp fist rapped on the attic flat door.

Gillian leaned closer to it. "Just a minute." She swung her chin in the opposite direction and spoke with pretend hushed tones to thin air. "Quick, Graham, you and the rest of the rugby team hide in my closet.

I'm about to become a married woman. No-one can know about today." She counted to ten, then opened the door to her best friend.

Deborah Rowling's flat smile left many unsure of her mood or intentions. Combined with disproportionately wide eyes the colour of lacquered mahogany glaring from a head of Germanic aspect, she could intimidate without a single utterance. Yet straight, soft walnut hair almost obscuring broad eyebrows and tickling the base of her neck, hinted at an emotional marshmallow centre only her pals understood. Deborah was a fierce friend who didn't suffer fools gladly; but sweet as apple pie, once you broke through that '*fuck off*' crust reserved for strangers. She raised an eyebrow so high it disappeared beneath her lampshade fringe. "If you can get Alresford RFC in your closet, you must have knocked through to next door." She tapped one sarcastic foot. "You might be many things, Gillian, but a tart isn't one of them."

Gillian kissed her on the cheek. "Busted. I knew I chose you to be my Maid of Honour for some reason or other."

Deborah kissed her back. "It's because I'm your bestie, Fairy Princess." She crossed the threshold and spied the glittering headdress by the window. Her face lit up. "Did you finish it?"

"About an hour ago. I've been tweaking it ever since; silly perfectionist that I am."

Deborah drew nearer in open-mouthed wonder. "Oh, Gillian, it's exquisite. You've outdone yourself this time. Please tell me you'll make something for my wedding, when I meet Mr Right?" Her tone shifted from wonder to sarcasm. "Or if I can find any half-decent, available bloke who doesn't run a mile at the first hint of commitment."

Gillian clasped her hands together. "You'll find someone. So, you got off early from the office?"

Deborah straightened. "I took short lunch breaks, four days in a row this week. The boss let me use some flexi. I thought I'd better check in with my girl before her parents arrive. Where are they staying, anyway?"

"The Swan. Right around the corner from the church. They're treating me to dinner, this evening."

"I like your folks. It's a shame they don't visit more often."

Gillian glanced out the dormer window. "One of these days you must come home with me for a long weekend."

Deborah grimaced. "Am I posh enough for the Crane estate?"

"Well, no. But we can always bed you down with the horses. Our stables are lovely." Gillian's elfin grin broke free.

"Cheeky mare." Deborah chuckled. "Fine. You're in good spirits. I've accomplished my mission. I wanted to check you were okay, ahead of the big day. Is the car meeting us here tomorrow?"

"Yes. Andrew and Coralie have allowed me to dress downstairs. Bring your gown over. Dad only has to cross the road."

"It's going to be a short drive."

Gillian toyed with a strand of hair. "Then I won't

have to worry about being late, will I?"

"Speaking of which, when is Brent arriving?"

"His Best Man, Larry, said he'll catch an early train from the city first thing."

Deborah frowned. "That's cutting it fine. Jeez, I hope there isn't a tree across the line in the morning."

Gillian gasped. "Don't say that."

Deborah tapped her wrist. "I meant nothing by it. Everything will run smooth as clockwork, I'm sure. Thank God they had the stag do last weekend. Did Brent wind up naked anywhere?"

"If he did, I wasn't privy to it. I couldn't marry a man standing half-cut at the altar. His vows would be meaningless." She fidgeted. "No, Brent assures me he'll be in bed early and staying off the sauce."

Deborah moved back towards the door. "Good. If he spoils your wedding day, he'll wind up singing falsetto courtesy of my high heels."

"Don't do that. What if I forgive him and still want children, one day?" Gillian followed.

Deborah hugged her. "You're adorable. Where have the last two years gone? It seems like we've been friends forever." She coughed and added, "In a good way."

Gillian half-closed her eyes. "The best." She opened the flat door. "See you tomorrow."

* * *

At almost five thousand square feet, the swanky, three bedroom London penthouse belonging to Paula

Norris cost a small fortune. As a city senior executive, this property 'feather in the cap' represented ho-hum normality for her cut and thrust, high-end corporate lifestyle.

A curvaceous, hourglass blonde, Paula worked as hard at maintaining a youthful appearance as she did in nurturing her lucrative career. In her twenties and early thirties, skill, talent, merciless backstabbing and an occasional spreading of her long, waxed legs skyrocketed Paula up the greasy, corporate pole. The fact she bore more than a passing resemblance to a popular 1980s page 3 girl familiar to many of her bosses didn't harm such prospects. Now the more intimate poles she'd ridden had turned flaccid and retired, attention shifted to her neglected intimate life. At forty-five and the pinnacle of business achievement, Paula wanted a man who'd behave without turning into a wuss. A young buck bursting with looks, stamina, and drive. In short, someone fit yet captivated by her professional power and intoxicating, mature sensuality. The day Brent Fawley accompanied his manager to a London board meeting, she ticked off another goal box on her internal life organiser. The time soon came to see how far he'd go to get ahead. As it turned out: all the way.

"Can you feel me clenching on you?" Paula gasped where she sprawled naked atop the master suite mattress as Brent eased himself deeper inside her.

If mullets were out of fashion, Brent Fawley didn't receive the memo. His thick, black hair suggested a wannabe fan of some old school, Scandinavian boy band, despite being too young to remember such things. A thick neck and penetrating, thousand-yard stare could be used to beneficial effect when needed. It wasn't wasted on Gillian Crane. When they'd first met, she remained unsure whether he was staring in shock as others so often did. A reaction provoked by her striking, elfin features. In that regard, she needn't have worried.

Superfluous to an office worker career, Brent loved to wear his shirt with the top button unfastened and sleeves rolled halfway up his forearms. He gave off the air of a thirty-year-old go-getter who got things done. Even those who delved deeper into Brent's soul often missed a well-concealed amoral disposition towards doing whatever he needed to get whatever he wanted. Most discovered that stable door unfastened, long after the horse had bolted. In the last few weeks, his fiancé, Gillian, became next in line.

Brent's reflection swam in Paula's enquiring eyes. Her blonde hair spread out across the soft, white pillow into which the back of her head sunk. He chose his response with care, opting for actions rather than words. Paula was someone you screwed, but didn't screw *with*. He gritted his teeth and juddered to suggest ripples of intimate, sexual pleasure. "Damn, that's hot." A final, wobbling vocal trill of approval avoided any chance of ambiguity. If the truth be told, Paula's womanhood had seen enough energetic action to drive a van through it without touching the sides. But Brent wasn't fool enough to let on. Besides, her cougar appeal, seductive power and business success drove his ambition wild with imagined possibilities.

Paula knew what she wanted and was never shy about laying her cards on the table. If she ordered, "Sex, now," you dropped your trousers and got down to business without asking dumb questions.

A panoramic array of ceiling-height glass windows and sliding doors overlooked a private roof terrace. Nighttime illuminations of the city skyline highlighted 'The Gherkin,' poking proudly above rooftops from way in the distance.

Brent cast a sideways glance at it, while one hand slipped from beneath his lover's back to send fingers wandering across her toned abdomen.

Paula intercepted his approach. "I've got it. You keep up the gentle strokes, Handsome."

Brent felt like an intern, untrusted with important office matters. He'd overseen multi-million pound projects. Surely she'd trust him with the correct operation of her clit?

Paula read his mind. She purred. "Mmm. I want you to enjoy yourself. We can't have you entertaining second thoughts on the plane tomorrow." She nuzzled his neck, then bit his right earlobe. Husky tones whispered with domineering but arousing authority. "I'd hate to see you throw your career away, right after that new promotion."

A man with scruples might have suffered from a guilty conscience. Brent couldn't care less. His betrothed had a weird beauty and her family were loaded. He couldn't believe his luck the night they'd met at *'The Horse & Groom'* in Alresford. He'd only popped home for a weekend visit to celebrate his friend Larry's birthday. Romance blossomed, Brent met her folks a month later, and all his ducks lined up. But then, her father was no fool. After their engagement, Mr Crane encouraged Gillian to obtain a prenuptial agreement to safeguard her future happiness. Brent realised the only family jewels he'd sample any time soon were Gillian's intimate, physical treasures or the kind she manufactured for a living. Pleasurable though she was, Gillian couldn't do anything to advance his career. The bloom was off the rose, with better - if more mature - offerings on the table. He didn't have the patience to waste another minute on that only child, little rich girl, after Paula Norris offered him the promotion of the century. Paula's price mattered little to Brent, though it gnawed at his insides. It was Gillian who'd pay.

Paula dug well-manicured fingernails into Brent's back and stiffened. Her mouth stretched to emit a wave of gasps that pulsed in time with a powerful orgasm. Wide eyes narrowed to the slits of a contented cat. She puffed out a satisfied instruction. "Go for it."

Brent picked up the pace. The rocking mattress emitted the only sound in an otherwise silent space of clinical white walls and cold, minimalist objets d'art. The sensation was sublime. He called out her name to demonstrate an overpowered, emotional core undone by pleasure as his intimate flood erupted.

Paula rolled over to pull a cigarette from a packet on

the nightstand. She flicked the wheel on a gold-plated lighter and took a long drag.

Brent lay with one arm draped across her midriff. "You're an incredible woman."

Paula's lips tightened to a stiff smile in time with a long exhalation of smoke. "That was sexy as hell." She watched him. "You remembered your passport, I assume?"

Brent nodded at a suitcase and carry-on bag resting beside her dressing table. "Of course. I'm looking forward to our getaway, though the timing is cruel."

Paula blew a stream of smoke into his face. Her voice grew tense. "Are you developing a conscience on me? Shit, I wondered if you had what it takes to be Senior Project Overseer."

Brent swiped the cigarette from her lips in a show of strength, took a puff and blew smoke back at her. "You know I'm the man for the job. And no, I'm not developing a conscience. Fuck, Gillian was fun, but there's no future with her. She's so tied to that arty boutique business, I'd never get her away from her insignificant life. She has access to incredible wealth with her family, but plays small in everything she does." He flicked ash into a tray Paula placed to cover his deflated nether regions. "It's harsh on her wedding day, that's all."

"Would you rather confront her to sever your ties in person? I'm providing you a straightforward way out. You're not going back to live there, are you?"

"No. I'm done with Hampshire." He passed the cigarette across. "It's a test, isn't it? You arranged things this way to see how far I'd go?"

Paula took another puff, face devoid of emotion. She scratched her left cheek with one pristine fingernail. "Smart boy. If you pull this off, your glittering future at Pearce McKenzie is assured. Then we'll see how life works out between us. You like my penthouse, don't you?"

"Are you kidding? Compared with my studio flat? Duh."

Paula smirked. She remembered their first tumble after a night out, heading back to his tiny, leased bolt hole in Tulse Hill. Its grand-a-month rent cost less than she spent on wine over a similar period. Shagging Brent in his pathetic digs offered further insight into his pressure points and net worth, or lack thereof. "The place looks good with you in it. If we get along in the Caribbean, we'll talk about turning this into a more formal arrangement. Something far better than stolen nights here and there."

Brent's eyes drifted back to the costly skyline terrace again. He kissed her neck and lifted the ash tray to expose the market recovery of his rising asset. "I like the sound of that."

Paula placed the finished cigarette and ashtray back on the nightstand, then reached to pull him in for seconds.

* * *

"You look amazing." Deborah Rowling smoothed down her copper coloured Maid of Honour dress.

Gillian turned to study the back of her bridal gown in a full-length mirror situated in a staff room behind the ground floor shop. The headdress glittered on her fiery gold and bronze hair. Those locks still hung loose, tamed by an open veil kept in place by the custom jewellery piece. A series of matching faux pearl inlays followed the chest line of her simple, white, off the shoulder gown. "It all came together, didn't it?"

Deborah passed Gillian her autumn bouquet of pink ice protea, peach peony roses, Clooney Ranunculus, trailing amaranthus and agonis. Their warm reds and oranges of various shades echoed the turning leaves of the season. "It's official: you're a knockout. Really, Gillian, you should be on a magazine cover."

Gillian wrinkled her nose. "Love you. It's funny, I've something old, something new, something borrowed, but I've not found anything blue. My pale eyeshadow, I suppose. Although that's more silver."

"As long as the 'something blue' doesn't arrive courtesy of unforeseen calamity, I shouldn't worry. Not everybody follows that tradition," Deborah replied.

Andrew and Coralie escorted Gillian's father through from the shop.

Coralie pulled out a handkerchief and blubbed at the sight of Gillian in her finery. Andrew stepped aside with a quiet, "Wow." Her father stopped in his tracks, unwavering admiration and a hint of moisture softening his transfixed gaze.

With a toned bearing, graced by the faintest evidence of good eating and slowing down towards retirement,

Bertram Crane appeared in rude health for a sixty-three-year-old man. Black hair provided natural highlights to a grey, cropped tidy cut smothering his square head but fading above the ears. Subtract a decade and emerging grey had produced such highlights, as if in a negative photo image of present physical reality. Bright, beady hazel eyes squinted through rectangular framed spectacles perched on the bridge of a sizeable, bulbous hooter. Those eyes were filled with laughter to match a straight, toothy grin of gentle positivity. At over six foot, two inches tall, her father always felt like a giant to Gillian. Most men did, but none with the awe and wonder she held for this man who occupied a place in her heart reserved for no other. Life as a self-made, commercial refrigeration magnate agreed with Bertram. Pressure and stress washed off his shoulders like water off a duck's back. He had faith in who he was and what his company could do. Solutions always presented themselves to problems. He applied the same relaxed patience to every other area of life. At that moment, in the rear room of The Tennyson Gallery, all the world disappeared for him.

"Hello, Pixie." Words came at last, pushed out with a subtle tremolo of emotion.

"Hi, Daddy." Gillian clutched her bouquet between nervous fingers. "A bit different to my appearance last night."

"Can this be my little girl?" Bertram addressed nobody in particular.

"She's beautiful." Coralie wiped her eyes and

sniffed.

Bertram approached his daughter, eyes scanning every inch of her appearance to record it for mental posterity. "Your headdress is stunning."

Gillian flushed. "A lot of work, but worth it."

Andrew Tennyson disappeared into the shop, then emerged clutching a printed paper notice. "Once you're in the car, we'll close up and nip across to the church. I've made a sign for the window."

Coralie checked her handbag for a compact digital camera.

Bertram smiled at Gillian. "Take all the time you need. Bride's prerogative."

"I'm ready, Daddy," she replied.

Outside the gallery, pedestrians parted to applaud when Gillian emerged on her father's arm. Cars taking the junction honked their horns in support. An immaculate chauffeur in tailored grey cloth opened the rear door of a white, vintage 1937, Rolls Royce Phantom III. Gillian slid in beside her father, while the chauffeur folded down one of the comfortable, occasional seats for Deborah.

Andrew and Coralie locked the gallery door and hurried across the road to disappear down an alleyway leading to St John's.

Bertram inclined his head towards the driver as he was about to secure the door. "Twice around the town before we head over to the church, I think."

The chauffeur tipped his cap. "Very good, Sir."

Promising weather from the day before carried into Saturday afternoon. Gillian realised she could have walked to the church. It seemed pointless driving around Alresford, only to arrive back within sight of the point she'd boarded the lovely old Rolls. But her father promised a vintage car, and she was glad of the ride. Besides, bride and groom would require conveying to the reception in style afterwards, so it made sense when she took that into consideration. People waved, making her feel like royalty during their ten minute cruise. She smiled at each in response. In one hand, Gillian clutched her bouquet. With the other, she held tight to strong loving fingers of the man who'd shielded her from the cold, cruel world for a quarter of a century before she left home.

On the path outside St John's, Deborah made sure her bestie's dress hung free without crease or blemish.

Gillian took a deep breath and tilted her head upward to take in the tall church tower.

One of the ancient wooden doors opened a crack. Larry Downes emerged in top hat and tails, a white carnation puffing from his lapel. Long sideburns chased down to neat designer stubble. His slender form hurried forward while he removed the hat with one hand.

Gillian froze. "Larry? What's going on? Why aren't you inside with Brent?"

Larry grimaced. "He hasn't arrived."

"What?" Gillian, Deborah, and Bertram chorused in perfect unison.

Bertram placed a hand in the small of Gillian's back. "Where is he? You're the Best Man."

Larry pulled a smartphone from beneath his grey, sharkskin morning coat. "I know, I know. I'm sorry, Mr Crane. I drove to collect him from the station in Winchester this morning, as arranged. He wasn't on the 7:39, 8:09, or 8:39 from Waterloo. I've been calling his mobile, but it goes straight to voicemail. When he didn't show up by ten, I decided to head home and get dressed, in case he'd made other last-minute arrangements and went straight to the church."

Deborah studied Gillian's stunned expression. She stomped a foot. "I'll kill him. So help me, Larry, if Brent spoils her day I'll rip this throat out with my bare hands. Did he get drunk last night? He promised Gillian he'd go to bed early." She ground the demonstrative foot into flagstones of the church path. "Why didn't he catch the train yesterday and stay with you?"

Larry shook his head. "I offered. He hasn't spoken to me much since the stag do. Brent is more in with his London crowd, these days." He hung his head. "I'm so sorry, Gillian. I don't know what to say. Should I call the Met Police and tell them we're concerned for his welfare? You know: have a copper knock him up at the flat to check he's okay?"

Bertram Crane swallowed. "It's a tad late for that."

An elegant woman emerged from the church. Her face brightened for a moment upon spying the bride. "Darling, you look lovely." Lines of concern returned to strain her forehead. Gillian inherited her defined facial aspect and bone structure from her mother, Felicity Crane. Felicity, or 'Flick' to her society pals, embraced life with gusto, counterbalanced by a healthy dose of common sense and good breeding. Her husband was already on his way to setting up a successful company when this pretty woman, eight years his junior, caught his eye at a charity fundraiser. At fifty-five, Felicity's short, white-blonde, cute two-tone undercut meant mixed colouration from advancing age provided natural tints requiring little attention from her stylist. It was the only sign of ageing for a woman who could pass for mid-forties without breaking a sweat. Good exercise, healthy eating and hydration, combined with an effortless (although active) lifestyle kept the dreaded wrinkles and dryness of maturity at arm's length. Felicity's blue/green eyes danced with an ever-present intelligence, always surveying the environment or reading people she encountered. A generous spirit and tender nature made receiving such scrutiny far less intimidating than it could otherwise have been.

"Hi, Mum." Gillian felt lost and alone, despite the love surrounding her.

Larry's mobile phone chimed to announce a text alert. He swiped it open. His watering eyes bulged outward with every line he read. "Good God. Brent, you shit." He noticed the older woman, who'd now reached his shoulder. "Oh, excuse me, Mrs Crane."

Gillian shut her eyes tight and took a deep breath. "What does it say, Larry?"

The phone jiggled in Larry's quivering hand as he

read aloud. *"Sorry about today. Had a change of heart. Off to St Lucia to clear my head. Be a mate and let her down easy. Cheers."*

Deborah's cheeks glowed the colour of beetroot. "You've gotta be fuckin' kidding me? It sounds like he's blown off a casual acquaintance from a night out at the pub."

Gillian's head throbbed. Her eyes rolled upwards to the church tower again. Its rose-coloured upper portion blurred before it and the surrounding trees whirled and everything turned black.

Felicity Crane sat on a chair beside Gillian's attic bed in the hours after dark. Gillian lay atop the mattress, still wearing her wedding dress, face to the wall in a zombified stupor. On the bedside table, a later text message sent to her own mobile phone sat open beneath the contact name: *'Brent Fawley.'* It read: *'Got to do what's best for myself. We both know it wouldn't last. Keep your chin up. Have a good life. Brent.'*

Gillian buried her nose into a pillow, devastated and humiliated beyond measure.

3

Buried Feelings

Mad female shrieking interspersed with gruff male responses jolted the eleven-year-old boy from restless slumber. His parents' fights grew in volume and physicality by the day. Enid always initiated the arguments with her passive, patient and frustrated husband. The child pushed his covers aside. He flexed his feet at the shock of cold, bare wooden floorboards coming in contact with his blanket cosseted soles. Two minutes passed while he waited for his eyes to adjust. If either he or Sally switched a light on in their rooms at night, their mother flew off in a fit of rage at such flagrant disregard for generator running costs. A pencil-thin sliver of dancing flame cast shadows beneath the bedroom door. The boy wandered over and twisted its cold brass knob with cautious fingers. He opened the door a crack. Two animated silhouettes, projected by a candle lamp Enid always used after dark, played out their scene of conflict on the landing wall.

"Enid, you need help. Maybe it's the atmosphere at the house, but your health is suffering." Derek pleaded with his wife.

"Looking to lock me away in a mental institution, are you?" Enid's shadow retracted.

"No, Love. Tell me: are you happy here? You seem angrier each week. If we visited a doctor-"

"Get away from me," Enid screamed. A bulky, tensing arm thrust forward to shove her husband aside.

Derek lost his footing on the top step of the staircase. He tumbled headlong, crashing and bouncing with reverberating bangs all the way to the bottom.

The boy opened his door wide. He drew in a sharp, involuntary and resonant breath. Sally poked her head around the jamb where she'd observed from the doorway of her own room. To the lad's eyes, her face sparkled with curious glee.

"Did you see that, Little Brother?"

The boy nodded without a word. He drew back as the candlelight brightened.

Enid shone her lamp towards the children from the stairway. "What are you two doing out of bed?"

"We heard you and Dad fighting again, Mum," Sally replied.

Enid hurried over to them with a swish of her crinkled old dress. "What did you see? Did you watch your father fall down the stairs?"

"Fall?" The boy's sudden, loud response took

himself by surprise.

Enid crouched before him. "You know he fell, don't you, Son?"

The boy gulped. "Is Daddy okay?"

Enid rested a firm hand on his shoulder. "No, I'm afraid he isn't. He's not moving and I think he's left us. You're the man of the house now." No remorse flickered in her mad eyes.

"B-b-but you pushed him," the boy stammered in protest.

Now Enid put down the lamp. She gripped both his shoulders and shook him. Her voice grew stern and frantic. "I reached out to save him, but it was too late. Can you imagine if the police accused me of killing your father? I'd go to prison. What do you think would happen to you then? Who would look after you? You'd both wind up in care."

Sally touched her mother's vigorous arms with a delicate hand. "We know it was an accident. We'll say as much." She glared at the boy. "Won't we, Little Brother?"

The boy looked from one to the other. His head produced one hesitant nod.

*   *   *

Derek's funeral featured scant attendees. The white stone interior of St Peter & St Paul's church, awash with summer light, brought a cheeriness at odds with the sombre ceremony inside.

Enid rose from a pew on the left of the aisle beneath

a polished wooden pulpit. "Come, children. It's time to say one last goodbye to your father."

Sally followed in dutiful silence towards an open casket resting on two trestles before the altar. She looked back to where her younger sibling still sat, fingers whitening against the pew. "Come along, Little Brother." Sally spoke in a stern whisper, unsure what would happen if their mother - currently distracted by proceedings - spotted his failure to heed her instruction.

The boy licked dry lips. He used the pew for support to push himself upward onto shaky pins. His sudden elevation brought the tip of his father's nose into view above the coffin's edge. Piercing eyes of the scattered mourners in the rows behind, burrowed into the back of his eleven-year-old skull like parasitic insects. He didn't want to be 'the man of the house.' Not a house like Ashburnham. And he didn't want to approach the stiff corpse, which once blossomed with his gentle father's life essence. He considered the timing. Had this tragedy occurred more than a month earlier, nobody would have saved him from drowning. He wondered if Sally would display the same curious glee at *his* funeral, as the eager fascination which he now appraised to adorn her visage.

Enid's head snapped round. She glared at her son, then stabbed a finger at the church floor beside her like someone reigning in a disobedient dog and bringing it to heel.

The boy shuffled sideways into the aisle. His steps grew hesitant as the coffin drew nearer.

Derek's discoloured skin shimmered with a waxy appearance akin to a dummy at Madame Tussaud's. His face suggested a tranquillity uncharacteristic of its owner in life. Those who approached to pay their last respects would remain unaware of the cotton stuffed into his nose and throat, his mouth sutured shut, and the eyelid cups keeping their sockets from caving in. The mortician did a professional job. It was Derek, but not as most remembered him. Some would argue this fake facade didn't assist the grieving process. Within three days of death, a collapsing and decomposing body provided clear notice to any observer that the person within had moved on. That unfamiliarity of appearance on his father's face made the gruesome corpse feel a stranger. Such a realisation amplified tension lifting the boy's shoulders about his ears.

Sally crossed herself and whispered. "Goodbye, Daddy. I love you." She stepped aside.

Enid lingered, mad crimson face fixed on the well made-up remains of the husband she'd pushed down the stairs. Her head ached from a gin bender the night before. Back at their remote house, empty glass bottles still littered her bedroom floor. Each spoke of an attempt to drown her sorrows and dissatisfaction with the absurdity of life. Her son's silence agitated her. "Say goodbye to your father, boy. Are you so unloving and ungrateful? It's bad enough you tried to drown your sister."

The lad clenched his teeth. No words of support rode in to buttress or express his incredulity. If they had, would their valiant charge prove any more effectual than that of '*The Light Brigade*' his father had once spoken of? He squashed a rising emotional spurt and forced himself to look into the waxy face. "Goodbye, Dad. I'm sorry Mum murdered you." His follow-on statement escaped unbidden. No sooner had the words left his lips than he wished to reel them back in. However true the comment, veracity mattered little to the bulky woman heaving beside him in a seething mass. Restrained by propriety in the polite atmosphere of the church at her husband's funeral, Enid would bottle her anger. When she uncorked it, the boy feared to sample the wine, stranded in a house with this livid, crazed creature as his only parent and guardian. That and a sister determined to put him six feet under.

*   *   *

A common parental warning to children of the time: '*You wait until I get you home. You won't sit down for a week,*' took on fresh significance at Ashburnham after the funeral. Sally watched her brother limp from room to room, cruel red welts leaving his epidermis slick to the touch. He'd taken to shutting himself in his room or disappearing on long walks in the grounds, from which he always returned covered in dirt. The mere sight of his dishevelled appearance sent Enid into further rampages of self-righteous corporal punishment. She didn't spare the rod in dishing it out.

One Wednesday morning, Sally waited until her sullen sibling slunk out through the kitchen door. Ten minutes later she washed the breakfast things for her mother, then excused herself to play.

An industrious noise of loosened earth and stones greeted Sally's ears a hundred yards beyond the pond. In a clearing of ash trees, piles of disturbed soil littered overturned turves of succulent grass. Sally pulled herself tight behind one of the tree trunks. A fresh flurry of dirt tossed into mid-air from a concealed spot near the focus of activity. The blade of a shovel sparkled in a flash of sunlight. Warm, indistinct rays that melted into the landscape. Sally crept closer to the upturned soil. Her brother crouched in a shoulder-height pit. Careful preparation of a gentle, descending slope on one side of the depression, allowed him safe extrication from something that bore a passing resemblance to their late father's grave.

"Who are you planning to bury?" Sally's head poked over the rim of the crumbling hole. "Not Mum. Don't tell me you're intending to hurt her? Remember what she said about us going into care after Dad died, if we're left all alone."

The boy paused from his strenuous activity without looking up. "When she killed him, you mean."

"Don't you think I miss him, too? Mum says we must be careful with money now." Sally peered back towards their home, which already bore additional tell-tale signs of neglect amidst ongoing underinvestment. Tiles slid down the roof to allow rain into the attic. Wood peeled and rotted around doors and windows. Mortar dropped in crumbling chunks between dirty bricks. Ivy slithered in sly snail trails around the corners, ready to strike with a leafy stranglehold on its unsuspecting prey. "Not that Dad was free with the cash, while he was alive."

"What do you want, Sally?"

"Nothing. I wondered where you've been disappearing to each day. It's the summer holidays. A season to play with my little brother. What with home school lessons during term time and no friends, who else have I got?"

The boy slammed his shovel into the earth again. "I'm digging a camp, okay? Somewhere to escape the pair of you." He hesitated. "During the funeral, Mum said I tried to drown you. Can you believe it? I'm sick of her beatings. Why am I punished for your behaviour? Who did Dad pull from the water?"

Sally lay face down and leaned further over the edge. "Both of us. You don't remember, do you?"

"Oh, shut up. You're a monster and a liar, like Enid, the beast of Ashburnham."

Sally toyed with an unearthed rock, half buried on the heap of accumulating soil beside her. "Do you think our father would appreciate you calling Mum that? He loved her, you know. Despite her difficult ways, Dad loved her like he loved both of us."

"What do you know of love? Cold, heartless creature. I saw the joy on your face at his funeral."

Sally tossed the rock in the air and caught it with a carefree hand. "And you think *Mum* is unhinged?"

Clods of heavy earth pressed down on the boy's chest where he lay supine. Friable dirt filled his nose and ears, then stung his eyes as they read nothing but filthy blackness above. He opened his mouth to scream, only for it to fill with powdery, suffocating earth. Vague remembrances of a heavy object, like a rock striking his head, caused the lad to wince. He tried to lift his arms and touch the spot, but his entire torso remained pinned in an unyielding soil tomb. Its relentless grip instigated a spasm of uncontrollable panic that infused the boy's limbs with adrenaline fuelled power.

One small hand burst through a deep covering of earth. Like a vampire pushing clear of its grave to feed, the male child's head bulged then parted the soil. Dirt sprayed from nostrils and mouth in a choking gasp that descended into a bout of coughing. With a stilted series of tense jerks, the rest of his body eased clear, covered from head to toe in filth.

"I'm going to kill you." The boy stood in the open kitchen doorway, staring at his sister.

Sally sat at the table, her torn and sullied summer dress caked in mud. Cuts, bruises and smeared earth detailed normally pale cheeks. She clutched a glass of milk between both hands.

Enid stormed away from the sink and grabbed her son's wrist. "You evil little devil. First the pond, now you try to bury your sister alive. Is it not enough for you we put your father in the ground?" Enid slapped him around the face with her free hand. Its snap knocked the boy's head sideways.

He yelled. "She did it. Sally tried to bury me."

Enid shrieked. "Shut up, shut up, shut up. You vicious liar. Look at the state of your sister. First you struck her on the head with a rock. It's a wonder she doesn't need stitches. It bled something fierce. Then you tried to suffocate her with earth." Enid slapped him again. "All this time digging a grave ready to bury your murdered sister in. Why, I've a mind to call the police and ship you off to Borstal."

The boy shook himself free. He backed away and glowered at his mother.

Enid folded her arms. "And then where did you go? Wandering the grounds to devise your next act of wickedness, I suppose?"

The lad twisted and jerked in a sudden fit of overload. He squatted to bounce on the spot. A weird series of twanging noises at various pitches thrummed from his vocal cords.

Sally banged her glass on the wooden table. "What's happening now? Crumbs, he sounds like a banjo."

Enid folded her arms. "Trying to gain sympathy, the calculating demon." Her lips crinkled at the corners. She regarded Sally for a moment. "Banjo? I like that." Enid crouched to halt the boy's jerking with a rigid shoulder grip. "Hear that, boy? Since you refuse to act like a decent human being, you'll forfeit the right to a person's name. Banjo it is." She tugged his ear until he wailed, then pushed him towards the hallway. "Go upstairs and wash that muck off. Don't use all the hot water. Your sister still needs to bathe."

Banjo tossed and turned in bed, fighting a growing nightmare. The artificially shaped eyelids of his father's corpse drew nearer until they burst open to reveal milky white emptiness. He fell through those eyes as they collapsed into a bottomless mine shaft. Down he went, spinning out of control. The dream of falling wasn't new, but he always awoke before its feared impact. This time he struck something soft and came to a rest, nose buried in fabric laced with a formaldehyde odour. Banjo pushed down with both hands to lift his head. Pungent, sticky goo mushed between his fingers, while a wooden board restricted the lifting of his head more than an inch. An eerie light filled the enclosed space, enough to make out basic shapes in cramped surroundings. Banjo came nose to chin with his dead father. Ooze coating the child's trembling digits wafted gas from Derek's putrid, liquefying organs. The wooden board preventing movement was the coffin lid. Somehow he lay face down, buried with his deceased parent. Banjo thrashed. His yelps of terror muffled into the pillow as he jolted back to consciousness in his darkened bedroom.

Banjo rolled over on his back. Beads of sweat glistened on his brow in pale moonlight filtering through moth eaten curtains. He allowed his thundering pulse to settle at tick-over, then eased himself up. A fox cried out in the woods. Its eerie scream dominated the night. All else remained quiet.

Banjo reached into his bedside drawer for a small torch he kept for rare nocturnal bathroom visits. His tongue grated against the roof of his mouth with the abrasiveness of coarse sandpaper. His stomach tightened and spread upwards to induce heartburn. *I need a glass of milk*. He clicked on the torch and eased off the bed. Floorboards creaked beneath his torn and faded slippers. He hesitated, ears straining for any living reaction to the structural movement. In his own room, risk remained low. If Sally was restless next door, she might hear him. Then there would be hell to pay once she blabbed to their mother. He moved with delicate pigeon steps to the door. Each flexing of warped wood beneath his feet caused him to pause and listen again. Ashburnham enfolded him like a villain's cape, as though ready to tattle on his being out of bed at night, much like his older sibling would. Was anything in this world *not* allied against him?

Out on the landing, Banjo peered over the banister. Sometimes his mother felt wakeful and wandered the house at night with her lantern like a hag on some infernal quest. Darkness and silence - bar the odd scurrying rodent - offered the only sensory feedback. That and a chill, midnight breeze wafting down from the attic to ripple fine white hairs on his exposed arms. He set off for the stairs, but halted outside Sally's door. No sounds arose from within. Banjo gripped the doorknob and opened it with the delicacy of a professional safe cracker. He kept the torch beam aimed at the floor, so as not to rouse his sleeping sister.

Sally sighed and turned over, straggly light brown

hair matted against the pillowcase.

Banjo crept up beside her. She looked so helpless laying there at his mercy. How much pressure would it take to wring the soft rise and fall of breath from her delicate body? A surge of elation at the prospect caused Banjo to shudder. He grinned and bent forward until his warm breath blew strands of hair away from her right ear and teased the sleeping teenager's cheek. "Keep up the torture, and you're mine," he whispered in her ear. The overwhelming power of some dark intelligence within, fixed his gaze. He licked Sally's cheek with one long, vertical sweep of his dry tongue. Sally's brow furrowed, but she remained asleep. Banjo retreated to the landing hallway and secured her door with a gentle click.

The stairs creaked worse than his floorboards. He pushed himself against the wall, hoping to reduce their duplicitous report on his descent to the hallway. At the foot of the staircase, he froze on the spot where his father's broken body came to rest. How long had he remained alive there, or did the tumble finish him before he ever reached the bottom step? Banjo released a languid breath. His shoulders eased at putting some distance between the sleeping occupants and himself. Downstairs, with nobody around, he could almost imagine owning Ashburnham himself. Nobody would punish him, then. He'd be king of the metaphorical castle. In that moment, his attitude towards the lived-in disrepair of that draughty abode softened. Would this home be his one day? What if something happened to Sally and his mother? He wandered into the kitchen. A refrigerator was one of the few items at Ashburnham connected to their Heath Robinson power supply. Banjo opened a wall-mounted kitchen cupboard. One hinge dropped halfway through its travel. Wood splintered, and the door hung slack from the remaining brass fitting. Banjo gritted his teeth. He swiped a cloudy highball glass from inside, then lifted the broken door back into place. How long would it stay shut without tearing free and crashing to the floor? He couldn't tell. Delicious visions of his mother or Sally opening the cupboard door next morning, only to suffer a nasty wallop from its demise, added to his relaxing posture. Banjo tugged open the fridge. Its interior light bulb blew years earlier, but the appliance still kept provisions fresh and cool.

After he poured himself a generous serving of milk, Banjo stared out the kitchen window, across the garden to the pond with his pit beyond. Something probed his innards, willing him out to the scene of his most recent waking nightmare. Part of him wanted to dash back upstairs and hide under the blankets. Anything other than experiencing an encounter with that camp which almost became his grave. But the feeling remained insistent. He gulped down a last mouthful of milk. The thought occurred that his mother would know he'd been up if she came down in the morning to find a dirty glass in the sink. He rinsed it under the cold tap, wiped round the inside with a tea towel, then stood before the broken cupboard door again. *Here goes.* Banjo eased it part way open enough to squeeze the improperly cleansed drinking vessel back onto its shelf. The door held on with the last efforts of a terminal patient awaiting some promised hospital visit from their nearest and dearest, before shuffling off this mortal coil. Banjo stepped away and took a deep breath. No sign of imminent collapse from the cupboard.

He slipped into outdoor shoes, then unfastened the kitchen door and stepped out into the night.

The garden and surrounding woods of Ashburnham offered a novel experience at this hour. He'd never been downstairs after bed time, let alone sampled the heady thrill of a midnight ramble. It was naughty and forbidden by his mother. That simple fact piled on pleasures aplenty as he skirted the pond. Was it the cool night air or memories of almost drowning that sent a shiver down his spine? Were it not summer, he'd tremble to within an inch of his life, roaming around outdoors in nought but his nightwear. A familiar collection of ash trees lured him onward. Somewhere in the dark, his excavated pit still waited like the cavernous maw of a basking shark, hoovering up plankton. Far enough away from the house to not draw attention, Banjo illuminated the torch again. An effort to avoid twisting an ankle or tumbling back into the hole. He swept the beam from side to side until it fell upon the pile of earth and the discarded rock Sally played with before everything in his memory went blank. He squatted beside it for a better look. No dried or caked blood encrusted the stone. Banjo touched the back of his head again. It remained free of cuts or bruises. "I must be a quick healer, like my father." He spoke the sentiment aloud.

Derek's rasping voice seeped over the rim of the pit. "Even I can't heal from breaking my neck on the stairs." Two clawing, masculine hands dug at the loose earth to haul up a bloated, decomposing body. Flat pupils fixed on Banjo as the man's sutured mouth tore open its stitches to spit out lumps of cotton and clods of earth.

Banjo backed away, rising and ready to run. "No. No, you're buried in the churchyard. This can't be happening." He spun to lock stares with Sally. She stood in her nightdress, oblivious to his presence. Both eyes rolled upward into her unconscious head. Arms hung limp at her sides.

The combined shock of both encounters freed a tremulous wail from Banjo's voice box. He glanced over his shoulder to find the pit empty, with no sign of his father.

Sally's eyes screwed tight, like someone waking from deep slumber. When they reopened, the jolt of finding herself no longer abed - combined with her brother's wild facial expression on the edge of his erstwhile shallow grave - forced a shrill, air cutting scream from her pipes.

At the same moment, the sagging kitchen door gave up the ghost and tore free of its other hinge. The heavy wooden object dropped to the floor with an echoing bang. Shock from its sudden release disturbed several glasses on shelving inside. A round of crisp, shattering impacts accompanied the crashing disturbance.

Upstairs in Enid's room overlooking the rear garden,

a candle flame flickered to life. Her feet shuddered into the floorboards with similar force to the collapsing kitchen cupboard door beneath.

Banjo spied the dancing flame across the pond. His mother always slept with the curtains open. *Oh, no.* His mind raced. *What should I do? There's nowhere to run.* He opted for an attempt at subterfuge and bolted for the sideway, hoping against hope to duck out of sight before his raging lone parent made the kitchen door. If she'd heard Sally scream and hurried to investigate, he'd nip back inside and make a break for his bedroom. Even had it worked, Banjo knew the plan lacked merit. Enid could find him feigning sleep and still not believe her senses. Once Sally came to hers and registered her brother's actual presence - rather than branding it the product of a sleepwalking dream - his goose was cooked.

Banjo got within ten feet of the sideway before dancing candlelight spread throughout the kitchen. Orange flame washed Enid's furious features and electrified brush of red hair. Her bulbous eyes fell upon the scrambling boy and she tore open the back door. One savage, talon-like hand grabbed him by the scruff of the neck. From the far side of the pond, Sally's startled screams continued unabated. Banjo realised another judgement day had come. He hated both females with a passion.

4

Cutting the Cord

ALRESFORD - OCTOBER 2019.

In the absence of that vital spark which infused Gillian with her bubbly power and creative drive, she fell back on the automatic patterns of daily routine. Numb to the core, her morning strolls along the River Alre lacked their usual joy. Often she forgot her regular food scraps to feed the waterfowl.

On a dull Monday morning, nine days after Brent jilted her, Gillian started walking in a daze and didn't stop. She'd run the entire gamut of emotions from guilt and self-blame, through anger to grief and her present, all pervasive sense of hopelessness. Beyond the old fulling mill, she vanished inside her own head. One foot pounded the path in front of the other until the Alre fed into the Itchen. Gillian didn't stop there, nor for a further eight miles of the meandering watercourse, until the squat tower of Winchester Cathedral appeared above red and golden treetops on the horizon.

"It can't be." She almost staggered off the riverbank in time with her sharpening wits. Now an ache in her ankles from feet ill shod for such a hike, caused her to crouch and rub them. She remembered this spot. Further on into the picturesque city near the cathedral, the River Itchen commenced one end of 'Keats' Walk.' Two centuries prior, legendary romantic poet, John Keats, used to follow that stretch during a sojourn in Winchester. It was here amidst striking seasonal colours like those of today, that he composed his oft-quoted masterpiece 'To Autumn' on 19th September 1819, after an evening constitutional. Published the following year, its opening line: 'Season of mists and mellow fruitfulness,' would become one of the most beloved in English literature and synonymous with autumn around the world.

The only mist Gillian experienced beyond a soft haze off the river was a constant fogging of her mind and emotions. She felt neither mellow nor fruitful. Nature's beauty engulfed her, but her wounded soul revelled not in its awesome grandeur; inoculated from all joy by her heartless betrothed.

Lacking the energy to turn back, Gillian gave her ankles a final rub, then pressed on into bustling streets. She pulled out her phone to check the time. *I wonder if Deborah fancies meeting up for a chat?* She scrolled to her bestie's work number and initiated a call.

"Hey, Gillian." Deborah couldn't conceal the concern in her voice. "It's good you called. I was thinking about you while I zoned out at an office meeting this morning."

"I'm in town. Fancy an early lunch?"

"Winchester? Hey, you should have told me first thing. Are you pitching your wares to a shop or gallery?"

Gillian cleared her throat. "No. It was err... a last minute surprise."

"Hang on a sec." The line muffled as Deborah consulted with a colleague at the other end. "Yeah, okay. I can do that. Where are you?"

"Outside the school of art."

"Are you teaching now?" Deborah's voice returned to its default, cheeky lilt.

"No."

"Well, you should. You've some serious talent. I'll meet you halfway. Do you know 'The William Walker?' That's pretty central."

"Err..."

"Head south on Upper Brook Street until it bends. Take the alleyway straight on to cross High Street into Market Street. The pub is on a corner right outside the cathedral. You can't miss it."

"I'd miss a worldwide alien invasion this morning. My head is a mess. Okay, south on Upper Brook Street, down the alley and keep going until I reach the cathedral. Got it."

"No need to rush. It's about the same distance from here for me. I'll see you soon."

"Bye." Gillian hung up. In truth, she wasn't familiar with any of Winchester's street names, despite occasional visits. She pulled up an electronic map and keyed in 'The William Walker, Winchester' as a destination. The app suggested a distance of half a mile, requiring twelve minutes to walk. She had eaten nothing for breakfast. Now a distinct stomach rumble from her unintended, vigorous exercise made Gillian touch her gurgling tummy. *I suppose it will hearten Deborah to see me eat something.* She set off south. As the quiet, red brick terraces of Upper Brook Street fed into the busy B3331, Gillian caught another glimpse of the 11th century cathedral. *Thank goodness I'm still with it enough to follow basic directions.* She walked on, feet and ankles protesting from further activity.

Deborah had estimated the travel time with precision. She waved from a broad, tree-lined thoroughfare forming part of the cathedral precincts, as Gillian reached the corner of Market Street and The Square. 'The William Walker' stood an elegant, whitewashed Victorian structure covering two floors, plus attic dormers. Pigeon grey sash windows lined both main storeys, while lettering atop a painted band of masonry above the upper dining floor declared it: 'Circa 1860.' An old, brass deep-sea diver's helmet jutted out of the upstairs corner, providing more visual interest than the typical flat, painted pub sign. This nautical theme continued inside, with abundant seafaring memorabilia, a brass topped bar and fresco of a struggle between a deep-sea diver and tentacled beast from the ocean depths.

Gillian glanced around the bar. "This is nice. What's the story with a diving themed pub in Winchester?"

Deborah grinned. "William Walker was a deep-sea

diver who worked underground in water to shore up the cathedral, after cracks appeared in its stonework. His expertise made him the perfect choice for the task. He used hundreds of thousands of bricks and concrete blocks to make it sound. Otherwise, Winchester Cathedral would have crumbled a century ago from river ingress to its foundations."

Gillian blinked. "Wow. It's nice they commemorate him at the pub. Man, I could eat a horse. I've had little since Sunday lunch yesterday. I didn't eat much then. Andrew and Coralie insisted on having me down for a roast. They're worried I'll starve myself, otherwise."

"They're not the only ones. Do you want to grab a drink first, or head straight upstairs to the dining room?"

"Let's go for the dining room."

They ascended to the upper public floor and found a pleasant scrubbed pine table occupying a sash window facing the cathedral. "You didn't tell me why you're in Winchester. Where are you parked?"

"I walked."

Deborah almost fell over the chair she'd pulled out to sit on. "What? That's gotta be eight or nine miles. What inspired this?"

Gillian sat down. "I didn't intend to do it. My morning stroll by the Alre sort of morphed into a hike." She rubbed her eyebrows. "I must have zoned out. Next thing I knew, the cathedral popped up on the horizon."

"You walked for three hours, unaware of your surroundings or progress? Shit." She plonked herself down on the seat. "Gillian, that's worrying."

"You're telling me."

"You've no recollection of the journey at all?"

"Not beyond the fulling mill in Alresford."

Deborah hunched over the table. "What did you think about?"

"There's the other thing: I can't remember *that* either."

A female staff member appeared clutching two menus. The friends took them and ordered two glasses of Prosecco while they browsed today's offerings.

Deborah flitted between reading choices and stealing worried glances at Gillian's lost facial expression.

Gillian pressed her forehead into stiff fingers, a picture of mental and emotional struggle. "So much to choose from."

Deborah put her menu down. "You're going to hate this suggestion, but have you thought about seeing a doctor?"

Gillian frowned further. "I got stood up on my wedding day, I'm not coming down with something. Not other than a serious case of disappointment and chronic embarrassment."

"What about depression?"

"Wouldn't you be depressed if your fiancé left you near the altar?" Gillian winced at her abrupt delivery. "Sorry. I didn't mean to snap."

"Forget it. And yes, of course I'd be depressed. Anyone would. That's my whole point."

"Are you a psychologist now?"

"No, but it might help for you to consult one."

Gillian didn't make eye contact, focusing instead on the list of dishes. "You think I've lost the plot? That I'll become that smelly old woman pushing a shopping trolley containing eight hundred empty plastic bags around Sainsbury's car park?"

A crooked half-smile teased Deborah's left cheek. "Nice mental picture. Think about what happened this morning with your walk, then tell me you wouldn't benefit from some professional advice."

Gillian brushed the side of her nose. "I'm processing everything, that's all." She waved a loose hand at the ceiling. "Like some pub undergoing a refit, normal business will resume once I complete the interior work."

"Some people don't like it when their local gets a refit."

Gillian shrugged. "Then they can bloody well drink elsewhere, can't they?" Her pale cheeks rouged in anger, while moisture rimmed her eyes. "Oh, God. Deborah, I'm so sorry." A tear ran down her right cheek. She fought to hold in a veritable detention block of sobbing, desperate for a prison break.

Deborah sighed. "You see what I mean? This isn't the Fairy Princess everyone who meets you falls in love with."

Gillian wiped the escaped tear aside with slender fingers. "I've no idea where that girl has gone. Ever since Prince Charming slipped off his charger, she's been AWOL. Now I'm an empty shell. I can't work. My passion has vanished. Sleep comes in fits and starts. Food has lost its taste, yet my body still requires nourishment." She shook her head and gazed out the window at Winchester Cathedral. "If you can imagine wrapping your head in cotton wool and wading through treacle, that's how laborious and dull everything has become."

Deborah gripped her hand across the table. "There's light at the end of the tunnel. You'll see."

Gillian hung her head. "I can't even see the tunnel, let alone imagine a light."

"So you'll get help?" Deborah sat up straight in her seat.

"No."

"What?"

Gillian bit her lip. "I love you, Deborah. Like Mum and Dad, Andrew and Coralie, your concerns are genuine. But I've got to work through this myself. When I consider telling a stranger what happened, I feel like I'd die of shame and heartache."

"It's not your fault, Gillian. Brent is the shitbag responsible. Jesus, if I ever meet that guy again, I'll wind up inside for murder."

Gillian chased her teeth with a curled tongue. "Can you do me a favour?"

"Anything. Name it."

"Could we change the record and enjoy a quiet meal without dwelling on the subject? It's on my mind 24/7, even if I'm so distracted and catatonic I don't realise." She nodded at the road outside. "Or I wind up walking to Winchester."

Deborah puffed out her cheeks. "Okay." Her resigned response followed an uncomfortable pause in which she found nothing better to counter with.

"Thanks. If I'm lucky, we'll even discover something to laugh about." Gillian banged her menu against the table. "Hey, did you hear the one about the girl who spent ages making a jewellery headdress for her own wedding?" Her eyes watered again and her voice wobbled. "We all know the punchline to that, don't we?" This time the grief tsunami would brook no refusal over its release. Gillian burst into tears, hurriedly muffled as Deborah rounded the table to hold her close.

Their server returned with a tray holding two glasses of chilled Prosecco. She hesitated at the awkward scene played out in an otherwise empty dining room.

Deborah looked up. "Man trouble."

The staff member set the tray down on the next table and toyed with a smart scrunchie, securing her dark blonde hair in a short ponytail. "Say no more. I'll leave these here and come back for your order later."

"Thank you," Deborah replied.

Gillian went limp in her arms like a floppy rag doll, or life-sized figurine of the Fairy Princess Deborah once christened her on account of those elfin features. Her tight lips clamped shut. All Gillian wanted was for the turmoil and anguish to end. But nothing helped or highlighted an exit from her languorous labyrinth of lament.

* * *

It was mid-afternoon when Gillian alighted the

number 64 bus from Winchester Broadway to The Swan Hotel in Alresford. Hiking back wasn't an option. Combined emotional and physical exertion left her drained. Despite Deborah's generous offer of a lift, she didn't want to be a burden or create problems for her at work. She could handle twenty minutes on a bus without making a scene. Gillian forced herself to concentrate on her immediate surroundings throughout that brief journey, lest she wind up twelve miles down the road in Alton and be worse off than when she started.

Andrew and Coralie would be worried and filled with questions. Gillian hoped to God they didn't already have Hampshire Constabulary dragging the river for her body. She'd left for her morning stroll and not returned. It was the first time thoughts of their potential turmoil interrupted her confused mind. *I should have phoned them from Winchester.* An interrogation - even a well-intentioned one - was more than her delicate shred of sanity could handle. Morning mist transitioned over lunch to fine sunshine. Gillian decided her landlords could wait a little longer while she composed herself. After biting Deborah's hand off at the pub, she hated the idea of a repeat performance with those sweet gallery owners. The tower of St John's loomed behind the hotel, reigniting memories of her last moments before passing out at Brent's text message to Larry. *I've got to confront this, or I'm lost.* She entered the churchyard and wandered curved paths bordered with moss and ivy-clad headstones. Sizes and shapes varied, yet all bunched together in a continuous wall, as though the dead were shepherding pedestrians to follow the path. Gillian eased herself down onto a wooden slatted bench, soaking up the fading rays of sunshine that would soon be little more than a memory. She lingered several minutes before biting the bullet to enter the church.

Inside, colourful fabric flags depicting angels hung from stone pillars between rows of wooden chairs arranged where pews might once have stood. Gillian sat and stared at the deserted altar, its cloth illuminated in prisms of coloured light from an ornate, multi-panelled stained glass window above and behind. In her mind's eye, a ghost of her own form processed down the aisle on her father's arm. The jewelled headdress shone resplendent, admired by a packed church of family and friends. Brent's eyes glistened with love and admiration as he twisted to glimpse his beloved during her glorious approach. Then the figures faded to dust motes drifting in slanting rays of autumn sunlight glorifying the house of worship. The enshrouding love of those imaginary well-wishers vanished with their dreamy spectres. This place wasn't helping at all. It felt like someone had peeled her heart and massaged in a hearty rub of sea salt and lemon juice. Gillian rose and walked in silence to the door.

Andrew and Coralie emitted a shared outcry of shock and relief when Gillian entered The Tennyson Gallery across the street.

"We were so worried," Coralie bustled from the counter to check Gillian over as though parts of her might be missing.

Gillian sighed. "I'm sorry I didn't call. It was thoughtless."

"Are you okay?" Andrew made a cautious approach. "An hour after you should have returned from your morning stroll, Coralie had me run down Wayfarer's Walk for a look-see. We were just debating whether to phone the authorities."

"I'm glad you didn't." Gillian pulled at her clothing. "I had a lot on my mind, that's all."

"Where did you go?" Coralie asked.

"Winchester."

"On foot?" the pair said together.

Gillian nodded. "Before I knew it, there I was."

"Have you eaten?" Coralie eyed her flat tummy.

"Yes. I stopped for a pub lunch with Deborah. Sorry again. I should have phoned."

Coralie rubbed her shoulders. "That's all right. We're relieved you're safe and well." Her mouth drooped. "Oh dear. Gillian, I wish there was something we could do. I suppose this will take time."

"Thanks. I stopped at the church on the way back. Thought if I confronted my demons after never making it to the altar, that might help."

Andrew sank into his right hip. "And did it?"

Gillian swallowed. "No. It amplified the pain and made things a hundred times worse."

"A brave choice, though," Andrew offered an attempt at bolstering her flagging confidence.

"Or dumb. I'm not sure." Gillian touched her brow. "I'm tired and have a headache. If you'll excuse me, I'm going to lie down for a bit."

Coralie stepped aside. "Good idea. Have a nice nap. Gosh, after a walk like that I'd need one myself."

Gillian wandered through the staff door into the back room. At the foot of the stairs she caught the shopkeepers' worried follow-on exchange.

Coralie sniffed. "She was so full of life before. Did you notice how empty her gaze has become? Poor girl."

Andrew grunted. "Mmm. Dead eyes. If they're the windows of the soul, we've received the faintest glimpse at how devastated she must be inside."

Gillian squeezed her 'dead eyes' tight for a moment, then trudged upstairs to the attic flat.

The last grey light of day illuminated a framed watercolour print of Alresford on the garret wall. Gillian started, awakened by the solid thud of Andrew setting security bolts on the gallery door way below at street level. Rain clouds hovered on the horizon. Combined with dismal fading daylight, they de-saturated everything in the flat. Colours drained to drab shades of black, grey or dirty pewter. As Brent's betrayal had sucked all chromatic variety from each aspect of Gillian's life, so the early evening environment on that day hammered one last nail into her coffin of resistance.

Gillian didn't stop to ponder. She knew if she did,

fresh power coursing through her veins might be thwarted and leave her forever in anguished limbo. She moved with robotic stiffness to a box of craft supplies and retrieved a length of nylon cord. An open-backed wooden chair wobbled as she stood on it to climb onto her tiny, square kitchenette table. Gillian looped the cord around a characterful, bending roof truss pockmarked with woodworm to present an appearance of flaky chocolate. Determined fingers tied a slipknot at the anchoring end. Then she fashioned a similar loop with the remaining cord and lowered it about her neck.

"God forgive me." Gillian wasn't religious, but in that moment where she intended to destroy the greatest gift given to us all, it seemed a reasonable statement. Was she hedging her bets? She closed her eyes. No, her spoken phrase bore no other connotation than to advise the universe: *this state of constant overwhelm has outstripped my resources to cope.* She was checking out of 'hotel mortality,' in hopes better places awaited somewhere beyond. One foot stepped forward to hover in mid-air above the kitchenette floor. Her thoughts turned to her parents and the cruel news they would soon receive. *How selfish am I? Will Mum and Dad ever forgive me? I can't go on.* Gillian wavered inside, the same way she wavered on the edge of the table. It was the table that gave resolution to events, rocking on a wobbly leg, then toppling from beneath her.

The nylon cord snapped taut around Gillian's windpipe. She swung in midair, but her neck didn't break. Panicked feet danced a hideous jig, while her tongue protruded in a morbid raspberry through gagging lips. Those emerald eyes swelled enough to almost pop from her ashen face like champagne corks. Both arms flapped, unable to grab the roof truss, so near and yet so far from reach in her present, regretted state of helpless horror. Airway restricted, she passed out unaware of the fraying cord torn by a rough section of splintered wood above the beam. Her swinging body tugged and sawed the makeshift noose into its ragged grasp.

On the ground floor, Coralie totalled the day's takings. A resounding crash from the attic shook both ceilings beneath it.

Andrew ducked on instinct, as though the entire roof were about to collapse. "What on earth was that?" He read the terror in his wife's face, then ran for the rear stairs.

Coralie followed hot on his heels, panting and whimpering throughout their furious ascent.

Andrew knocked on the attic flat door. No response.

Coralie called out. "Gillian?"

Again, silence.

This time Andrew hammered until the door shook, but no sounds emanated from within. He pushed past his wife, back the way they'd come. "I'm fetching the spare key. She can't have slept through that crash. Something's wrong."

When he returned two minutes later and opened the door, Coralie shrieked.

Gillian lay in a heap beside the overturned kitchenette table. Frayed ends of severed nylon cord hung like a leash from a neck turned blue to match her face.

Andrew swiped up a landline extension hanging beside the door. "Let's hope we're not too late."

*   *   *

"Respiratory distress, pulmonary oedema, convulsions, raised intracranial pressure and unconsciousness are all common during a suicide attempt by hanging." Dr Alice Carruthers' voice had lost none of its broad Scottish character, despite more than a decade living down south.

Bertram Crane found those tones soothing while the medical professional ran through her checklist of nasties. His wife evidenced no such reassurance, catching herself at the last minute before biting a nail on account of an uncharacteristic flap.

"What about brain damage?" Felicity pleaded.

Alice adjusted large-lensed spectacles. Rich ginger hair flopped about as she weighed up the question. "Permanent brain damage can be an unfortunate side effect due to lack of oxygen in some cases. Timescales are a significant factor. I understand your daughter's landlords were on the scene within three minutes of her falling to the floor. A lot depends on how long she hung suspended, unable to breathe. Paramedics resuscitated Gillian and gave her oxygen, but she drifted in and out of consciousness afterwards. She's still out at present and we've put her on a ventilator."

"Can we sit with her?" Bertram asked.

"Yes. She's in a private room along the hall. Number twelve."

"Thank you, Doctor." He pulled his wife close.

The couple locked hands, fingers intertwined, as they made for the half-open door of room twelve.

Andrew Tennyson stood up from a chair in the far corner as the Cranes entered. "You made good time." They were the only words he could find. Andrew thanked his lucky stars he didn't throw out some random comment about the weather instead. Silence wasn't an option.

"We shot down as soon as you called," Bertram replied.

"Thank goodness Buckinghamshire isn't far," Felicity added.

Coralie got up from a second chair pulled close to the bedside. Gillian lay connected to a bank of monitors, a breathing tube anchored into her mouth. Normal colour was returning to her cheeks, but she remained comatose. Coralie embraced Felicity, who allowed the forward, intimate action in deference to the woman's kind spirit. "Andrew and I feel awful."

"How did it happen?" Felicity held Coralie in a gentle but insistent grip to stop her pulling away while she obtained answers.

"Gillian left for her usual morning walk along the river, first thing. When she failed to return, Andrew popped out looking for her. She's been quiet all week since you left."

"Under protest," Bertram added. "She wouldn't come home with us."

Andrew offered him a seat.

Bertram declined with a wave. "I'm okay, thank you. Did you find her by the river?"

"No," Andrew replied. "We didn't know what to do. I couldn't believe we don't have Gillian's mobile number. Two years she's lived with us and the need never arose. Stupid, when you think about it."

Coralie continued the tale. "Gillian came home mid-afternoon. She'd walked all the way into Winchester for lunch with Deborah, then returned on the bus, tired and suffering a headache."

"She also stopped at St John's in Alresford, to see if that would ease her suffering," Andrew interjected. "Revisiting the scene of the crime, so to speak."

"That must have been difficult," Bertram replied.

Coralie proceeded. "She excused herself to take a nap. Her stare was so empty, it broke both our hearts. Right after closing up time, the building shook from the roof down. We ran upstairs but couldn't get a response from Gillian's door. That's when Andrew fetched the spare key and we let ourselves in. She was lying on the kitchenette floor beside a toppled table with broken nylon cord fastened about her neck."

Felicity let go of Coralie and moved to her daughter's side.

Bertram joined her across the bed. He stroked her matted, lava-like blonde hair with tender fingers. "Oh, Pixie. How deep must the hurt have run to bring you to this?" He leaned forward and kissed her forehead.

"She's up this morning and making excellent progress." Doctor Carruthers' Lothian accent carried down the hallway outside Gillian's room. "There are no indications of permanent neurological damage, and she's breathing without significant respiratory difficulties. Not what you'd call 'normal' yet, but on the mend and off the ventilator. A lucky escape." Her speech lowered in volume, causing Gillian to lean forward in her bed, hoping for a heads-up on the discrete disclosure outside. "So far, we've focused on her physical recovery. Attempted suicide is a serious matter. I *would* say people don't do it on a whim, but the reverse is true. They often do it on a whim without thinking, then regret it once a harmful chain of events start rolling."

Bertram Crane's voice muttered a soft response. "She was jilted on her wedding day."

Alice Carruthers drew in a sharp breath. "Oh my. That's enough to rattle anyone's cage. The poor young woman."

Felicity Crane joined in. "What do you suggest we do, Doctor?"

"I could refer Gillian for counselling, but a lot depends on where she's going to be once I discharge her."

"We tried to make her come home with us after the wedding fiasco, but she wouldn't," Bertram replied.

"Try again. Gillian has been given a rare, second

chance. It's possible she'll agree to your suggestion, after everything that's transpired." Alice paused. "You can't be with her every minute. Someone determined to take their own life will always find a way. But the support of her family in a setting removed from memories of that pain, could avert such an outcome. You may go in now."

"Hey, Darling." Felicity poked her head around the corner of Gillian's L-shaped private room, outside the en-suite bathroom door. She'd promised herself she wouldn't cry that morning at breakfast in Lainston House - an exquisite 17th century mansion hotel a short drive from the hospital. Upon seeing Gillian sat propped against pillows, looking lost and forlorn (yet alive), her resolve evaporated without hesitation.

"Hi, Mum." Gillian's voice croaked. A dark indentation stained her throat from where the nylon cord had incised and bruised the flesh.

Felicity reached the bedside to pull her baby close. Both women rocked and blubbed.

Bertram Crane appeared, clutching a fresh bouquet his wife had jammed into his hands when she ran for the bedside. He placed them on a nightstand beside a clear plastic jug of water. "It's good to find you awake, Pixie."

"Hi, Daddy." Gillian sniffed and wiped her nose on a paper tissue. "When did you two arrive?"

Bertram pulled up a chair beside the bed and sat. "The night it happened. Andrew and Coralie phoned us right after the ambulance took you away. We jumped straight in the car."

Gillian glanced around in vain for a calendar. She furrowed her brow. "How long ago was that?"

"Three days," Bertram replied. He leaned forward to share a mutual kiss with his daughter. "Listen. I know you wanted to confront the fallout from this situation on your own terms. But that hasn't worked too well. Much as I'd love to thrash Brent Fawley to within an inch of his miserable life, he's out of yours now. Don't throw everything away on a cad like him. You're smarter than that."

Gillian reflected on the subdued exchange with Dr Carruthers she'd caught at the doorway. Now her parents would struggle to broach coming home again, as though walking on eggshells. She'd put them through enough. It was time to redress the balance. "Would it be okay if I stayed at Retton for a while, after I get out of here?"

Felicity exchanged a watery glance with her husband. "We were hoping you would. Of course you can. If only you'd come back to begin with."

Gillian twisted the bedclothes between her fingers. "It's not Andrew and Coralie's fault, you know."

Bertram pressed a hand against her mattress. "Nobody is suggesting any such thing. They saved your life. Both have visited every day while you've been unconscious."

A gentle knock sounded at the open door, out of sight around the corner. Deborah Rowling's wide eyes peeped at the wall's edge.

"Deborah." Gillian sat up straight.

"They told me at ward reception that somebody is awake. Hello, Mr and Mrs Crane."

"Hello, Deborah." Felicity stepped aside to allow the new arrival clear access to their patient.

Bertram made to stand but halted at a raised palm from Deborah.

"Please don't get up."

Bertram settled back in his seat. "Here's another faithful friend who's been to visit every day."

A silent tear trickled down Gillian's left cheek. "I'm a lucky and ungrateful girl."

Deborah reached her side and the friend's embraced. "You're not ungrateful, Gillian. Hurting? For sure. Not in your usual frame of mind? Of course."

"I should have listened to you about getting some help."

Deborah sat on the mattress edge. "Don't fret about it now. Life's too short to have 'what ifs' getting in the way."

Felicity fetched a chair for herself. "Gillian has agreed to come home for a spell while she recuperates."

"That's great," Deborah said. "I'll miss my bestie. It's the right decision though."

Gillian reached for a glass of water. "If you've got any holiday leave spare, you should come and stay."

"Will I be sharing a stable with the horses?" Deborah raised an eyebrow.

"Stable? Horses?" Felicity frowned. "No, there's plenty of room in our guest wing, I assure you."

A faint cheeky grin chased Gillian' lips. It was the

first she'd managed since the day of her intended wedding. "I teased Deborah that she'd have to sleep in the stables if she ever visited."

Bertram chuckled.

Deborah brushed her work clothing with coarse strokes. "I'd best buy some smarter threads."

Felicity cleared her throat. "You'll be fine as you are. You're welcome anytime. The more friendly, supportive faces Gillian surrounds herself with now, the better."

"She spent time with my friendly, supportive face hours before jumping off that table. I'm not sure her doctor would prescribe a dose of me as medicine."

"That's not on you." Gillian clutched her hand. "Everything came to a head and boiled over. Almost a compulsion. I won't be trying it again. Thank goodness I didn't succeed. I'm so sorry, everyone."

Gillian's visitors gathered around in a tight arc of reassurance.

In the stillness of that private hospital room after dark, corridor lights still filtered across the far wall from a partially open door. Gillian stirred as its well lubricated hinges moved to allow more light into the room. The time was well after visiting hours. *A nurse coming to check on me, no doubt.* She still had trouble sleeping, and tonight proved no exception. Consciousness came and went. Inexplicable and confusing visions of a hospital ceiling from another room filled her befuddled brain.

"Where do I go now?" A young boy of around nine stood near the foot of her bed, clad in a hospital gown. Pallid cheeks sucked deep into a wan face, from which all the joy and optimism of youth appeared stolen.

Gillian lifted her head from the pillow, surprised at the odd intrusion. "What room are you staying in? Do hospital staff know you're roaming around alone?"

A warning buzzer sounded in the hallway. Feet thundered past, wheeling an equipment trolley. Someone called to the night desk staff in a gruff man's voice. "Which room?"

"Seventeen. He's gone into arrest," a nurse yelled back.

Gillian turned away from where she'd cast her face aside to the corridor wall and sound of commotion. The boy was nowhere in sight.

5

Chocolate and China

"Come on, Banjo, eat. Since you thought you could steal all my sweets, you might as well go the whole hog." Sally pushed three joined squares of chocolate into her brother's mouth between his bulging cheeks.

Banjo fidgeted against an old curtain sash, securing his hands together behind him on a broken-backed chair with loose joints. The damp, cobweb encrusted attic gained almost as much illumination from holes in the dilapidated roof as it did the two meagre, sixty watt light bulbs swinging from threadbare electrical cord stapled to the rafters. Banjo didn't recall how Sally overpowered and trussed him up like a trapped animal, but obviously she had. Now the bouncing chair, agitated by his ceaseless attempts to break free, dappled dust carpeted floorboards with fresh impacts. Most of the flooring hid beneath piles of junk and old wooden tea chests. Collections of long-forgotten treasures and sentimental memorabilia from former householders who'd passed away here. Derek had bought Ashburnham for a song after Enid's insistence they live a quiet life away from other people, their judgements and expectations. Even then it required serious money spending on it. In the years since, this crumbling shell, stuffed with historical bric-à-brac, sank further down the well of dilapidation towards oblivion.

Banjo attempted to spit out his mouthful of compacted confectionery. Sally clamped her hand over his lower face like a bung. Minor gobs of saliva and melted chocolate spluttered between splayed fingers to soil her ivory dress.

"Now look what you've done. Wait until Mum finds out you stole my sweets and spat chocolate all over this outfit. She'll lock you in the cellar."

Banjo jerked and fitted at her suggestion of punishment. His vocal cords twanged, causing him to half swallow the contents of his force-fed mouth. Scarlet of face, he banged the chair harder until its glue deprived joints gave up the ghost and collapsed.

Sally stepped back. The chair fell apart and her brother's hands slipped free of the tearing curtain sash.

Banjo writhed and choked on the dusty floor like a clockwork toy fallen sideways, spinning in hopeless arcs of releasing energy. He gasped for air with the dry, desperate attempts of someone in the worst throes of a chronic asthma attack.

Sally laughed and stamped her foot in sync with his gasps, mimicking some depraved fiddler at a barn dance keeping time. "Choke piggy, choke."

Banjo vomited a dark puddle of half-eaten chocolate and acidic bile onto the dusty grey floorboards.

Woodlice scuttled away from the disturbance.

A devastating cacophony of Enid's footsteps thundered onto the landing below. The attic door banged, and she stormed up the tiny creaking flight, bellowing with rage. "What on earth is going on here?"

Sally grinned at the gasping pile of arms and legs. "Now you've done it."

Banjo lurched upright in bed, cold sweat causing his now exposed upper torso to shiver. The memory of Sally shoving chocolate down his throat followed him into the realm of sleep. Enid had beaten him something fierce after discovering the broken chair and expelled stomach contents, reeking in an attic that already stank of mildew. Sally wasn't wrong about his punishment. He'd spent four hours locked in the cellar, jerking, fitting and uttering involuntary noises from his voice box. Ever since the garden pit incident, Banjo hated the cellar. Anywhere cramped and underground brought back those terrible memories in vivid, living colour. Still, something felt off about them in a way he struggled to fathom. Despite his protestations and an attempt to relay Sally's abuse, it was he who'd been punished again today. Enid appeared blind to her daughter's actions. He was formerly accused of almost drowning his sister. Their mother accused him of burying Sally alive and now of trying to choke her to death with chocolates. Enid's words still clawed at his brain. *"How could you tie your sister to a chair and almost choke her until she's sick?"*

Banjo turned over in bed. "I'm going to get you, Sally. One of these days you'll slip up. Then we'll see who enjoys the last laugh."

* * *

HIGH WYCOMBE - OCTOBER 2019.

Crowds milled about the High Street, stretching southeast from High Wycombe's elegant guildhall. Market day always found a bustling collection of traders on this section of the broad, block paved thoroughfare. 'Rough diamond' entrepreneurs hawking everything from fruit and veg to clothing, mobile phone accessories and household sundries. Further down on the northern side of the street, a smart parade of shops nestled behind arched porticoes of a three storey, red brick Georgian facade. One such shop was *'Cocoa Corruption.'* The owner of this artisan chocolaterie pitched his business from the unique selling proposition that his wares were so tempting, they could render the most resolute will helpless. It explained the title. How many people were put off rather than enticed by the word 'corruption,' was hard to quantify. It didn't matter to his full-time assistant, Tara Osmotherley, as long as they kept trading. The owner manufactured his confectionery at home and spent a mere token amount of time interacting with customers on site. Tara wondered about asking for a raise, since she ran all the day-to-day shop activity, aided by occasional part-timers. They worked late morning to early afternoon. At least their additional hours covered the shop's busiest periods and afforded Tara the opportunity to get away for a lunch break.

When it came to Tara's appearance, an ironing board frame, devoid of muscle tone with arms and legs the consistency of pipe cleaners, might turn any potential suitor away. But chest length fine blonde hair surrounding the most adorable, heart-shaped face with dimpled chin slowed any retreat. Glittering sapphire eyes and fruity coral lips pulling back to reveal a pristine smile, nailed those escaping feet to the floor. Angular and without curves she might be, sporting minuscule, 'fried egg' boobs; yet the twenty-five-year-old rarely went home for the day without acquiring at least one new phone number from a smitten member of the opposite sex. She'd tried dates with one or two, but excused herself early in the evening to go home and lay down in a darkened room.

Tara could be the life and soul of the party, but only in small doses. She adored helping customers discover new tastes in chocolate, or sourcing the perfect gift for a loved one. Yet once the day was over, her energy flagged. Where did people find the get up and go to entertain social lives or pour more of themselves out to family after work? She'd even visited her GP for advice. After blood tests for thyroid issues drew a blank, the doctors put her lack of energy down to a physiology which processed more sensory input than the majority. Now well documented thanks to the work of clinical psychologists and other medical professionals, this discovery brought some relief. What it didn't do was 'fix' what others often perceived to be a problem, but which Tara had since learnt to accept.

One side effect or 'gift' of her inherited trait (depending on your viewpoint), was an ability to connect with people and sense their needs. It amazed the part-timers how she could size a customer up, ask a few questions, then sell them a particular chocolate item with flavours so perfect a fit as to be the confectionery equivalent of a tailored suit. They left the shop delighted and soon transitioned into repeat customers. Another oddity of Tara's makeup came in the form of noticing subtle details and patterns in both her surroundings and the behaviour of others. On this particular morning, that oddity manifested as a prompting in her gut over a pensive passer-by who'd buzzed the shop exterior half a dozen times already. On each pass he peered through the window with stormy grey eyes set in a balding head. Scruffy and built like a brick shithouse, the man smoothed his stubbly, light brown beard while sizing up the shop, its patrons and Tara herself. No stranger to sometimes unwanted male attention she may have been, but something about that guy made her uneasy. He wandered off again. Tara hoped it would be for the last time.

A high cheek-boned, middle-aged woman pushed open the shop door with one hand. A girl no older than five clutched tight to the other, bundled up in warm clothing. If they sent children to join the British Antarctic Survey, Tara imagined they'd dress them in identical apparel to this kid. She squinted at sunlight intruding beneath the arched portico shadowing the storefront. *That's odd, it's pleasant out. Light jacket weather at worst.* She smoothed down her dress while the pair approached her wide, glass-fronted counter stuffed with trays of truffles. Spheres of white, brown and dark chocolate dusted with cocoa, lured patrons in for a closer look. The child pressed her nose against the cool glass, unblinking eyes spheres of pure wonder at the calorific treasure chest before them.

The woman accompanying her eased the girl back with a gentle hand. "Not so close, Mandy. You'll fog up the glass." She rubbed the back of her own neck as she addressed Tara, touching errant strands of coloured blonde hair. "Sorry about that. My granddaughter has suffered a severe chest infection for weeks. I'm looking after her while her mother is at work."

Now the heavy duty clothing made sense. Tara wondered if granny was killing her with kindness. They kept the chocolaterie at a constant, cool, air conditioned temperature; yet she couldn't imagine wearing a coat in here for long. "That's all right. I polish that counter front five or six times a day." Tara pulled out a spray bottle of chemical cleaner, then popped it back.

The child inhaled a dreamy breath. "It smells sweet and yummy in here, Nanny."

Tara leaned forwards. "What's your favourite sweet smell? Can you name any of the flavours?"

The child sniffed, tongue protruding from one corner of her mouth in deep thought. "Orange." She tried again. "And strawberry." She broke into a toothy grin upon this second assessment.

Tara performed a delicate, pretend clap by tapping fingers against one palm. "Very good. We sell both those flavours in a variety of chocolates."

"She adores anything strawberry," the older woman commented. "We had floods of tears once the season ended this year."

"Bless." Tara beamed, head cocked on one side. "What can I get you?"

"I brought Mandy in for a look. Yours is one of the quieter shops. She doesn't enjoy noise and crowds."

"I know the feeling," Tara nodded. "I'm not the biggest fan myself. Would she like to try something with strawberry in?"

The woman studied the artisan chocolates fronted by eye-watering artisan price tags in gold script. She gulped.

Tara's sensitivity radar registered her immediate discomfort. "We don't charge for a taster." Her eyes glittered and set the lady at ease. "I'm Tara."

"Gladys." The woman gave an appreciative squint.

Tara winked at the child. "And this is Mandy?"

The girl fidgeted on the spot, still entranced by the chocolate display.

Tara squatted behind the counter and pulled out a tray of dark chocolate blobs with bright red nipples. She straightened up to place them on top.

"They look a tad racy," Gladys smirked.

"My boss calls them 'Strawberry Seduction.' I have no idea whether the anatomical similarity of their appearance is deliberate, though they fit his marketing strategy. Each is formed from a high percentage cocoa dark chocolate."

"Isn't that bitter?" Gladys asked.

"It depends on the quality. Cheap, high cocoa percentage chocolate from supermarkets tastes bitter because it's inferior. These have no aftertaste, but contrast with the rich strawberry cream filling to deliver a balanced experience on the palate. The red nipples are strawberry sherbet, to tingle the tongue." Tara noticed Mandy wore woollen mittens attached to her coat sleeves with strips of white elastic. She slipped out from behind the counter to crouch before the child, one Strawberry Seduction chocolate clasped between thumb and forefinger.

Mandy stood on tiptoe and opened her mouth without further prompting.

Tara popped the treat onto her extended tongue. Hairs rose on the back of her neck, drawing her face towards the street. The weird, balding hulk had reappeared. He scowled at her through the window. His taut face reddened with inexplicable rage, intent on her action of feeding young Mandy one of the shop's wares. *He must be a vagrant or on drugs.* Neither explanation satisfied Tara's busy mind, but a slurp of childish delight returned her focus to the happy, overdressed child. "Did you enjoy that?"

"Mmm. It was scrummy." She tugged at Gladys' skirt. "I'd love some of those to take home, Nanny."

Tara caught Gladys' worried expression as she rose.

Gladys grimaced. "I'm afraid you've done it now."

She fumbled in her handbag. "I suppose I could take half a dozen."

Tara rummaged in a box out of sight behind the counter. "I've an idea. Would she mind having some if they're less than perfect?"

"Do you sell those?"

"No. My boss would have a fit if I did. There're always some 'runts of the litter' in a large batch that he wouldn't put on display. Most people can't tell the difference, but he's a particular man so we don't question it. Staff receive them to take home or eat on the job as a perk." She showed off her trim figure. "I don't indulge often, so I'm owed a few. Here we go. I can let you have eight Strawberry Seductions with wonky nipples. Even better than six."

"Eight will be fine. How much?"

Tara read the relief on Gladys' brow. "No charge. But please don't tell people we're handing out free odd chocolates, or I'll wind up looking for another job." She dropped the treats into a small paper bag and leaned back over the counter. "There you go, Mandy. Here are eight strawberry chocolates as a get well present for you."

Mandy clutched the bag between her mittens, face a picture of rapture.

Gladys nudged the girl. "What do you say?"

"Thank you," Mandy gasped.

Tara licked her lips. "You'd best let Nanny put them in her handbag, so they don't melt."

Mandy passed the package to Gladys as though it were The Holy Grail.

Gladys tucked them away in her handbag. "There's not much chance of melted chocolate outside today, despite the sunshine. Still, she won't drop or squash them this way." She zipped the bag again. "Thank you, Tara."

"You're welcome." Tara shifted into professional mode with an eye to her employer's bottom line. "Should you require a tasty gift for a special someone on a future occasion, perhaps you'll consider us?"

"I'm sure I will. Say goodbye, Mandy."

Mandy waved as Gladys led her to the door. "Bye. Thank you for my present."

Tara watched them depart, relieved the male weirdo outside had vanished again.

Harry Perrino the business owner arrived as Tara was cashing up alone. The part-timers had left three hours prior, as per usual. A mid-forties, slick haired, second generation Italian immigrant, Harry brimmed over with infectious enthusiasm for his chocolate passion.

"Hello, my lovely. How was your day?" He scanned the shelves and counter to ensure no items sat out of place or at jaunty angles. Nothing was allowed to confound his idea of retail confection perfection.

"Takings were up on an average Tuesday."

Harry rubbed scratchy designer stubble. "With folk buying for themselves, rather than as gifts?"

Tara bit her tongue. "It's scary how you know that. Are you psychic?"

Harry laughed. "A sign of the season. The weather

turns grey and light levels drop. People lose the higher Vitamin D offered by summer sunshine to enhance their mood, so they seek an alternative endorphin release."

"Chocolate being the natural choice as a feel-good food that's also indulgent?"

"Esattamente." Harry waved his right index finger with a flourish to accompany that sudden diversion into Italian with overdone pronunciation. Tara had observed Harry use this technique whenever he wished to make a point, or close the deal on an undecided customer wrestling with his extortionate prices. The fact he was born and grew up in Fulham mattered little.

The final warning tones of the shop burglar alarm halted, announcing it had set. Harry Perrino watched passers-by on the High Street, hurrying off home with their shopping. He nudged Tara. "I'll see you first thing in the morning. I've created a new truffle with ginger and caramel that I'm going to bring in."

"Does it have a name yet?" Tara zipped her jacket.

"Autumn Fire. I thought the warmth of ginger mixed with caramel sweetness would conjure up images of the season in the minds of our customers."

"Nice label. Clever. I can't wait to try one."

"Ciao, Tara. Have a good night." Harry sauntered off, hands stuffed into his trouser pockets.

"You too." Tara walked away in the opposite direction.

Despite tired decor adorning shabby rooms afflicted by a faint, musty aroma air fresheners never overcame, Tara's rented garden flat remained her cherished sanctuary. It occupied the rear ground floor section of a tidy Edwardian villa in a quiet, residential backstreet. Here she could decompress from the day's physiological overload and reach sensory equilibrium again. She paused at the gate beneath a streetlight to retrieve her keys. The jangling bunch slipped from her grasp to clatter on the pavement.

"Shit." Tara crouched to retrieve them. When she looked up, the tall, dark man with the domed head and angry eyes stood four feet along the footway, intense stare fixed upon her every movement. Tara straightened and attempted to make herself appear larger than the obvious reality of her slight form. Her jugular pulsed hard. "Who are you?"

The figure remained silent.

Tara pushed open the front path gate, slipped through and closed it behind her. It was a futile gesture, considering an average person could step across the low fence without stretching. But creating a barrier bolstered her courage. She glanced across her shoulder to find the street-facing, ground-floor flat lights on. *Thank God Gary and Angela are home. They'll come running if I yell.* She faced forward again and released an involuntary yelp. The sinister, stocky witness stood before her on the other side of the gate, two feet away.

Tara gritted her teeth. "What do you want? I saw

you watching me at the shop today. If you don't leave, I'll call the police."

An intimidating smile crept across his silent face.

Tara pointed up the road. "Get stuffed."

The man lingered a moment longer, then hurried away into the night. One amusing concept rose to prominence above the convoluted mass of mental images haunting his soul: *That's just what I was thinking about you.*

*   *   *

ALRESFORD - OCTOBER 2019.

Gillian wrapped a dainty, bone china teapot in grey packing paper. She deposited it beside other crockery in a sturdy cardboard box resting on the limited worktop space in her attic flat kitchenette. That teapot had been one of the first household items purchased during those initial heady weeks setting up home on her own, two years prior. She'd found it at the Alresford Craft Show on West Street, where exhibitors purveyed an array of handmade finery. It was at this show she first met Deborah Rowling, who'd fallen in love with a blue glazed pottery vase. Deborah bore the item in the crook of her arm like a proud mother with a new-born baby. The women laughed at how funny each looked, guarding their treasures. They went for drinks afterwards, then an excursion on the '*Watercress Line*' heritage steam railway a few days later. From that moment on, the pair became firm friends.

Gillian stroked the packaging.

"Knock, knock," Deborah's voice called from the landing hallway. The door remained open. Andrew and Coralie were nervous about leaving Gillian alone in the flat for extended periods after she came home from hospital. Now she kept the door ajar whenever possible, for their peace of mind and her own.

"In here," Gillian answered.

"There you are." Deborah appeared next to the righted table from which Gillian had taken her fateful plunge. She grimaced at the item of furniture. "Does it feel morbid or scary coming back here?"

Gillian shook her head. "I freaked out when I first saw that table. Andrew and Coralie were with me. They asked if I'd like it removed."

"You said 'no' then?"

"That's right. I've eaten so many heart-warming meals here. Once the initial shock wore off, it became nothing more than a table again. The memories remain, but their power has lessened. Although, for the first couple of mornings I confess I ate breakfast in bed."

"I'll bet you did."

Gillian lifted the teapot back out of the box and pulled aside enough paper for Deborah to identify it. "Do you remember this?"

"Aw." Deborah touched her heart. "We were like two young mums showing off our kids at a village social."

Gillian forced an awkward smile. "Especially you with that jolly vase."

Deborah stuck her nose in the air. "Some loves last a

lifetime. I fell headlong that day."

Gillian swallowed, tone flat. "Some loves last a lifetime." Those repeated words whispered to the wall. She scanned Deborah with sad eyes. "And some don't."

"Oh, Gillian. I didn't mean to bring all that up again." Deborah reached for her.

Gillian accepted a momentary embrace, rubbing her friend's shoulder blades. "I'm okay. I've got to quit thinking about Brent and what he did. Time to move on with my life and stop wallowing. Self-pity is a most unattractive quality."

Deborah prodded her upper arm. "It's a good job you've *some* unattractive qualities. They give the rest of us a sporting chance with the opposite sex, Fairy Princess."

Gillian's eyes sparkled. "Flatterer."

Deborah sighed. "Brent's not worth another thought. I hate the bastard, but even I'm tired of fallout from his betrayal monopolising my attention and emotions. And he wasn't even my fiancé. If I found myself alone with him in an empty room except for my vase… Well, I'd smash it over his head."

Gillian grinned. "What happened to 'some loves last a lifetime?' That changed in a flash."

Deborah re-packed the teapot for her. "No, it didn't. Love for my bestie takes precedence."

"I hope you get away and come visit, soon."

"Now Mummy Crane has extended the royal invitation? Try to stop me." Deborah put on a faux, haughty air. "I can cut caviar with the best of them."

Gillian snorted. "You don't cut caviar. It's fish eggs."

"Well, whatever," Deborah batted the comment aside. "Will Andrew and Coralie rent this place out after you leave?"

"Not right away. They're insistent on holding it, in case I return."

"Oh, the darlings. Can they afford that?"

"No idea. I suppose. Every time I encourage them to let the place, they put up a conversational brick wall."

Deborah wandered into the main living area. "That's because they love you. There's a lot of that going around, in case you haven't noticed. Amongst decent people, anyway."

"I know. I'm sorry I forgot and rode roughshod over it." Gillian rested against the small kitchen table. "What a selfish bitch."

"Don't run yourself down, Gillian. We've been over this before." Deborah stiffened. "Besides, can you imagine Andrew and Coralie interviewing some poor soul as a prospective tenant? The candidate could qualify for sainthood, and it still wouldn't suffice. As far as those two are concerned, you're a tough act to follow. Impossible, even."

"Daddy's little rich girl?"

"Daddy's warm, sensitive, artistic girl more like." Deborah snapped her fingers to wake Gillian from a dreamy daze. "Hey. If you don't knock it off, I'll string you up from that bloody roof truss again myself."

Gillian bit her lip and flushed. "I'll behave. Promise."

Deborah moved to one of the dormer windows, where Gillian always sat to work on her jewellery.

"Are your craft supplies packed?"

"Yes. I loaded them into my car earlier. There are two bags of clothes, one of toiletries, and these kitchen items still to lug downstairs."

"I'll give you a hand. We should manage it in a couple of trips. A nice step aerobic workout on two flights of stairs. No need for gym membership."

"When have *you* ever joined a gym?"

Deborah shrugged. "Never. Can you imagine me on a treadmill? That's not a pretty picture."

"When you visit, I'll take you riding."

"On one of those horses I was supposed to be sleeping with?" A wicked light danced behind Deborah's eyes. "Not in the literal sense, of course."

Gillian played along. "Oh, I don't know. Dad's stallion, Troy, is hung better than any man I've ever seen."

"Bestiality? Ew, now I know your sense of humour is returning." She hesitated. "That's a good sign."

Gillian lifted her box of china off the worktop with a puff. "There you go. Your presence is balm after all."

Deborah reached her side and forced the box down again. "I'll take that. You grab one clothing bag."

Gillian rested both hands on her hips. "I'm not an invalid or weakling."

Deborah hoisted the chinaware container into her own arms. "It's a question of build best suited to the job. If we're still using that horse analogy, you're an Arabian or Lipizzaner."

"So what does that make you?"

Deborah staggered towards the open flat door with

her heavy burden. "A Shire or Suffolk Punch." She blew out strawberry cheeks. "An out of shape one."

Gillian shouldered a soft bag of clothes. "I've always thought of you as more of a Clydesdale."

Deborah frowned at her from the landing. "You'd better run like a bloomin' Arabian or Lipizzaner once I put this bag down."

Gillian stuck out her tongue. "There, there. If you're a good mare, I'll treat you to a nosebag of oats once we get downstairs."

Deborah gave Gillian a pretend kick up the backside as she squeezed past to take the lead. The act of exchanging their signature cheeky remarks eased understandable concerns she still harboured for her best friend's wellbeing. Gillian wasn't out of the woods yet, but it heartened Deborah to see her transition from gloom and despair to evidence the healing presence of good spirits.

When Gillian left Buckinghamshire, her father insisted on buying her a brand new car. He'd stressed the importance of owning a reliable motor. Ever of a practical mind, Gillian opted for a black Nissan Qashqai, eschewing offers of a more expensive Mercedes M-Class. She'd have been happy with a used five-year-old model, but Bertram wouldn't hear of it. Gillian liked the crossover vehicle for its ride height, capability on English country lanes, sporty looks, sensible boot and versatile cabin space. It hunkered down like a puma ready to pounce, even with the engine switched off. Yet Gillian still found its 'face' friendly. A career producing jewellery that required a keen eye for aesthetics, meant such details mattered to her visually inclined temperament.

The car sat outside the gallery, large silver alloys and matching door mirrors gleaming in low autumn sunlight. Gillian had folded the rear seats forward to allow a full 860 Litres of cargo space. Half of that now remained after her earlier trips to load up.

Gillian fed her clothes bag into the storage area, then helped Deborah deposit the chinaware in a secure spot. "One more trip and we're done. I can fetch the last bags of clothes and toiletries myself."

"Don't be silly, I-"

Gillian halted Deborah's protest with pleading eyes. "I know it's silly, but I want a moment to say goodbye to the place."

Deborah's tone softened to a flat calm. "I understand."

Gillian stepped back onto the kerb, pausing at her friend's follow-on comment.

"Hey, you've packed the nylon cord away already, right?"

Gillian blew her a sarcastic kiss, then disappeared back inside.

Upstairs in her garret, Gillian moved from area to area. Each sang with abundant memories of life in her first independent home. "I'm going now." She had no idea who the statement was addressed to. A desire for closure saw her take one last, loving look before shutting the door and descending stairs from The

Tennyson Gallery attic one final time.

Andrew and Coralie were waiting beside Deborah on the pavement by the car when Gillian reappeared, bags in tow. Andrew clutched tight to his wife, whose attempts to put on a brave face scrunched her countenance into a bizarre range of unreadable muscle spasms.

Gillian dumped the last two luggage items into the Nissan and closed its boot with a soft but reassuring clunk. She'd envisioned this goodbye many times during the last few days. Its reality proved an impossible burden. Gillian struggled to get any words out without blubbing, rather than coming off as the picture of movie star poise she'd presented in her daydreams. She hugged each of the three. They'd spoken enough words in the period leading up to this event. Even Andrew resisted an urge to remind her she was welcome back; that her flat would be waiting, and that they wished for her return, in time.

Gillian started the engine and wound down a window.

Deborah stuck her head through, unable to let her friend drive off in silence. "Remember not to drink tea with your pinkie extended. You've got to take some of my slob ways back to Buckinghamshire with you."

Gillian brushed lips against her cheek. "If you're a slob, there's no hope for anyone."

"You take care. I'll see you soon." Deborah stepped back from the vehicle, eyes misting.

Gillian waved and released the handbrake.

The shiny black Nissan Qashqai pulled away into a hazy street sprinkled with falling leaves of red and gold.

6

A Spiritual Home

Gillian shifted down and signalled right off the A40 at Beaconsfield, heading north. She followed the undulating, tree-lined road across a rolling landscape towards Amersham. Along the way, her left foot tapped to chart music resonating from the Nissan's impressive Bose audio system. An initial heaviness at leaving Alresford and her friends behind eased once she passed a welcome sign for her home county.

Gillian skirted Amersham to drive northwest towards the picturesque and prosperous settlement of Great Missenden.

Great Missenden was an affluent village nestled in the Chiltern Hills area of Buckinghamshire, populated by approximately 2,000 residents of the Misbourne Valley. The busy A413 London to Aylesbury thoroughfare bypassed the village's narrow and historic High Street, cutting its centre off from an ancient church. Most worshippers now accessed their sanctuary via a bridge across the aforementioned bypass.

Gillian wasn't old enough to remember Great Missenden's most famous resident, legendary author,

Roald Dahl. He passed away a year before her birth. But she was raised on his wonderful children's books and visited the museum and story centre many times. Her mother once took her on a trip to the grounds of his former home, *'Gipsy House,'* on *'Roald Dahl Day'* when that tradition was still available to the public.

The village's reputation as one of the richest in England was well deserved. Country piles dotted folds of the Chiltern Hills, owned by bankers, stockbrokers and company directors like Bertram Crane.

Gillian pulled off onto a subtle, sweeping private tarmac drive skirted by trees and topiary hedges.

Set in twenty-three acres of land, Retton House — built in the early 18th century — was a fine example of Georgian architecture, harnessing proportion and symmetry. Ivy coated, the building could be vertically bisected into identical halves. Its chimneys and curved walls were mirror images of each other. A section in the back comprising staff quarters betrayed the architectural balance of the main formal house. Its interiors weren't ostentatious, but featured generous proportions. Doorways, windows, and the central hall staircase were all expansive, adding lightness to a desirable home. Three storeys plus an attic and cellar, the building appeared as tall as it was wide. No doubt a deliberate design choice summoned from the skilled depths of an ordered mind belonging to its architect.

The black Nissan Qashqai rolled to a halt before a tall, arched door the colour of faded peaches, accentuated by a glossy white surround. Classic bar windows occupied the two floors immediately above, with the top storey comprising a frame half the height and number of panels (two rows of three smaller panes, rather than four rows of three). This reduction in proportions relative to the two equal sized lower floors was a common design feature of the period. Either side of the doorway, the house bulged outward in matching tower-like sections the height of the structure. Each stood crowned by slate capped, shallow domes melding into classic angles of the main roof behind. Combined with the less interesting square bulk of the building, featuring attic skylights and two identical red brick chimneys, Retton House presented a footprint from the air similar to an old cartridge of photographic film. Each semi-circular bulge included three windows per floor, allowing light into those rooms from a variety of angles throughout the day. In a time before electric illumination, this stylistic element did more than ease the blandness of what might otherwise appear a dull block of a building. It enhanced light levels for rooms that would otherwise receive daylight in a single direction.

Felicity Crane's face appeared in one of the ground floor bays. As Gillian hopped out of the car, the faded peach front door opened. A furious but friendly series of barks accompanied a flurry of curly ears flying free, as a Blenheim Cavalier King Charles Spaniel charged between Felicity's legs. The friendly pooch darted across the threshold to make a beeline for where Gillian squatted with outstretched arms.

"Hello, Mace. How are you, boy?"

The dog hit her with such force, Gillian toppled backwards onto the driveway, giggling in time with a face full of licks while she clutched the energetic animal. The spaniel's tail spun like some deranged, out-of-control propeller. His barks softened to whines and whimpers of delight and heartsick affection, released at last after an absence he didn't understand.

Bertram Crane joined his wife on the doorstep. "Need we say Mace has missed you?"

Gillian clambered to her feet. Mace reached up on hind legs to prod her knees with his forepaws, tail still rotating. Gillian played with his ears. "We gave him the right name. Is there anyone he hasn't knocked over when he's pleased to see them?"

Bertram chuckled. "Mace had a better ring to it than '*Battering Ram*.' The label fits." He stepped down onto the driveway. "We're glad you're home, Pixie."

Gillian kissed him on the cheek, then welcomed her approaching mother in for an embrace.

Felicity walked Gillian towards the door. "I had housekeeping spruce your room up. There's a heavenly aroma of lavender beeswax polish on the furniture and shelving in there now."

Gillian pursed her lips. "Housekeeping. That'll take some getting used to again after life in my attic flat."

Bertram detached the overjoyed spaniel from Gillian's left leg. "You mean you didn't have housekeeping in Alresford?" He winked.

Gillian screwed up her face. "No, I did. It was called a Dustbuster and an old rag. Cleaning my garret took fifteen minutes. That includes freshening up the toilets, bath and basin."

Bertram stroked Mace's back in long sweeps. "Well, if you get bored, you may recall we've plenty of toilets, baths and basins to keep you occupied."

Gillian paused on the doorstep. "That would freak the staff out. They'll think you're fixing to get rid of them."

Bertram let Mace go. The act of stroking had tamed his exuberance. Now the dog padded over to Gillian and sniffed at her shoes. "I've never sacked anyone in my life. I don't intend to start. They know that."

Wealth never went to Bertram's head. His wife shared a similar, down-to-earth ethos. While their impressive home included devoted employees, the couple utilised staff as a life enhancement to spare precious time rather than something relied upon. Felicity loved to cook and cater, yet retained help for whenever she was too busy or the company too numerous and required her attention as hostess. A married couple acted as housekeeping for all chores about the immediate property. Beyond the house, a stable manager regulated the health, wellbeing and day-to-day upkeep of their horses. Retton's twenty-three acres were managed by a head gardener, assisted by occasional temporary assistants. Bertram liked to help interview those. If he found someone down on their luck, looking for any work they could find to put food on the table, he took great pleasure in offering them employment. One such previous helper - made redundant after fifteen years at a city logistics firm -

became a regional manager in his refrigeration company after the gardening post ended.

In the two years since her departure, Gillian had only been back to Retton House for the odd long weekend. Now, childhood memories of sliding down the impressive wide banister (to her mother's horror), flooded back as she gazed around the expansive main hallway.

"Good to be home?" Felicity whispered in her ear.

Gillian absorbed every nuance of the interior. "Yes." Her voice trembled.

"You sound uncertain."

"I'm glad to be home. Of course I am." The last word stuck in her throat. "It's just that I feel as though I'm in retreat. Like I set out to build a life of my own and failed."

Bertram entered the hall carrying two of Gillian's bags from the car. "Don't knock retreat. Sometimes pulling back to regroup is the best way to win. Think of the British Expeditionary Force. If our little ships hadn't pulled them off those beaches at Dunkirk, we'd all be speaking German and walking around like we'd over-starched our trousers. Anyway, you're recovering from a cruel injustice beyond your control, not a failure at daily life."

A beanpole of a middle-aged man appeared from a side corridor. "Goodness, Mr Crane. Why didn't you call? Let me help you with Miss Gillian's luggage."

Bertram dropped the bags. "Thanks, Gerard. There're plenty to take up to her room."

"Very good." The man smiled at Gillian. "It's heartening to see you home again, Miss."

"Thank you, Gerard. Is Katie well?"

"Tolerably, thank you. She's changing the linens on your bed as we speak." He passed her and followed Bertram outside to unload the Nissan.

Gillian and Felicity moved into a sumptuous living room occupying one of the front ground floor bays. Mace padded over to curl up before a crackling log fire with an antique brass fender. He rested his head on a thick rug, shiny eyes watchful but content.

"I'll have Jenny fix us a pot of tea. She's making your favourite soup for lunch," Felicity said.

"Lobster Bisque? Aw. Thanks, Mum."

"Back in a tick." Felicity popped along the corridor.

Gillian stood in the bay watching Bertram and Gerard retrieve her belongings. Gerard lifted the heavy box of chinaware as though it weighed nothing. In that moment, Gillian's adventure in self-sufficient solo living seemed a small and unimportant existence. Yet she missed the simple scale and cosiness of it.

"Was it very hard saying goodbye to Deborah and the Tennysons?" Felicity reappeared in the living room doorway.

"None of us had any words. Well, Deborah managed a quip at the last moment."

"Your father and I are so glad you met her. She's a solid friend."

"She is that. I can't wait for her to come and stay."

"In the meantime, given the season, we've arranged a little Halloween soirée to take your mind off things.

Fine dining, fancy dress. The kind of party you always used to enjoy."

"That's grand, Mum. Only..."

Felicity coughed. "Most guests will know what happened on your wedding day, but nothing thereafter. We've not discussed it with anyone, including the staff. They believe you're here to recover from an unpleasant experience. True, if not a comprehensive explanation."

"That's a relief. It'll be bad enough occupying the centre of attention after getting jilted. I'd die if our guests knew about my suicide attempt." She frowned. "No pun intended."

"We'd better find you a high-necked dress. Either that or cover that mark with a necklace." Felicity approached and indicated the bruise at the base of Gillian's throat. "Is it fading? It doesn't look as bad."

"Slower than I'd like, but yes."

"Hello there, Miss Gillian." A portly, fifties woman in kitchen whites deposited a tray of tea atop a low, mahogany table set before two plush blue sofas. "Your Bisque is ready and warming whenever you feel like it. Say the word and I'll have Katie set the dining table."

"Thank you, Jenny." Gillian deposited herself on a sofa.

Jenny disappeared back down the corridor.

Felicity poured out the tea and handed her daughter a cup and saucer. "There you go. Let me see if your father will join us." She walked to the doorway and called through into the hall. "Bertram? Tea."

Bertram emerged, tucking in his trousers from the

exertions of hauling Gillian's luggage. "Gerard is taking your last few bits and bobs upstairs now." He sat down beside his daughter.

"Thanks, Daddy. I'll move my car round to the garages after I've drunk this."

Felicity poured her husband some refreshment. "I was telling Gillian about Halloween."

"Marvellous. Thank you." Bertram took the offered cup. He nudged Gillian. "That's assuming a social with all those people under your feet isn't too much? We'll cancel if necessary."

"I can manage one evening. It might do me some good."

Bertram lifted the cup from his saucer and hesitated. "That's a relief. I've sourced twenty pheasants from Martin Naismith's shoot for the main course. He's hung them up to draw for me. Your mother will turn into Superwoman, no doubt: preparing food with Jenny all afternoon, then transforming like a butterfly into Cinderella to welcome our guests."

Felicity shook her head. "Charmer."

Gillian sipped her tea, knees pressed together in a demure pose. "It's kind of you to do this. I don't know how long I'll be back." She glanced at Mace watching her from the fireside. It was a relief he didn't understand a word, though Gillian wondered how much the dog picked up on instinct and emotional vibes.

Felicity set down her drink. "There's no expiry date on your stay. I know it's a jolt after two years building something for yourself. We both realise you're keen to return."

"Not until I've found my gumption again. I'll miss it there, but life became an empty hell after the wedding. Or lack of wedding."

"Quite." Bertram shifted on the sofa. "What we're saying is: take all the time you need. Go back only when and *if* you feel like it. Nobody is judging you. This is your home too. It always will be, as long as we own it."

* * *

Gillian sat down beside a lamp at her bedroom dressing table, taming those wild locks with a limited edition Mason Pearson brush featuring silver inlaid handle. It had been a present for her tenth birthday and was one of several items she'd unpacked before bedtime. A short, glass Art Deco vase of seasonal Scented Pinks sat on the opposite table end to the lamp; its blooms a 'welcome home' present from Joe, the head gardener. Gillian halted the brushing. Her emerald eyes stared back from the tilted table top mirror. Its hinges emitted a gentle whine as the reflecting device pivoted backwards.

Gillian put down her brush and set the mirror straight. An errant breeze from no definable source caused her shoulders to shiver. She cringed and rubbed them with her opposite hands, glancing about for moving curtains or other signs of atmospheric disturbance. All remained still. She rose and crossed to pull back thick drapes and check the windows were secure.

Below, between the trees and topiary bushes, a slender white figure flitted for an instant and vanished. Gillian drew in a sharp breath, fogging glass panes chilled by nocturnal autumn temperatures. She let the curtain fall and stepped away, rubbing her neck. She was still rubbing it as she turned to discover the dressing-table mirror had tilted upwards again. Gillian sighed and spoke aloud. "I must ask Gerard to tighten that for me tomorrow, or it's going to get annoying." She left the mirror at its odd angle and clicked off the table lamp. Now only a bedside light offered any illumination in the high-ceilinged room. Gillian pulled back the covers to slide underneath. *Who roams the grounds at this time of night? It looked like a woman.* She extinguished the final light source, then plumped a pile of soft pillows before allowing her head to sink into them.

Gillian awoke in the small hours to a resounding crash on the floor above. A puff of powdered plaster drifted down like fragments of sleet on a north wind to speckle her face in the darkness. Gillian rubbed her eyes and listened. A stamping of feet thundered across the upper storey, with the incongruous rambunctiousness of an excitable child at play. Gillian pushed herself up against the padded headboard. A rigid paralysis anchored her legs to the mattress beneath a heavy tog duvet. *There shouldn't be anyone on the top floor. That sounded like a reckless kid.* The footsteps thudded again. This time they descended the upper staircase to the middle landing. *My folks must have heard that. It was loud enough to wake the dead.* Gillian rubbed her numb shins to restore circulation. The sound of heavy running circled the landing outside her room like a horse at full gallop. Gillian swung her legs clear and inserted both feet into a pair of lambswool lined moccasins. Heating efficiency at a residence the size of Retton House always left much to be desired. She shivered and clicked on the bedside light. The running feet continued their unsettling derby. Gillian hobbled with uneasy steps towards her door. The cold brass knob twisted in her hands. She waited until the circling commotion came back around, then yanked the portal open.

The middle landing lay in silent stillness, washed by mild moonlight from the central atrium windows and dappled with shadows from the boughs of trees nodding in a gentle breeze. Gillian's mouth went dry. *What is going on? Am I seeing and hearing things now?* Her mind drifted back to the morning after that boy appeared at her bed in the hospital. When a nurse informed her a nine-year-old lad down the hall had passed away in room seventeen during the night, she'd almost choked on her breakfast. *Have I lost my mind or are my senses heightened since that brush with death?* She remained unwilling to consider the latter, but somehow it was less scary than the former. *Little rich girl goes to the funny farm. No thanks.* Gillian pulled back inside her room and closed the door.

"Why are you out of bed?" A boy's sudden,

vocalised question caused Gillian to shriek as she turned. No older than that child at the hospital, this youngster wore a smart shirt and trousers. He looked for all the world like a costume drama extra.

Gillian's shoulder blades pressed back into the wooden door, desperate to melt through the barrier like the ghost she feared this child to be. "W-who are you?" Her vocal cords strained.

"I'm Gareth," he replied with the indifference of someone asked to pass the salt at table. "This is the first time you've ever spoken with me."

Gillian fought for control of her bladder, fearful a trickle of urine might provide warmth from an unwelcome source to her ice cold, gooseflesh covered legs. "I'm Gillian. I've never met you before."

"You've always ignored me." His eyes appeared sad and hollow. "You're much older now than you used to be."

"Used to be?" Gillian's bottom lip quivered.

"When I tried to play with you before. Why are you in my room again?"

Gillian sank down on her haunches, unable to support herself in a standing position any longer. She wracked her brain for ideas to answer this impossible apparition. Hallucination or reality, she couldn't sit there like a stuffed lemon and ignore it. "How old are you, Gareth?"

"Nine. But I'll be ten soon."

"Where are your parents?"

"Mother had to visit her sister. Aunt Helena was taken ill, so I've been alone with the staff. Though, I've only seen Avril lately. Father is fighting for the King in the war."

"Which war?"

The boy tutted. "The only war, silly. The war to end all wars."

"And you've watched me grow up?"

A shadow of unwilling realisation and confusion fell across Gareth's brow. "Y-y-yes."

"So how can you still be nine?"

The boy backed away from her. "What's happening?"

Gillian pushed a fist against her mouth. "I wish I knew. But you can't be alive. The war to end all wars finished over a century ago."

Gareth scowled, eyes filled with fury and rising grief. "It's a lie. The war will end soon and Father will come marching home."

Gillian swallowed hard. Should she blurt out the truth, or let this tragic creature continue in his spiritual limbo of delusion? She opted for the former, inspired by a hesitant attempt at kindness and a desire to help. "Your mother and father are dead, Gareth. So are you."

Gareth sobbed, then yelled. "Liar! Dirty liar! Leave me alone. Get out of our house." He swiped Gillian's silver inlaid hairbrush from the dressing table and hurled it at her. It smacked her square on the forehead, then dropped to the floor. When she scooped it up and looked back towards the table, Gareth had vanished. She reached for the dressing table chair and used it to leverage her unresponsive legs into a hunched over, standing position. Her matted night hair hung in a straggly bush like some wizened hag as she gazed into the mirror. "Oh fuck, I'm in deep trouble."

*   *   *

"How did you get that bruise on your forehead, Darling?" Felicity Crane poured ice cold milk from a jug onto her muesli.

Gillian picked a slice of toast from a metal rack beside a choice spread adorning the circular, eight person conservatory breakfast table. A shiny black and white checked floor reflected ample sunlight streaming through the structure's curved glass roof to fill its fifteen foot high space with a cheery glow.

"A careless moment involving my hairbrush." She pushed vague truth telling to breaking point. Gillian hated lying to anyone, least of all her beloved parents.

Bertram lowered the top of his '*Financial Times.*' "Did you wallop yourself? It's all swollen."

"Something like that. I'm fine. Don't worry, I haven't regressed from suicide to self-harm of a non-terminal nature."

Bertram's eyes laughed, but he said nothing. He recognised his own sense of humour on display, reflected at him.

Gillian buttered her toast, leaving a pause before her intended cautious inquiry. "Has anyone ever experienced odd happenings at Retton House?"

Felicity hesitated with a spoonful of muesli held halfway between bowl and mouth. "In what way?"

"Unexplained phenomena."

Bertram put down his paper and poured out a steaming cup of black coffee, before scooping in two brown sugar lumps. "You mean ghosts?"

"Or unseen happenings nobody could account for. Noises, smells, draughts, moved objects and such."

Bertram stirred his coffee with a clang of the rotating spoon. "A house this size and age is full of noises, smells and draughts. As for moved objects, we're a family of three with a permanent and tidy staff of five plus occasional temporary help. It's a given objects won't always remain where you leave them."

Felicity finished a mouthful of her breakfast. She eyed the welt on Gillian's forehead again. "Have you experienced something unusual?"

Gillian cut her toast in half, unwilling to offer full disclosure of the previous night's events. Gareth had looked and sounded real enough. Nobody could deny the injury to her brow, so how could it have been the product of a mental breakdown? Not wishing to worry her parents further without more to report, she opted for a lesser truth. "I checked the windows before I went to bed, and could have sworn I saw a woman in white darting through the gardens."

Bertram blinked. "Really? That's interesting. I've not seen anything like that, although our room lies on the other side of the house."

Gillian took a delicate bite and flicked crumbs from her spare fingers. "After everything I've been through, I could have imagined it. I grew up here, but it dawned on me last night that I know so little about our home's history."

Bertram locked his fingers together and sat back in his chair, tongue pushing out one cheek in thoughtful swirls. "Retton has changed hands many times in its two hundred year history. Your mother and I moved in right before Christmas '89, almost two years to the day before you were born. The family we bought it from had owned Retton since the late fifties. There are odd documents knocking about in dusty business ledgers, but no comprehensive history of the house and its many residents that I'm aware of."

Gillian shrugged. "Not to worry."

Felicity sipped Earl Grey with a slice of lemon. "You could ask Old Joe if he knows anything. He spends so much time roaming the grounds at all hours in every type of weather."

"I'll do that. Thanks, Mum."

Bertram snorted. "Don't fall for any of his wild yarns. I won't thank our head gardener for winding you up with a prank. You know what a joker that fellow is. A dry sense of humour, when he lets it out to play."

"He hasn't pulled the wool over my eyes since I was twelve." Gillian left the rest of her toast. She folded a white linen serviette and placed it beside her setting.

"Darling, you've hardly eaten a thing. Two bites of toast. Is that it?" Felicity lifted in her seat.

"I'm not hungry. A little fresh air and an exploration of my old haunts might build an appetite for later." She got up and pushed in her chair. "The leaf colours are fabulous this morning. I'm going to take a walk and visit Joe for a chat."

Bertram shook his head dismissively at his wife's concerned face while they watched Gillian leave. "She'll be fine. A good roam around the great outdoors will do her a power of good."

"Roaming all the way to Winchester from Alresford didn't, if you recall?"

"She's in a better place mentally, now," Bertram said.

"What about this new interest in the supernatural?"

"Wouldn't you have a few questions about the great beyond, if you'd stolen a kiss from death like our Pixie? We'll keep an eye on her."

Gillian found Joe digging up spuds in the walled kitchen garden behind their stable block. At seventy-three, the white-haired man with bushy eyebrows and a mischievous twinkle in his eye showed no signs of slowing down. Despite drawing his state pension, he remained active and in the Cranes' employ. Bertram was happy for this to continue however long the old boy wanted, providing he asked for help as required and didn't push himself.

Joe rested one foot on the blade of his shovel. He removed a Tweed flat cap and mopped sweat from his wrinkled brow with a white pocket handkerchief.

"Thank you for my Scented Pinks." Gillian halted ten feet away so as not to shock their faithful horticultural retainer.

Joe twisted round. "Bless my soul, if it ain't Miss Gillian. However are you, young lady?"

Gillian inhaled a pronounced stream of air through

her nostrils. "Bearing up. It's nice to be home."

Joe stuffed his handkerchief back into a pocket of threadbare black trousers that matched his dark wellington boots. "Brave words a'ter what happened." He yanked the shovel free of loose earth with the strength of a twenty-one-year-old, then clutched it menacingly in both hands. "Why I'd like to get a swipe at that no good, slimy toss-pot wot left you at the altar." Joe's thick, rustic accent and wonky grammar ran as rich and earthy as the soil he tended.

Gillian couldn't hold back a smile. "I'd enjoy seeing you have that opportunity too."

Veins in Joe's cheeks turned into scarlet rivers matching the tonal quality of autumn berries. He puffed out a cloud of hot air which condensed to merge with the chill, damp morning mist. "Daft bugger must have a screw loose. You're better off shot o' him, Miss. Mark my words."

"Consider them marked, Joe. I was curious about something I saw in the garden last night."

Joe grumbled. "Not more bloomin' foxes? A'ter they banned the hunt, Retton's swarming with them bushy tailed ruffians. Broke into one of the coops last week and killed every chicken there. I came along to find nothing but blood and feathers, next morning. Bold as brass they are now, 'cos they've nothin' to fear. It wouldn't surprise me if I got back to my hut and found the little bastards drinking tea and 'elping themselves to the gingernut biscuits." He doffed the flat cap upon recognition of his profanity in Gillian's presence. "Beggin' your pardon for my language, Miss."

Five minutes in the old gardener's presence and already Gillian felt burdens falling from her shoulders. Joe brought a fresh perspective to any situation. "Think nothing of it. That's awful about the chickens. No, I saw a woman in white running through the bushes. Call me crazy, but I believe she was a ghost."

Joe's face steadied. His twinkling eyes flashed like diamonds reflecting in a torch beam. He jammed his shovel back into the earth and stepped onto the path. "You've seen her then?"

"Her?"

"Avril."

Colour drained from Gillian's cheeks. Gareth's statement the previous night: *'I've only seen Avril lately,'* resonated in her head. "Avril who?"

Joe shrugged. "Can't say. We wouldn't even know her first name, were it not for Katie."

"Gerard's wife?"

"That's right. It seems Avril was also a maid, back in her day. The Edwardian era or right after, I'd say from the look of her."

"You've seen her too?"

"Most of the staff have. She lived in our apartments, once upon a time."

"How did Katie discover her name? Has Avril spoken with her?"

Joe rubbed the back of his neck. "You'd best ask Katie that yourself."

"So it *was* a ghost?"

Joe nodded. "There's many as don't believe in 'em. Fools, I say. Any idiot who thinks people are nought but skin, bone and blood is as daft a prat as you'll find anywhere. We're souls, spirits, call it whate'er ya like. We don't cease to exist when this feeble vessel stops working." He thumped his sturdy chest. "There's some wot don't move on. Avril's one. Sad she is, when you get close enough for a look."

"What about a young boy?"

"Boy?"

"Around nine."

Joe squinted. "Can't say I've seen one. I've caught the sound of feet running around the bushes once or twice. Like a child at play, the spit of what you were nigh on twenty years back. Never could explain it, though."

"Thanks, Joe. I'll see Katie."

"She's got a pile of ironing going, over in the laundry room."

Gillian kissed him on the cheek, then giggled and hurried off with a spring in her step.

Joe flushed and removed his cap to watch her leave. "Well, I never. Ain't that the biggest perk a gardener ever received?" He turned back to his spuds, muttering under his breath. "Sweet girl. God bless her."

Gillian pushed open a cream, wood panelled door into the spacious, red-tiled laundry area. Sheets and garments hung airing. Gerard's wife, Katie, paid great attention to ironing a crease line in a pair of Bertram's trousers. Slight of frame with neat, short brown hair, Katie's forty-plus years didn't show on her creamy complexion despite a job requiring intense physical labour. She reached the crease end in time to notice Gillian enter.

"Good morning, Miss. How was your room? Everything all right?"

"Marvellous, Katie. Thanks." She studied the results of serious industry. "I hope I'm not intruding, but I wanted to ask you something?"

"No intrusion at all. I was about to take a quick break and a spot of fresh air in the garden. It gets hot in here with all this steam."

Gillian's blouse clung to her moistening skin. "I see what you mean."

Katie walked outside with her. They ambled along a curved path beside a bed of Dahlias.

"What can I do for you?" Katie asked.

"I saw Avril last night. The first time, for me."

Katie gasped. "In the house? She spoke with you?"

"No and no. She was down in the garden when I looked out of my bedroom window."

"How do you know her name?"

Gillian gritted her teeth. "I was about to ask the same question. Joe told me a little. He said she was a maid, and that he only knew her first name on account of you."

Katie pulled at her overalls. "That's right. When Gerard and I first joined the household as youngsters out of school, Mrs Crane was very patient with us. We both had a lot to learn."

"I remember when you arrived. I was only a little girl."

"That's right. One day you spilled some blackcurrant

cordial on the living room fireplace rug. I had a devil of a job getting it out. Nothing worked. Mrs Crane called me away to help Jenny serve lunch to company. When I came back, there was a pitcher of milk and a cloth beside the fire. Someone had written something with their finger in the unswept grey ashes."

Gillian leaned closer, fingers balling into her palms with anticipation. "Written what?"

"The message read: *'This will help - Avril.'* I daubed milk onto the stain and blow me if it didn't come right out."

Gillian touched the base of her neck. "Oh my goodness. Are you serious?"

"No word of a lie. It was after that I saw her in the grounds one night. I've not experienced her inside the house again, which seems odd. One night Gerard and I found her peering through our apartment window. I let out such a shriek, but my shock soon faded. She looked so sad."

"Joe said something similar."

Katie stopped to gaze across the grounds. "I've no idea why she runs through the gardens after dark. Something bad must have happened here, long ago. She's never harmed me. I wish I could help her."

"What about a boy in the house?"

Katie sighed. "I've experienced nothing else unusual inside the house, since Avril helped me with your blackcurrant stain."

Gillian halted at the path's end. "Thanks for your help, Katie."

"Pleasure." Katie turned back towards the laundry.

"Oh, Katie?" Gillian called.

Katie pivoted on the spot.

Gillian fumbled her fingers together. "I'm sorry about the blackcurrant."

Katie smiled. "No bother, Miss."

7

Terminal Treats

Relief came on swift wings to Tara Osmotherley the day after her encounter with the leering beast. Wednesday dawned with intermittent passing showers and breaks of sunshine. She made her bed and ensured everything was neat and ordered in her musty but appreciated garden flat. Stepping out onto the street where she'd faced down the balding menace, forced her to scan for signs of his presence. Her head remained on a swivel all the way to open up at Cocoa Corruption, but her stalker was nowhere in sight.

Tension eased in her neck while she prepared for another day of trading.

Harry Perrino arrived early as promised with his *'Autumn Fire'* truffles. As soon as the caramel and ginger sample coated her tongue, Tara knew they were onto another winner. That boded well for the shop's continued trading in a competitive commercial environment with substantial business rates. Or, from her practical point of view, it meant she'd keep her job, pay rent on the flat and be able to eat the basic but imaginative meals she cobbled together on a tight budget.

The day passed without incident. A few kids with moneyed parents visited the shop to purchase a range of upmarket Halloween treats Harry had created. Soon Tara was on her way home once more, delighted that Gladys also visited the shop again (alone this time) to purchase something special for an unwell, elderly neighbour.

Back at the flat, she dropped her house keys in a bowl and hung up her jacket in the postage stamp sized hall. A cardboard box of cheap, assorted mass market chocolates sat beside the door. She always kept some on hand in case of young Trick or Treat visitors. *Either I'm not feeling the benefit, or my boiler is on the blink.* She hugged herself at the chill atmosphere, then checked on a combi boiler mounted to the wall inside a shallow cupboard. *The pilot has gone out. That figures. It must be time for a service.* Tara held the reset button. The burners reignited without issue. *Thank goodness for that.* She entered the main living/kitchen/dining space, which opened onto the overall property's back garden via a pair of single glazed French doors with peeling green paint. Tara knelt beside a compact, tiled fireplace. A romantic at heart, she always kept the (usually unlit) fire stacked with a log or two and some kindling for those rare treats when she savoured the company of dancing flames. *Not so much for atmosphere as a necessity this evening.* A gust of wind unlatched one of the French doors. "What on earth?" She started from the disturbance. Tara left the unlit fire and hurried to secure the doors. A sharp blade or other metal object had shredded more paint around the lock, whose bolt now rested in a semi-retracted state of travel. "Oh, God." *Has someone broken in?* She shot her cheap TV and portable radio rapid fire glances. Both remained untouched. *Could someone have disturbed an intruder, causing them to run off? I'd best change my clothes and phone the landlord.* Tara dragged one of two worn dining chairs across to wedge the doors shut as a temporary measure.

She walked into the bedroom and unbuttoned her work blouse, before turning to open twin louvered white doors of a built-in wardrobe. Fierce grey eyes flared in the darkness between hangers of clothing. That balding monster from the day before surged out of the cupboard. One giant mitt of a hand clamped across Tara's mouth as the man pinned her to the mattress with his bulk. Hot air blasted from his nostrils against her cheek. Tara's sapphire eyes bulged in panic. Her attacker raised a leather cosh with his free hand. Its approaching, bulbous end was the last sight she registered in the confines of her intimate sanctuary.

* * *

ASHBURNHAM - OCTOBER 2019.

Blurred images of worn and chipped floor tiles swam before Tara's half-lidded eyes. Their character resembled something from a modest, rundown

National Trust property, pre-renovation. Her head ached above the right temple where the cosh had struck its effective blow. Plastic cable ties cut into her wrists, locked behind her back on a wobbly kitchen chair. Similar restraints lashed each ankle to the chair legs, with an old bicycle security chain running between both shins for good measure. A twisted cloth gagged Tara's mouth, fastened in a tight knot pressing against the base of her skull. The natural build-up of saliva from a mouth she couldn't close saturated the rag between her molars. Its accumulated fluid dripped a rank flavour from the dirty material onto her flexing palate.

Tara's focus sharpened. She sat in the kitchen of some sprawling, derelict house. The sort Victorian parvenus might inhabit on their way up a social ladder they'd yet to scale the full height of. Total darkness beyond windows set above the sink, suggested a lack of streetlights. That hinted at a possible rural location. No traffic sounds nor any noise disturbed the setting. Only a breeze rattling casements and shifting roof slates far above, accompanied Tara's auditory sweep for whatever information her subdued senses might glean.

The sudden, definite stomp of feet on a staircase descended above and behind her into what she assumed must be a hallway of some description. Deliberate hesitations between those steps drew out further, following each footfall. A tense wait for the next impact infuriated and agonised Tara in equal measure. What did this man want, and what would happen when he reached her?

"Woo. Woo. Woo." Every new 'woo' grew in pitch and volume, like a child playing at spectres. Yet this chorus arose from the voice box of a middle-aged man.

Tara craned her neck towards the hallway door, a faint whimper pressing against the foul-tasting gag.

A cavorting shape covered in a white sheet swooped into the kitchen. Strong arms raised beneath it to enhance the ghostly noises seeping from a bulge where the head must be. The figure spun, wild eyes glaring through two rough triangular holes. He stopped still as a statue before Tara. This spontaneous lack of activity unnerved her more than his insane ghost impression, because she couldn't see his face to read it. If a human stare could freeze, her abductor's would transform her body to the depths of cryostasis in a heartbeat.

"Trick or treat." The words muffled without emotion beneath the fancy dress shroud. His eyes burrowed into Tara's head. The ghost leaned forward to drag a cardboard box of cheap chocolates into view on a table beside her. Tara recognised the item without hesitation as the one she kept by her flat door for kids out on a Halloween frolic. The heavy, mitt-like hands reached behind to unfasten her gag. Tara seized the moment to summon the loudest scream her lungs allowed.

One meat hook slammed her jaw with such force, her head snapped left and almost broke her neck. Tears of agony flooded Tara's eyes, reducing her outburst to a heavy sob.

"Dirty witch, telling lies to our mother." The ghost spat from inside its sheet.

A crinkling of foil wrappers drew Tara's agonised face back around in an arc of stilted jerks. Those strong, banana fingers raised one of the chocolates. The triangular eye slits focused on it like a precious jewel.

"Do you remember when you accused me of taking your chocolates?" His voice rang cold, laced by a sinister undertone dallying with nostalgic bliss.

Tara blinked multiple times to clear saltwater from her eyes.

A sharp pinch of the nose forced her mouth open. The ghost stuffed his chocolate inside and clamped her jaw shut. "Now eat."

She chewed. The moment he released her head, she spat the chocolate out.

Another hand-whipping sent her face in the opposite direction. Blood seeped from beneath her lower gums, mingling salt with the sweet aftertaste of supermarket confectionery. In a bizarre moment of reflection, it occurred to Tara that Harry Perrino might make something special out of those two flavours, given enough time in his creative kitchen. What a place and situation to ponder it.

"You will eat every chocolate I feed you." Menace coated this new statement with an insistence that brooked no refusal. No soft centre lurked under that hard shell. He unwrapped another chocolate and inserted it between her lips.

Every motion of a now semi-dislocated jaw burned with searing fire down into her neck. This time Tara chewed. She couldn't endure another strike. There were worse fates than being tied to a chair and fed sweets. She hadn't finished the tubular, chocolate coated caramel toffee, when her abductor pushed another into her mouth.

"Chew. Don't stop unless I say, Sally, or you'll never use that lying mouth of yours again."

Sally? Tara shed a silent tear, fearful of the consequences if she deviated from instructions. How long would this continue? What happened when she reached the bottom of the box, if that were even possible in her present state?

Rough hands crammed two more chocolates into her mouth. Each fresh addition made swallowing those already undergoing mastication, an arduous task.

The ghost whipped round to stare into a corner. He hissed. "No, Mum. Sally deserves it. She needs to be punished. You never believed me when I told you what she did. Now she'll understand what it feels like." He threw his sheet aside to reveal the stalker who'd broken into the flat and abducted her.

Tara risked moving her head a fraction. Did another figure lurk in the shadows? The kitchen was dim, illuminated by a single, grimy incandescent bulb encircled by moths. She squinted through stinging eyes hard enough to reveal a mop propped into an empty corner. No other soul appeared from the dullness.

More chocolates went into her mouth; enough to make progress impossible.

"Chew." The ghost barked his order, hands clamping against her aching jaw to mash top and bottom parts together. When he sensed Tara's inability to respond, he pinched her nose tight again while keeping her mouth closed. Tara attempted to swallow, but the lack of air forced her to gag. Chocolate overwhelmed her windpipe. Choking erupted. Tara's restrained limbs shook with violent force against the chair.

The man knelt on the floor. In doing so, he pulled the chair and its restrained occupant over backwards.

The rear of Tara's head pressed into cold floor tiles. Panicked eyes stared at her upended feet, ringed by a halo from the dim ceiling lamp and its cloud of worshipping, paraphyletic insects. The man clamped her mouth tighter like a vice. Tara's body jolted and trembled, desperate for oxygen. A sick gurgle of delight from the balding monster chased each of her choking spasms. Her captor's own fitting limbs kept time and an eerie twanging noise flowed from his throat.

* * *

RETTON HOUSE - OCTOBER 2019.

Gillian sat at her dressing table before the mirror Gerard had examined. He'd found no loose hinges and the item of furniture now behaved itself. Gillian couldn't shake the thought Gareth had moved it in those oblivious moments before she encountered the boy's spirit face to face. Now prosthetic rubber ear tips expanded her elfin features. Folds of emerald green cloth in a puffed sleeve dress matched her eyes to present an image of the 'Fairy Princess' Deborah often referred to her as. The headdress Gillian made for her wedding day would crown her resplendent in such an outfit. But she couldn't bring herself to look at the decorative piece, let alone wear it. She sighed. *No. That's staying packed away in a box with my other stuff.*

Two gentle knocks sounded on the door.

Gillian looked away from the mirror. "Come in."

Felicity Crane entered the room, a slim, rectangular blue jewellery case clasped in one hand. "What a vision you look, Darling."

"Thanks, Mum. You're not so bad yourself." Gillian eyed her mother's figure-hugging black strapless one-piece, decorated with ebony lace spiders and bat motifs. "If they print a *'Coven Couture'* edition of Vogue, you'll make the front cover. Best looking witch outfit ever."

Felicity chuckled. "Thank you." She stood behind Gillian and placed the jewellery case on the dressing table.

Gillian nodded at it. "What's that?"

"Something I ordered from town. I hope you like it."

Gillian opened the case. Inside lay an intricate red and black velvet choker, from which hung a gold charm in the shape of a fairy with broad wings. "It's beautiful, Mum."

"I thought it would match your outfit and cover that mark on your neck like we discussed. Unless you've something else planned, or it's not quite right."

Gillian fastened the adornment around her neck. "Perfect. I love it. You can't see the bruising with this on."

"It should keep prying eyes and awkward questions at bay. The first guests are due any moment. Are you almost ready?"

"Five minutes. I've some glitter paint to daub on my cheeks." She hesitated. "Mum?"

"Yes?"

"Is Regina Pontefract coming?"

"I'm afraid so. I had to invite her, what with such an in-crowd attending. She still chairs the pony club."

Gillian winced. "I guess. She's as subtle as a sledgehammer. I'm in two minds whether one of her snipes would send me into a flood of tears or make me punch her lights out, right now."

"Neither of the above, I hope. We'll have sufficient guests to excuse yourself and mingle elsewhere for blessed relief." Felicity moved towards the door, then looked back. "You should see what your father has done to the family pooch."

"Mace?" Gillian grinned. Bertram had a wicked sense of humour and she loved it. "How did he take it?"

"With no small amount of whimpering at first. I wish you could have seen his little face. Gerard had to hold him still while... Well, you'll see."

Gillian bounced a little in her seat, trying not to spill her glitter paint. "I'll be right down."

"I thought that would stir you to action. You'll find me welcoming new arrivals in the hall." Felicity left.

When Gillian opened the door of her room, Mace sat

on the landing watching her with large, sad eyes. A pair of bright red fabric devil wings spread out from his back supported by strong wire. Two short, pulsing LED horns like emergency strobes winked from a comb fixed atop his head. A red painted sponge point clung to his tail. That tail sagged to match the confused animal's sullen mood.

Gillian clapped her hands together. "Oh, you are such a darling."

The pointed tail flicked in signs of hesitant life as the green fairy princess before him crouched to play with his fluffy ears. Mace opened his mouth in that way dogs often do that suggests a smile to onlookers.

Down below, beyond the foot of the sweeping staircase, murmurs of exchanged pleasantries grew in volume and number.

Gillian rose and patted her right thigh. "Come on, you adorable devil dog, you. Heel."

Mace obeyed the command without question. He walked beside her as Gillian descended the stairs. His daft appearance and winking horn lights elicited no small amount of chortles from canapé crunching attendees mingling in the hallway.

Bertram greeted Gillian at the foot of the stairs, clad in a shimmering wizard's outfit plastered with stars and crescent moon shapes. A pointed, matching hat sat back on his head at a jaunty angle. "Tonight nobody will question me calling you Pixie. Those ears suit you."

Gillian kissed him. "Thanks, Daddy. And thanks for my party."

"Do you like what I did with Mace?"

Gillian giggled. "I'm not so sure he does, but yes."

"From the noises he made, you'd think it was borderline animal cruelty. It's a good job Gerard is current with his tetanus shots. Mace gave his fingers a good old nip while he restrained our excitable spaniel."

Gillian's gaze wandered to the front door where Felicity stood beside an orange-haired, big boned woman dressed as a she-devil. If ever an outfit suited its wearer while providing an added hint of irony, that costume and Regina Pontefract were a match made in heaven. *'Or should that be - hell?'* Gillian wondered.

Felicity waved her over. Gillian gulped. She crossed the hall, accompanied by Mace.

Regina looked her up and down through mauve cosmetic contact lenses applied to round off her demonic costume. She sipped from a flute of champagne with floating blackberry, then swirled a taster around her mouth above a neck wattle of rippling puppy fat. After swallowing, her eyes twinkled at Gillian. "There she is: the spurned fairy."

Gillian clenched her teeth. She fought not to tighten agitated facial muscles and so give this overbearing woman the satisfaction of triggering her. *Regina Pontefract. Regina Pontefract. Regina Pontefract.* Gillian forced herself to mentally recite the woman's correct name, hoping to stave off an embarrassing social blunder. She despised her so much, in private she'd taken to referring to their local pony club chair as *'Vagina Ponceyfat.'* On one occasion she'd let the term slip out in person, but was saved by a hurried and skillful recovery on her mother's part.

Felicity cleared her throat with a polite cough. "I was remarking earlier how lovely our Gillian looks in her costume."

Regina scoffed. "Unfortunately appropriate. Poor Gillian. Fairies also remain loveless and unwed."

Gillian tried not to drill through the woman's head with a sudden, unblinking stare. "Oh, I don't know. Titania got all the action she wanted from Oberon, if memory serves."

Regina drummed black painted fingernails against her champagne flute. "What a base assessment of Shakespeare. Is that a Hampshire trait you've picked up? Where is it you live again? Al-rezz-fud or some such place?"

"It's pronounced 'Ulsford,' not the way it's spelt: A-L-R-E-S-F-O-R-D."

Regina's eyes narrowed. "How quaint. Well, it's a blessing Flick and Bertie were here to run home to, after your would-be husband found a better deal. Still, you've a few good years in you yet. That's what happens when you chase self-made types rather than sticking with society."

Gillian flushed. "I didn't chase Brent, he pursued me. And regardless of what happened, my father is also a self-made man. We're all the better for it."

Regina rocked on her heels, shook her head and turned to Felicity. "I've never understood you 'marrying out,' Flick." She glanced around Retton's impressive hallway. "Still, Bertie hasn't done badly."

"He prefers Bertram, Regina." Felicity's frame

stiffened at the cold barbs directed towards Gillian during her attempted recovery from near-terminal loss. Her mind wrestled with visions of ejecting this callous creature. She pondered how close Regina's behaviour drifted towards that as a justifiable course of action. But Regina knew her place all too well. She could skate along a knife edge of brusque impropriety, while retaining the balance of acceptability.

It was Mace who came to the rescue. Waiting with calm attentiveness by Gillian's leg, his enormous eyes had become mesmerised by a bouncing, pointed tail attached to the rear of Regina's dress. Humans weren't supposed to have such features. Somewhere amidst the firing neurons of his doggy brain, the spaniel decided Regina's tail would make a far better chew toy. He pounced without warning, gripped the tail between his teeth, then pulled and growled in a bizarre tug of war with the shrieking woman.

"Get off me, you spiteful animal." Regina spun first one way, then the other, champagne slopping from her whirling glass to Gillian and Felicity's amusement.

A ripping of fabric. Then the tail came away with the hind quarters of Regina's outfit. Chunky red buttocks, the rare roast beef of old England, spilled around the periphery of her immodest underwear. Panties suited to a thinner woman half her age.

Regina roared, eyes aflame. "Look what he's done. Your dog has left me half naked. Exposed to the world."

Ever the gracious hostess, Felicity attempted to calm her with little success. "Why don't I see if I've something you can change into?"

Gillian scanned between her mother's toned figure and Regina's surplus folds of flesh. "Like a tent, you mean?"

Felicity glared at her, but had to bite her lip to avoid smiling.

Regina scowled. "How dare you?" Veins bulged in her neck. "Flick, I'll not stay a moment longer in a house where I'm attacked by dogs. Nor where I suffer personal insults from your JILTED daughter." She stressed the word 'jilted,' with forceful venom to grab the attention of anyone not already witnessing the drama. "My outfit is ruined. I'm going home."

Gerard opened the door for Regina to storm across the threshold.

Gillian hunched down beside Mace, who sat staring after the woman he'd taken a severe dislike to. Words meant nothing to the animal, but he sensed Regina's animosity towards those he loved. Regina's costume tail still hung in his closed mouth. Gillian patted his back and pulled him close. "Good dog," she whispered. Her eyes registered Felicity's shoe tapping with faux impatience on the floor tiles.

Gillian straightened to meet her mother's discretely amused stare. "At least you invited her, Mum. Even if she chose not to stay."

Felicity wagged a finger in the air. "I'm in for a roasting at the next pony club meet up."

Bertram hurried over, distracted from an in-depth discussion on the volatility and net gearing of a favoured stock with a man his own age. "Is everything okay? I heard a commotion."

Felicity nodded towards the door. "Regina Pontefract stormed out."

"After being rude and spiteful to me," Gillian muttered.

Bertram frowned. "What caused her to leave?"

Felicity sighed at the tail hanging from Mace's dribbling jaws. "Mace took a chunk out of her costume."

Bertram gasped. "He did?" He squatted beside the animal and stroked his back. "Good boy. Pixie must have sprinkled you with fairy dust."

Felicity laughed. "You're incorrigible."

Bertram shrugged. "I only ordered twenty birds from Martin Naismith. Now there'll be plenty to go around, without Regina's gluttonous appetite. Speaking of which, Katie said Jenny is ready to serve. We'd best shepherd our guests through to the formal dining room."

Gillian signalled to Gerard, then turned to her parents. "Make sure Mace gets some choice scraps. He deserves a treat after that."

Smart, printed cards adorned each place setting in Retton's spacious formal dining room. Each listed the evening's three-course menu: '*Gazpacho, Pheasant and Chestnut Terrine with seasonal vegetables, Ginger and Rum Pumpkin Pie.*' Candles sputtered from the grinning faces of carved pumpkins adorning covered mahogany side tables. The lanterns added a fun, rustic air to sophisticated historical elegance.

Gillian sat with her parents on either side. Guests across the table remained far enough away to avoid in-depth conversation during the hubbub of dinner. None of the other attendees caused her concern. She'd grown up around many of them. In a curious emotional paradox, Gillian needed the bustling distraction of this party. Yet she still wished for a period of quiet, solitary introspection.

The diners were halfway through their main course when events took an extreme turn toward the bizarre and macabre. Gillian rubbed her eyes. The room appeared to fog and fade, despite her feeling wide awake. Food in her mouth swelled until it overwhelmed her ability to keep pace with chewing and swallowing. What went in as Pheasant and Chestnut Terrine adopted a peculiar cocoa flavour: like over-sweetened, budget supermarket chocolate, crammed with unnecessary fat, palm oil and milk powder. Gillian coughed and spat a mouthful onto her plate. It came out as terrine.

Felicity touched Gillian's arm. "Goodness, Darling. Are you all right?"

The room blurred further. An angry face with fierce grey eyes set in a balding head, thrust a handful of something towards her face. The dining room dissolved into scenes of a dirty kitchen, viewed through another's eyes. Again her mouth experienced the sensation of filling to near overwhelm. Gillian spat once more, but nothing came out. The kitchen scene flipped backward to reveal a dirty light bulb encircled by moths, like children round a maypole. The viewer's feet swung upward, chained and fastened to chair legs. In the dining room at Retton House, Gillian's chair tipped over backwards to accompany her desperate physiological response to the vision. The image's angry man clamped sausage fingers around her face. Gillian choked. A blue pallor coated her glittered cheeks as she gasped for air that failed to reach bursting lungs.

Bertram kicked his chair aside, then knelt over his daughter. "She's choking. It must be a bone. She can't breathe. Maurice?"

Maurice Gange, a private physician and family friend, darted across to join his hosts. "Hold her while I release that choker."

Gillian's eyes rolled in her head; sometimes showing her the dirty kitchen, while at others the closing crowd of diners and faces of her worried parents.

The choker clasp unfastened.

A shared gasp from assorted guests rippled through the dining room. Whispered comments of *'Look at her neck'* were difficult to ignore.

The kitchen scene dimmed to a black tunnel before Gillian's eyes. Maurice Gange lifted her enough to perform the Heimlich Manoeuvre. No obvious obstruction dislodged, but Gillian coughed, received air, then vomited down the front of her dress.

"Pixie?" Bertram's voice filtered in soft tones through the wood of Gillian's bedroom door.

Gillian lay on her side, facing towards the window with a vacant stare.

"Pixie?" Bertram called again.

"Come in." Gillian didn't move.

Her door opened and closed. The mattress sagged. Tender weight from her father's hesitant hand rested atop the duvet. "How are you feeling?"

Gillian remained fixed on the window. "Like a stupid, helpless little child." She shut her eyes for a moment. "Have you come to tuck me in, *Daddy*?"

Bertram released a reflective snort. "Not unless you want me to. I tuck your mother in when she's unwell. Imagine that: a fifty-five-year-old woman. What's your excuse?"

Gillian looked round.

Bertram continued. "And I hope you never stop calling me 'Daddy,' no matter how old and crusty you become."

Gillian sat up and flung her arms around his neck.

Bertram rubbed her back. "What's going on? I'm no expert, but that was more than a pheasant that flew down the wrong tube at dinner, wasn't it?"

Gillian held tight. Her head bobbed in acknowledgement.

"Do you want to talk about it?"

"I saw something. More than saw… felt."

"Saw and felt what?"

"I don't know. It was like looking through the eyes of another person. A woman, from what I remember of her shoes."

"What was this woman doing?"

"It's more a case of what was being done *to* her."

Bertram pulled her back in front of him, concerned

155

where this tale might lead. "Something bad?"

Gillian wet her lips. "I saw an angry man. Middle-aged with receding hair. He was stuffing something into her mouth. I... I mean, *she* was so scared. He was force-feeding her chocolate."

"Chocolate? Where was this?"

"I don't know. A kitchen. Old, dirty, dark and moth infested. She was chained to a chair. When it fell backwards, I couldn't breathe."

"You tipped your own dining chair over."

Gillian's stare flitted from side to side, brow furrowed. "That must have been the same moment. Hands clamped onto my jaw. The image faded to black. I saw you and Mum, then came round and threw up. Sorry. What a mess."

Bertram took a deep breath. "It was a Halloween dinner party to remember."

Gillian fidgeted. "Somebody removed my choker, didn't they?"

"Dr Gange. He was attempting to clear your airways."

Gillian touched the bruise on her neck. "The guests saw...?"

"I'm afraid so. Hey, better that than us losing you." Bertram looked away. "To their credit, nobody asked your mother or me about the mark. We won't be offering an explanation if any do. That's a private matter. None of their concern."

"I hope I didn't spoil everything."

"Mum ushered everyone out of the room to mingle. Gerard and Katie served slices of dessert in the hallway. An informal third course for people to enjoy at their leisure, between conversations. Many expressed concerns and offered well wishes for your speedy recovery."

"Thank God Vagina, err, I mean Regina wasn't there. The bush telegraph would work overtime around Great Missenden."

Bertram smirked. "Vagina? You still call her Vagina Ponceyfat?"

"Only to myself these days, after I embarrassed Mum that time."

Bertram stroked her hair. "So what do you reckon that vision was about? First ghosts and now this."

"Do you think I've lost my marbles?"

"No, Pixie. I don't think that. You've been under a tremendous strain of late." He rubbed his chin. "Do I believe your overloaded brain and nerves could produce the things you've experienced? Yes, that's possible. But you said our staff have all encountered that ghost you witnessed running through the garden. I can't put everything down to stress."

Gillian minced her palms together. She wanted to add, '*I spoke with the ghost of a young boy in here, too. I've never mentioned that before. I didn't want to worry you.*' Instead she went with a more conservative, "I've seen and experienced some weird stuff since I left hospital. I haven't covered the entire list."

Bertram raised an eyebrow. "Nobody is suggesting you have to tell us everything. But, we'd like to feel trusted. Bottling concerns up and not sharing them can be dangerous."

"I learnt that the hard way already, Daddy."

"So you did. Well, let's hope tonight's waking nightmare was nothing more than a side effect or bump on your road to recovery."

Gillian slid further under her covers. "That's a nice thought. Is Mace okay?"

"That episode was difficult for him. He knows he's not allowed into the formal dining room. The poor dog stood whining in the doorway while Maurice attended you. He's settled down in his basket now." Bertram stood. "Oh, you'll never guess what?"

"What's that?"

"He's still got Regina's tail in there with him. A trophy from a vanquished foe."

Gillian smiled. "Goodnight, Daddy. Thanks for checking on me."

"Goodnight, Pixie." He leaned over and kissed her forehead. "Try to get some rest."

8

Rising Revelations

AMERSHAM - NOVEMBER 2019.

Paul Drummond spun the wheel left in the cab of his gargantuan yellow sewage treatment lorry. Beside him on the bench seat, colleagues Phil Harrison and Stu Webb studied the quiet, tree-lined side street for a suitable parking spot.

Phil clocked their dashboard mounted, work sat nav with the job location georeferenced onto a street level basemap. He pointed through the windshield. "There's the manhole, halfway down."

Paul signalled and pulled in. "It looks quiet enough. Should make signing, lighting and guarding a doddle for this job." He switched off the engine.

Stu crossed his arms. "As I was saying: I reckon England only lost to the Springboks because of the Yokohama climate."

Phil frowned. "How do you figure?"

"Simple. It's Japan, innit? Those South Africans are more at home in warm temperatures."

Phil unfastened his seatbelt. "So you're saying their fly-half, Pollard, landing six penalties and two

159

conversions had nothing to do with it?"

"No. I'm saying he landed them because he was well acclimated."

Paul retrieved the ignition keys. "32-12 is a big difference for nothing more than familiarity with playing rugger in a warm environment. How much did you put on the World Cup?"

Stu flushed and lowered his eyes. He muttered. "A monkey."

Phil's mouth dropped open. "Five hundred quid? Are you mad?"

Paul opened the driver's door. "Does your missus know?"

Stu shook his head as he and Phil decamped the other side.

Phil clapped him on the back. "If I put more than a pony on the rugby, Carol would file for divorce. Even if I bloody well won! It's the principle. You won't be celebrating Guy Fawkes with extra fireworks this year. Not unless they're the marital kind."

Paul stretched and sniffed the air. "Make the most of that clean smell, boys."

Stu grinned, relieved to focus on something other than his gambling loss. "Why us? It's your turn in the hole."

Paul squinted, then slapped a palm across his forehead. "Shit, you're right."

Phil unhitched a road sign from the enormous vehicle with its smelly, tubular tank reeking of stale excrement. "Shit is the word. You're about to be waist deep in it."

Within fifteen minutes the trio had arranged signage and barriers appropriate to the New Roads and Street Works Act 1991. Each man having over fifteen years' experience in sewer engineering, they set up a configuration appropriate to the thoroughfare without a second thought.

Phil and Stu erected a steel tripod for their winch across the opened manhole, while Paul donned his white overalls and matching hard hat. He clipped a mobile gas tester to his chest rig and checked its battery level.

Stu connected the harness rig to the winch. "It's a mess down there, Paul. Looks like a fatberg with a bung of wipes and nappies."

Paul leaned over the edge. "All the usual suspects. I'll take a shovel along."

Phil helped him into the harness and Stu eased their colleague down into a chamber twenty feet by twenty feet, fed by large pipes in three directions.

After a decade and a half wading through faeces and unmentionable sludge, Paul's nose had desensitised to the aroma. His legs disappeared into a brown goop, on which floated mashed together detritus cemented with congealed fat, grease and cooking oil. His disturbance of the mismatched surface dislodged waves of tiny, yellow floating fragments. *Sweetcorn. Yep, another day on the job with nothing out of the ordinary.* The human body couldn't digest sweetcorn kernels. Buoyant objects, they often floated in the rank chambers that served as 'office' for the day. Paul didn't know another colleague in his line of work who still ate sweetcorn.

"Hose coming down, Paul," Stu called from the rectangle of grey daylight above.

"I'm clear. Send it through." Paul wedged his shovel against three vertical pipes caked in a grey crust. *Once we reduce the liquid level, I'll see how much of that I can free up.* He stepped aside, red rubber gauntlets pushing past a bung of wet wipes and used condoms.

Stu fed a ribbed green hose, around the diameter of a human head, into the manhole.

"Ready when you are," Phil's faint voice called from somewhere on the other side of the truck above.

Paul caught hold of the strong but flexible tubing, then held it close to the soupy brown surface. "Start her up."

Powerful suction pulled the bung of wipes and condoms into the hose, followed by the bobbing plastic head of a child's baby doll. Some stuff they'd found in sewers over the years was so surprising, each engineer kept a list of their top ten favourite oddities.

"How's it going?" Stu shouted above the din.

"The fluid level is subsiding. Part of the fatberg is caked-" Paul was interrupted by a sudden buzzing from his chest worn gas detector. He raised his voice in an authoritative tone "Hold up. Hydrogen Sulfide alert."

Stu signalled to Phil, who cut the lorry's suction pump. "Sit tight, Paul. We're bringing you up."

The three engineers sat for ten minutes on the roadside, each enjoying a thermos of tea.

"That gas must have been trapped beneath the fatberg," Phil said.

"Same old, same old. Still, it gives us a chance for a cuppa. The air should have cleared by now." Paul drained his white plastic cup lid.

Stu replaced a thermos screw cap. "Off to work, then."

When Paul plunged back into the brown sludge - now reduced to knee height - it relieved him the gas alarm remained silent. He gave Stu a thumbs up and retrieved his shovel from the vertical pipes. A floating crust of fat and household junk which should never have found its way into the drainage system, wedged into a mass half the width of the manhole. Paul had long since ceased to admonish people over what they tipped or flushed away. It got annoying after a while and they rarely changed habits. Plus, their behaviour kept him among the gainfully employed. What did it matter in the grand scheme of things? Paul attacked the crust with his well-used tool. Memories of his father chiding a teenage Paul that he wasn't fit to shovel shit, creased a smile across his grim, weathered face. Schoolwork had never been his forte, but now he could shovel shit with the best of them. Dad was wrong.

A chunk of the fatberg broke free. *Smashing. Five more minutes of this and we can go back onto suction without gumming up the lorry.* Paul chiselled a clinging mess like albino moss on a tree trunk, clear of the pipes. Satisfied with his work, he returned to slicing through the buoyant crust. Three more wedges split, then broke apart. A bobbing mass floated clear from beneath. *What's this?* Paul tugged at more used condoms and disposable nappies. A final foam of freed sweetcorn parted as the pale, bloated face of a mid-twenties woman broke the surface. Her cheeks puffed like a hungry squirrel orally transporting nuts. Brown sludge filled her mouth to overflowing. Paul didn't want to guess what it comprised. He let out a short, involuntary wail that surprised him with its girlish tone.

Stu's head poked back over the rim. "Are you all right, Paul?"

Paul's back pressed against the shit encrusted underground wall. "There's a body down here."

Phil chortled. "Yeah, yeah. Pull the other one. It's November, mate; not the first of bloody April."

Paul barked an angry retort. "I'm serious."

Stu retrieved a high-powered torch from their kit bag, then shone the beam in a cutting arc across the depths. The light fell upon two sunken eye sockets. Strands of golden hair - once this young woman's glory - floated around her head adorned with the rectally ejected braids of undigested sweetcorn. Fatty white globs of wet wipes and discarded prophylactics traced the silhouette's periphery in a perverse aura.

Stu almost overbalanced and tumbled into the opening. "Fuck me."

* * *

RETTON HOUSE - NOVEMBER 2019.

Gillian tramped through a patch of dew-soaked grass in her stiff, black riding boots. Seven A.M. mist blew in puffy waves across the grounds. Beyond, beneath a pitched roof topped with a white wooden cupola, brisk noises of subdued industry told her what she would have expected: Lorcan the stable manager was already hard at work.

Lorcan Donnelly hailed from County Cork. A broad-shouldered, late thirties equine genius with dark curly hair; he also evidenced a light-hearted, easygoing temperament. Animals in his care sensed and responded well to his soothing energy. Yet with humans, Lorcan displayed a rapier wit and was blessed with a gift of Blarney appropriate to his home county.

Gillian adjusted her riding hat and tugged at the white jodhpurs she hadn't worn in an age.

The Irishman pushed a stiff bristled broom across a concrete floor, passing the half-open double doors as Gillian appeared.

"Hey there, Gillian." Lorcan's eyes twinkled.

Lorcan was the only member of staff not to prefix her name with the title 'Miss.' Gillian appreciated this. Her mother and father were also 'Bertram' and 'Felicity' whenever he addressed them, rather than 'Mr Crane' or 'Mrs Crane.' Nobody displayed a problem with it, so Lorcan didn't change his ways.

"Is Nellie ready to ride?" Gillian peered through bars into a stall. A chestnut Cob mare poked her head above its door.

"She is that. Poor girl had some thrush in the frog of one foot last week. Black slime and everything. I can't think how it happened. I pick all their feet out with care. Warm water and an antimicrobial spray sorted her out. She's well recovered. Do you want me to tack her up for you?"

"That's okay, I'll do it. Where's the grooming brush?"

Lorcan indicated a bench of equipment. "I treated your saddle and stirrups when I heard you were coming home. There's a fresh pad with them, too."

"Thanks, Lorcan." Gillian brushed Nellie to avoid any unnoticed dirt rubbing the beautiful animal once she applied the saddle. "Have you been home to The Emerald Isle since I was last here?"

Lorcan leaned on his broom. "For a few days the other month. My grandfather passed away, God rest his soul. I went over to attend his funeral."

Gillian looked at him for a second. "I'm sorry."

Lorcan shrugged. "It was the best thing. He never recovered after losing my Nan. They're together now." He tilted his head. "Mary and the Saints be praised." He watched Gillian brush the mare with attentive sweeps and unbroken concentration. "I hear you've had a rough time of your own?"

"Oh?" Gillian touched the top of her riding jacket to make sure it was buttoned over the tell-tale neck bruise.

Lorcan propped his broom against the stable wall. "Tell me to mind my own business if you will, but we've a term for bad bastards like your ex-fiancé where I come from."

"You mean other than '*Bad Bastards*?' I'd love to learn it."

Lorcan shook his head. "I'd like to slap him into the middle of next week. What a fruit loop. Fancy doing that to another human being?" He ran a hand through his mop of curly dark hair. "Fancy doing it to a gorgeous young woman such as yourself? He's proper mad. The lad is touched in the head, so he is."

"Thanks." Gillian put the brush away. She always enjoyed Lorcan's musical Irish accent and quaint turns of phrase, underscoring his honest humour.

Lorcan admired her attractive figure. "If I thought there was a chance, I'd propose to you myself." He grinned. "If you'd convert, of course."

Gillian grinned. "Sorry. Not happening."

Lorcan chuckled to himself. "I'm only joking. But what a catch you'd make."

"I'll tell my father you said so." Gillian winked.

Lorcan's nostrils flared. "I hope you're joking. Being employed by Bertram Crane is like winning the lottery of life."

Gillian lifted her saddle. "I thought that was being born an Englishman?"

Lorcan's grin crept up one side of his face. "Don't be daft now. Why would I say something like that about a Limey?"

Gillian passed him and prodded his ankle with a pretend kick. "I've missed our banter."

"Me too. Anytime you want to pop out on hack, let

me know. I'll fix Nellie right up. Now if you'll excuse me, I've some home-baked soda bread with my name on it back at the apartment."

Lorcan always fed the horses before he fed himself.

Gillian rode Nellie across Retton's twenty-three acres and out onto public bridleways crisscrossing woodland on the surrounding hills. The Cob had been a perfect choice for Gillian's frame, weight, strength and riding ability; most of which remained consistent. She trotted the animal through a cutting, surrounded on both sides by leafy, long forgotten earthworks. Here the forest grew dense and dark, with quick-growing conifers crowding the upper banks. Gillian couldn't wait to get out of that glorified trench. Maybe it was the summation of so many recent weird experiences, but she couldn't shake an uncomfortable sense of being watched. The trees all about seemed to close in, as though lifting their roots and shuffling forward whenever she looked away. Ahead, a landslip had tumbled a sturdy tree and an assortment of rocks and earth into a heap barring onward travel.

Gillian brought Nellie to a halt. "Crap." She dismounted and patted the horse's neck. "Easy, girl." Ten seconds scanning the obstruction left Gillian in little doubt of her inability to clear the bridleway. She led Nellie back around in a tight, opposite turn. The cutting left little wiggle room, making the manoeuvre a chore.

A twig snapped high on the hill to her left. Gillian froze. Birds fluttered through the oppressive canopy.

Some predator must have disturbed them. No doubt one of those foxes Old Joe was bleating on about. She hooked her left foot into a stirrup and swung aloft.

Another sharp crack of breaking wood cut through otherwise silent air, further down the bank towards her. *That's it. I'm getting out of here.* She urged Nellie onward as fast as she dared in the close terrain. Back along the cutting she rode, towards welcome, open ground and rolling hills beyond the forest. Stirrups flared and Nellie surged forward with mounting speed.

Back near the earthworks, another twig snapped far beyond Gillian's range of hearing. Chunky fingers pulled branches aside, so their owner could watch her gallop into the distance.

* * *

Gillian wandered into the living room, accompanied by Mace.

Bertram sat on one sofa, jangling an ice cube against a tumbler of single malt scotch. In a corner to the left of the fireplace, two ebony doors of an ancient cabinet hung open. The antique now served as a tasteful receptacle to conceal their television whenever it wasn't being watched. At first Bertram's wife had baulked at the concept of so elegant a piece of quality furniture re-purposed in such a manner. On further reflection, she recognised the aesthetic benefit of banishing a modern, technological monstrosity from sight in their exquisite living and entertaining area.

The local evening news broadcast announced itself with familiar music.

Felicity followed Gillian into the room. "How was your ride this morning?"

Gillian sat down on the sofa opposite her father. "Fine. There was an obstruction across one bridleway."

Bertram diverted his attention from the news presenter. "On our land?"

"No. East of here near the old woodland earthworks. That narrow stretch like a trench skirting the rise."

Bertram nodded. "I know the one. What sort of obstruction?"

"A fallen tree and some rocks. It looked like a landslip."

Felicity sat beside her husband. "The bank must have given way. It's so steep. I don't like that route."

"I'm not the only one, then. It's oppressive. I was glad to turn Nellie around and leave," Gillian added.

Bertram jangled his ice again. "Have you reported it to the council? They must clear the bridleway."

"No. I spent the rest of the day shopping, then reading in my room. That and taking Mace for a jolly good walk around the grounds."

Felicity watched the spaniel sink down in front of crackling logs in the fireplace. "I thought he looked healthy and calm."

Gillian stretched. "Give him five minutes and he'll be fast asleep."

Felicity pointed at the television. "Goodness, what's this? Turn it up, Bertram."

Bertram aimed a slender remote at the box to

comply.

The female news presenter adopted a grim expression relevant to her imminent unfolding story. Beside her, a photograph of an attractive, if gangly blonde woman with deep blue eyes faded into view. A line of white text on a shimmering blue banner beneath her read: *'Missing High Wycombe woman's body found in Amersham sewer.'*

Gillian twisted on her cushion for a better view of the screen.

The presenter paused a moment to clear the air after her previous spiel over education reform, then commenced with the new article.

"This morning, sewer engineers working to clear a fatberg in Amersham, turned up more than they bargained for. The body of twenty-five-year-old Tara Osmotherley, who disappeared from High Wycombe on Halloween, was found floating amidst the blockage. Thames Valley Police have launched a murder enquiry. Our sources reveal a preliminary inspection of the body indicated forceful restraint and deliberate choking, with traces of chocolate coating the lungs. Tara worked at a boutique chocolaterie called *'Cocoa Corruption'* in High Wycombe. Police have arrested business owner, Harry Perrino, on suspicion of murder. They are appealing for witnesses who may have seen anyone accompanying a woman matching Tara's description, away from the shop on or around the 31st of October. The force wouldn't comment further, but we grabbed a quick interview with Paul Drummond, who made the unfortunate discovery."

The scene switched to a haggard face, twitching from minor indications of delayed shock. In clear discomfort, the sewer engineer stood at the side of the road in his overalls. An on-site reporter invited him to describe his morning.

"I'd just gone back into the manhole after a gas warning cleared. We'd already pumped a lot of junk into our lorry, and I was breaking up the fatberg with my shovel. After a sizeable chunk fragmented, this woman's body floated free. It didn't half make me jump."

The reporter grilled him further from off-camera. "Can you describe the body?"

Paul scowled. "Are you serious? Who'd want to hear that? Not her relatives, I imagine."

"No specifics. Anything out of the ordinary?" the reporter pressed.

"Finding a body down a sewer was out of the ordinary for me, pal. What do you want me to say? She was bloated and covered in sh-" *(expletive bleeped out by the news editorial team)* "and other junk."

The view switched back to the studio presenter. "The investigation continues."

Bertram lowered the volume again, eyes never leaving Gillian's ashen, open-mouthed face.

Mace snored from the fireplace fender, then broke wind in a pungent, whistling fart, adding unconscious, olfactory resonance to the sewer news story.

Felicity gasped and batted the smell aside, still shaken from the awful television report.

Bertram cocked his head at Gillian. "Are you all

172

right, Pixie?" His tone hung hesitant with dread and uncertainty.

Gillian turned from the screen to face him. "Choked on chocolate. That *is* what they were suggesting? Did you hear that? Can it be what I saw at the party?"

Felicity fidgeted. "It's a grim coincidence, for certain."

Gillian rubbed her eyes. "There's nothing I can do, is there? I can't phone the police and tell them I experienced a vision on Halloween of a woman being choked on chocolate. They'll brand me an attention seeker, time waster or lunatic."

Bertram sipped his scotch. "You saw the attacker's face during your episode, didn't you?"

"Yes. But that doesn't help. If I tell the police they're looking for a balding, middle-aged bloke with piercing grey eyes, they'll want to know how I came by that information."

"True." Bertram put down his glass on a low side table. "Let's hope it *is* pure coincidence or puts an end to the matter. They've arrested that Perrino chap. This could prove an open and shut case."

"What if it doesn't? What if the arrest is nothing more than a routine part of their investigation?" Gillian wobbled to her feet. "I'm going to skip dinner, this evening."

Felicity leaned forwards. "You must eat something."

"Sorry, Mum. I'm tired and I've lost my appetite. All I want is to sleep."

Mace stirred and looked round. He watched Gillian leave the living room, then settled back down to snoozing before the fire.

Up in her bedroom, Gillian followed the dog's example of seeking some shuteye. Fresh, unfolding dreams depicting life at Retton House during the second decade of the twentieth century, sapped rather than boosted her energy levels.

* * *

RETTON HOUSE - AUGUST 1918.

"Did you hear, did you hear?" An excitable Gareth Morrison hurried into the living room, flapping a newspaper.

Avril the maid knelt before the fireplace, scrubbing a stubborn stain from the rug with a milk drenched cloth. She didn't look up from her task while speaking. "Did I hear what, Master Gareth?"

The nine-year-old boy waved the paper around as though it were a messenger of great fortune. "An assault on Amiens has begun. The British III Corps have attacked north of the Somme. The Australians, Canadian and French, are joining in support. I know Father will be home for Christmas. The war is going to end, Avril. I'm sure it is."

Avril finished scrubbing. "I pray you're right, Master Gareth. Is there any word from your mother?"

Gareth hung his head. "No. Aunt Helena is very sick. It may be awhile before Mother returns home."

Avril wrung her cloth into a white enamel bowl and

stood. "At least they won't have a stained rug to greet them on arrival. Not unless you're careless again, young Master."

Gareth studied the immaculate fabric. "You got it all out. Avril, you're a wiz!"

Avril's cheeks rouged. "Nothing to it. Good old cow's milk. A trick I learnt from my mother."

Gareth clutched at the paper again. "I'm going to tell the rest of the staff." He hurried from the room in search of an audience.

"Right you are, Mas-" Avril looked round from where she'd examined a dull patch on the fireplace mirror up close. Gareth had already left. Avril smiled to herself. "He's a good lad."

A midnight shower tinkled against window glass in the servants' apartments. Avril lay awake in her bed, hoping for the deluge to cease. It was Wednesday; the evening she always snuck outside to meet her beau, Ted Yates, from the gardening staff. *I'll get proper drenched if I'm caught for long in this.* Avril yearned for these nights. Their liaisons began with two or three hours of chatting they could never enjoy during daylight hours. Relations between unmarried staff were frowned upon, irrespective of how innocent. From their conversations about dreams and the world around them, the couple progressed to holding hands. Last week, as she was about to leave the greenhouse where they always met after dark, Ted kissed her on the cheek. She could still feel the warm, wet brush of his lips against her face. Their lingering physical memory aroused other warm, wet sensations she tried hard to ignore in the more intimate regions of her fertile body.

The rain eased to a light patter; dripping gutters announcing their need of attention. Avril slipped from beneath her sheets and tiptoed to the door. If James Farrell, the head butler, caught her out of bed at such an hour, there would be hell to pay. She edged along a corridor wall towards the rear, communal apartment block door. Outside, a bold, clipped male voice exchanged pleasantries with another man. She recognised the first as Farrell. No chance of sneaking past unnoticed that way.

Avril reversed course to check for sounds by the front entrance. When all remained still, she hurried from the block, ran the full frontage width of the house, then disappeared down the far side. Her billowing white nightdress fluttered in a gentle summer breeze as she darted between trees and bushes in a wide curve to avoid detection from the head butler. Only Master Gareth had any chance of spying her journey from here. He would be long since asleep, rather than watching from his bedroom window.

The greenhouses came into view. White panelled window frames set atop low brick surrounding walls, they ran the entire length of the kitchen garden's right-hand side.

Ted didn't dare light a lamp, but the stars and moon shone with enough silver brilliance through abundant glass panes for their burgeoning romantic trysts to unfold with reasonable clarity.

A fresh downpour opened from the heavens without warning. Avril gasped. She dashed along slippery paving slabs, trying not to lose her footing. By the time she reached the middle greenhouse, her nightdress and hair were soaked through. An unpleasant sensation to the touch, yet compensated for by heady, fresh aromas of abundant precipitation on verdant grass in her nostrils.

"I'll have a tough time explaining this if anyone finds my nightdress still wet," she whispered into the darkness between a row of raised beds. Musky grapes hung in bunches from vines positioned to make the most of robust light and warmth provided by the horticultural structure. A shadow emerged from the far end.

"I'm sure you'll clean and dry it with the other laundry before that happens."

Butterflies tingled Avril's stomach. She skipped forward, hands reaching to clasp Ted's.

Over six feet high with dark, soulful eyes, Ted's powerful digits moved from the tender grasp of her pale fingers to rub the length of her drenched arms. Avril's white nightdress clung to her sodden body, translucent from the soaking. Ted's gaze traced the outline of her bosom and protruding nipples. He also couldn't banish that stolen kiss on the cheek from his mind. Now the memory, combined with Avril's unintentional, seductive appearance, inflated his ardour. Blood flowed to swell the extremities of a fleshy tool with which he yearned to tend her womanly garden. Ted pulled Avril close, locking his mouth onto hers. At first she resisted, but passion soon melted her resolve into embracing the forbidden joys of clandestine fornication.

Outside, a hedgehog snuffled along the base of the middle greenhouse wall. Rain pattered against the many panes of glass in a romantic symphony. Beneath that covering, two lovers gasped and moaned to the musical accompaniment of nature's orchestra. Moonlight fell across the pale, undulating buttocks of a well-built gardener. Beneath him, shapely feminine calf muscles splayed out and flexed with every rhythmic, driving impact.

Avril knew her nightdress would be filthy by the time she returned to bed. But the stretching joy of Ted's vigorous intrusion into her virgin womanhood cast all other cares aside. Stars whirled above and heaven came down to earth amidst mutual cries of joy and release.

At the end of August, Gareth Morrison's optimism flourished. Philip Gibbs, the British war correspondent stated, *'There's a change also in the enemy's mind. They no longer have even a dim hope of victory on this western front. All they hope for now is to defend themselves long enough to gain peace by negotiation.'*

Despite the boy's growing excitement, Avril harboured concerns. There'd been no letter from Gareth's father in over a month. Avril knew other families from the locality who'd heard news from loved ones after Amiens. It didn't bode well, and she prayed for a miracle.

Worries over Gareth's happiness and family wellbeing weren't the only distraction from her customary attention to detail. On more than one occasion in the last few weeks, James Farrell had reprimanded her for sloppy work. Avril couldn't help herself. Wednesdays blossomed into mind scrambling encounters of loving sexual bliss with Ted Yates. She knew it was wrong, but she loved him so. Matters grew more complicated upon the cessation of her normal reproductive cycle. Even before a doctor confirmed it, Avril realised she was carrying Ted's lovechild. The night of Wednesday 28th August, found her determined to deliver that fateful news.

Ted rushed to embrace her in the darkened greenhouse. He smothered Avril's neck with kisses and pressed his bulging arousal into the crotch of her nightdress.

Avril pulled away. "Ted, there's something I've got to tell you."

Ted took a breath. "Can't it wait until we cuddle afterwards?"

"No, Dearest, it can't." She clasped her hands together. "I'm pregnant, My Love."

Ted blinked and took a step back. "Are you sure?"

A warm smile rippled to lift her rosy cheeks. "Yes. We're going to have a baby."

"How can you be certain?"

"I saw Doctor Baker in the village." Her face fell. "What's wrong?"

Ted scraped the back of his neck. "We'll lose our jobs. How can we provide for a child?"

Avril stepped forward to bridge the distance between them. Ted recoiled.

Avril's face paled, yet her eyes still swam with hope. "I'm sure we won't lose our jobs. Once the Morrisons know we intend to wed, they'll be all right with it."

"Wed?" Ted gasped. "When was that arranged?"

Avril's pupils dilated. "You love me, don't you? I mustn't be an unmarried mother, Dearest."

"You can't keep your job as a maid while bearing children." Ted folded his arms.

"They might give you a raise and let us stay. You told me how happy the gaffer was with your work. Other gardeners have families. Why not us?"

Ted remained silent.

Avril reached a trembling hand towards him. "Say something, Ted."

"I need to consider this. Weigh everything up." Ted's face displayed no emotional cues. "We'll talk again another time. Goodnight, Avril." He whirled and marched from the greenhouse without so much as a kiss or farewell.

Avril stood motionless in the grape-shadowed moonlight. Snuffling and grunting noises beyond the wall indicated another hedgehog who'd got lucky with a second mate at the end of the season. Those sounds mocked Avril's ears while she lifted quivering fingers to touch her pregnant belly.

9

Entombed Empathy

Tall and slim with athletic thighs, Claire Walker could be mistaken for a professional netball player. Her long, layered hair the hue of weathered teak swept back from a prominent brow and firm, triangular jaw. A young single mother, she lavished as much attention on her wellbeing and presentation as she did her adorable, four-year-old son, Tony.

Waiting for a session to finish at '*Launchpad into Learning*,' her local pre-school group could sometimes get fractious. Claire didn't hate her ex, Ashley, despite his penchant for getting drunk with his mates and attending every football game going. By the time their marriage ended, the only thing the couple had in common was their biological offspring. Both loved him, but it wasn't enough to sustain their relationship. Claire sold the house and moved into a rented first floor, two-bedroom flat. She took the basic maintenance upkeep for their son from Ashley, and nothing more.

This gracious approach to what she believed had

been an amicable split aside, the wives of Ashley's drinking buddies took umbrage at her ending the relationship. Most of them also had children at the same pre-school.

Today was a 'Cold Shoulder Day' as Claire dubbed them. Appropriate, given the plummeting temperatures. 'Cold Shoulder Days' were times when the other women spotted Claire, then turned aside to engage in conversation as though she weren't present. It came as some relief, since Tony was full of spirits and proved a handful when she'd dropped him off earlier. He'd reached that age where kids understand what happens at Christmas. With that holiday little more than a month away, infantile excitement levels were building. The last thing Claire needed was a session of verbal sparring with people she once considered friendly peers. Those 'Pub Widows' - another of her mental labels - could prattle all they wanted, as long as they left her and Tony out of it.

Doors opened for Heather Watson, the pre-school manager to reunite the correct children with their mothers, assisted by two staff.

"How was he?" Claire asked Heather.

Tony reached backwards towards a series of fresh paintings taped to the far interior wall. His brow furrowed at a blue, yellow and black stick figure walking its dog beneath a sunny sky.

Heather followed his gaze. "I swiped one of his paintings before he could destroy it, today. See. I told you he had a talent for composition."

Claire peered into the room and squinted at the

picture. "It's lovely. Tony doesn't seem too pleased."

"He made a fuss when I took it away. Insisted he wasn't finished." Heather adjusted thick-rimmed black glasses on a broad nose. "We all know what that means."

"Hmm," Claire replied in a tone suggesting this outcome proved less than helpful. She understood what Heather was getting at. Ever since her breakup with Ashley, Tony had developed a habit of producing beautiful paintings, then covering them over with layers of dark paint in black and brown. The result always resembled chestnut wood panelling, with nothing to hint at the fine scene concealed beneath. When she'd asked him about it at home, Tony said he liked to tell stories with his paintings. Claire thought she understood: rather than capturing a moment in time, he was playing out a series of events through paint. Whether those results represented an understandable inability to add anything extra to paper already splattered with colour, or something darker, Claire couldn't be sure. From the expression on Heather Watson's face when she repeated his statement, it was clear the pre-school manager suspected the latter.

Claire reached down to take Tony's hand. "What do you say to Mrs Watson, then?"

Tony tore his gaze away from the painting to regard the bespectacled woman. "Thank you."

"You're welcome, Tony. See you next week," Heather replied, then leaned closer to speak with Claire in a subdued voice. "He's become insular of late.

Tony never used to be that way. I'm not sure he likes to play with the other children."

"Or vice versa," Claire shot a sarcastic side-glance at the *'Pub Widows,'* entertaining no doubt of the instructions they'd forced upon their offspring regarding her son. She directed a flat smile at Heather. "Thank you. Come on, Tony." They passed the other mums without a glance.

"Can we look at the swans on the river, Mummy?" Tony tugged Claire's sleeve.

"Are you sure you're not too cold or tired?"

"No. I want to see the swans. They're always happy."

Claire pulled him close for a moment. Was this an innocent comment or indicative of the child suffering some undisclosed inner turmoil he couldn't vocalise? "Come on, then. The river is this way." She swung his arm playfully to make the boy giggle. They turned off the High Street beside Marlow Canoe Club at the 19th century suspension bridge. Hand in hand, mother and son followed the riverside path southwest between private boat moorings for modest pleasure craft. Across the water, the village of Bisham squatted like a rustic echo of what Marlow might once have been before its explosion of growth.

"Can you remember the name of this river, Tony?" Claire stopped for the boy to admire a line of swans gliding past with effortless grace.

"The River Thames," Tony replied without hesitation.

"And which city does this river flow through, further on?"

"London." His follow-on answer came with no less of a pause.

"Good boy." Claire let go for a moment to adjust her long, layered hair in a rising breeze. She glanced left at the spire of All Saints Church, pointing like an arrow toward heaven. Less than a hundred yards distant, a solitary, bulky male figure stood watching her. It had to be her, since there was nobody else on the path. Claire shielded her eyes from the low sunlight. She could have sworn she'd noticed him in town earlier, on her way to collect Tony from pre-school.

A sudden splash and spray of water brought Claire back to the moment with terrifying rapidity. "Oh my God, Tony." She reached helpless arms towards the water.

Strong currents carried the flailing boy out into the river where he'd toppled over while attempting to reach out and stroke a swan. The ivory waterfowl skittered away, disturbed by his panicked splashing.

An approach of racing footsteps echoed along the footpath. That hulking great man threw himself into a headlong dive, sending a sheet of water to half soak Claire's frozen form. Powerful arms pulled at the strong forces carrying the child further from reach. Claire followed the accomplished swimmer's balding pate, tilting from side to side in a determined front crawl until he reached the stricken but stilling form of her son. Tony's modest strength was almost gone and he couldn't swim. How much water had he already taken down?

Claire almost lost her footing at the water's edge. The gasping man swam to shore. Tony coughed and clung onto him. He was alive but shivering.

"Thank you. Thank you. I don't know what else to say." Claire grabbed hold of Tony.

The man released him and clambered to his feet, clothes sodden and skin pale from the cold.

"You must both be frozen."

Tony cried.

Claire pulled him close. "It's all right. You're safe now."

Tony pointed a nervous finger to his rescuer. "I was trying to pet a swan when I fell in. This man saved me."

"I know, Darling. Shh, now. It's okay." She rubbed his shoulders. "Goodness, we'd better get you inside and dried off before you catch your death of cold." She fixed strained, shadowed eyes on the welcome stranger. "We don't live far. Would you like to come home and dry off with us? I've still got a t-shirt and pair of trousers from my ex-husband in a cupboard. He was about your size."

The man shivered and nodded.

Claire was entranced by his eyes, dark with the intensity of a thunderstorm. Something about them made her cringe. Or was it the ice cold body of her shivering son and shock induced by his ordeal? *Jesus, Claire, you've become paranoid since you broke up with Ashley. Don't you trust anyone these days? This random stranger risked his life to save Tony, and you've never met him before.* Claire moved the quaking child away from the bank, still focused on his rescuer. "Home is this way."

Claire opened the flat's communal entrance door and led her two bedraggled companions up to the first floor. Two minutes later they were inside, whereupon she tugged fluffy towels from the linen cupboard.

"Tony, strip your clothes off in the bathroom if you can. I'll be there in a minute." She passed a blue towel to the dripping man. "There you are. I'll fetch that change of clothes as soon as I've towel dried my boy."

Four minutes later, the bathroom door opened again, following happier sounds of Tony being patted down and tickled by his mother.

The man stood in the hallway facing the front door.

Claire spoke without paying him much attention. "Sorry about that. Those fresh clothes are in her-" She paused at the entrance to her bedroom.

The man slid a security bolt across the flat's entrance.

Claire inclined her head. "What are you doing?"

The hulking figure didn't turn. His voice hissed with spiteful venom. "It's payback time, Sally."

* * *

ASHBURNHAM - NOVEMBER 2019.

Claire awoke with a groggy head. Everything happened so fast after her challenge to Tony's rescuer in the flat, she struggled to put the pieces together.

Whatever occurred next, she was no longer at home. And where was Tony?

She shook herself and glanced about. A smell of industrial grade plastic mixed with damp earth invaded her nasal cavity. Claire found herself secured, hands behind her back in a kneeling position. Yet her legs couldn't stretch away. Instead, they'd been folded vertically towards her bound wrists, as tight as the human musculoskeletal structure would permit. She viewed the world from inside a dark blue, tubular plastic tomb. Claire recognised it as a bulk storage keg, similar to those from a warehouse she'd once performed a temporary stock control job at. Her shoulders pressed against its sides. Cramp from both pinioned thighs shocked her muscles with relentless agony, but she couldn't move. Wet earth from the partially filled tub reached her waist. She was half buried inside it like a potted plant. At present no lid had been fastened onto the container. Claire stretched her neck to peer across its rim. The barrel rested amidst ash trees near a woodland pond. Beyond, a crumbling, detached derelict Victorian villa looked out of place in such a wild and remote setting.

A flurry of soil sailed past her face, dirtying her already splattered cheeks. It settled atop the earthen contents into which she was set.

Claire twisted her head. The balding man stood clutching a shovel. His pitiless grey eyes settled on her terrified features.

"So you thought to bury me in my own camp, did you, Sally? You won't get away with it, no matter how many lies you tell our mother."

Claire called out. "What have you done with my son?"

A curious twanging noise warbled from the hulk's throat. He bent down out of sight, but his voice carried over the keg's lip. "You want a doll to keep you company in your grave, do you, Sally?"

A heavy object dropped into the container. Its sudden addition left little room to spare.

Claire found herself face to face with Tony's lifeless, staring eyes. Earth filled his open mouth like a re-stuffed teddy bear into which not another strand of kapok will fit. She vented her anguish in an unrestrained scream.

Banjo shovelled extra earth inside. "Not much more to put in, now. I must press it down good and tight." He chuckled and appeared to speak more to himself or some distant memory of a person long gone than Claire. "Scream, Sally, scream. Mother won't hear you now. Nobody is coming to your rescue."

Dirt reached the base of Claire's chin.

Banjo's firm hands compacted the surrounding earth, forming a solid bung inside the barrel. He returned to shovelling. Claire's screams muffled as dirt filled her mouth. She spat it clear.

Before the earthen cargo reached the base of her nose, Claire had shut her mouth without taking surplus soil into her throat. Flaring nostrils provided her final lifeline of air. Her shadowed eyes stretched wide, level with the empty stare of her child's corpse. In another minute, the barrel would reach capacity and her end would come.

*　*　*

GREAT MISSENDEN - NOVEMBER 2019.

"I need some decongestant spray from the pharmacy," Felicity Crane pointed to a squat but sprawling building. She crossed a side-by-side entrance to the Greek temple-like Baptist church and rear car park of 'The Cross Keys' pub. At this end of Great Missenden's High Street, one could be filled with many kinds of spirit within the space of a hundred yards.

"Do you have a cold?" Gillian watched a red and white flag bearing the cross of St George flutter from a forty-five-degree shop front flagpole opposite.

"No, but I threw an expired bottle away yesterday, when I checked the medicine cabinet." Felicity pushed open the pharmacy's turquoise painted wooden door.

Gillian followed her inside. The shop interior blurred. Gillian fingered her jacket collar, head throbbing. She staggered forward. Her arms reached for support on a four tier, freestanding shelf display. Two canisters of shaving gel tumbled to the floor, catching Felicity's attention.

"Gillian, are you all right?" She left the decongestant medicines alone to reach her daughter's side and shore up her swaying frame.

Gillian gripped her forehead with one hand. "It's happening again."

The pharmacy shelving vanished, replaced by the dead, staring face of a four-year-old boy. His cheeks bulged; moist earth filling a mouth preserved into a never ending, unheard scream. Gillian's shoulders pressed in tight, held rigid by a source of invisible, compacting pressure.

A woman pharmacist dashed from behind the counter. "Is she okay?"

Felicity winced. "She's been ill and suffered fainting spells. Last time it happened, she had trouble breathing."

"I've a chair in the corner. Let's sit her down. Would you like me to call an ambulance?" The pharmacist helped Felicity guide an unresponsive Gillian towards the seat.

Felicity attempted to rouse her, but those emerald eyes registered nothing before them. "Can you breathe, Darling? Can you hear me?"

Gillian's mouth remained clamped shut, as though to open it would spell certain doom. Both nostril's flared like a horse given its head at full gallop.

Felicity eased Gillian down into the stiff-backed wooden chair.

Something blocked Gillian's nostrils, inducing a fit. Her bowels moved without warning in empathic fear transmitted through the vision. She defecated on the seat in a squirting release of loose fecal matter.

Felicity recoiled at the stench. Pleading eyes made contact with those of the pharmacist. "I'm so sorry."

The pharmacist already clutched a phone to her ear. She shook her head to cast Felicity's concerns aside. An emergency operator's voice crackled from the handset. The pharmacist spoke. "Ambulance, please."

Bertram and Felicity hurried into the A & E at Stoke Mandeville Hospital, Aylesbury. After the paramedics took Gillian away, Felicity raced home to Retton House for her husband. Now they found their daughter clad in a hospital gown, sipping tea in a curtained alcove of the emergency ward.

Gillian clutched her cup between both hands, eyes meek. "This is becoming something of a habit, isn't it? The three of us meeting in hospitals, I mean."

Bertram sat down alongside her. "At least you're not on a ventilator this time. Your mother said you stopped breathing again."

Gillian closed her eyes. "I could feel her terror."

"Your mother's?" Bertram asked.

"No."

Felicity sat down beside her husband. "Whose terror?"

"The woman."

"You had another vision of the girl who was force fed chocolate?" Bertram asked.

"No. This was different. Someone else. She was bogged down in a container, facing a dead child. A boy." Gillian's lips tightened. "His mouth was filled with earth."

Felicity pressed fingers against her own oral cavity.

Bertram continued his line of questioning. "Did you see that man again?"

Gillian shook her head. "Not this time. Somebody was piling earth into the container, though. First it covered the woman's mouth. I was too scared to open mine. I could smell damp soil in my nostrils. Then my nose blocked and I couldn't breathe. That must have been the moment my bowels evacuated." Gillian shivered. "Wherever that woman was, she did the same." She snapped back to her present surroundings. "Oh Mum, I'm so sorry. I must take some flowers along to the pharmacist. Was the shop a terrible mess? I stunk to high heaven when they brought me in. That's how come I got a hospital gown. They haven't decided whether to keep me in for tests yet."

Felicity sighed. "They're going to monitor you for an hour and see how things go. The pharmacist was wonderful. She's the one who called the ambulance. I left her fixing to scrub and disinfect that seat."

Gillian put her cup down. "I wish I knew what's going on. I can't get that dead child's face and the woman's terror out of my head."

Bertram touched the mattress. "There, there. It's only been a short time."

Gillian leaned back. "I wonder if we'll hear anything on the news, like with that girl from High Wycombe?"

Felicity's eyes reddened. "Don't worry about it for now."

* * *

ETON - NOVEMBER 2019.

"Dad, there's something in the water." Eleven-year-old Peter Ransome pointed across the prow of his father's white, 36.9 Grand Sturdy, 'Windsor Dream.' It coasted opposite 'The Boatman' pub at Eton on the River Thames. The round keep of Windsor Castle stood sentinel on an overlooking hill.

Kevin Ransome pulled a pipe from one corner of his mouth to exhale a cloud of smoke. He throttled back the chugging vessel and leaned over for a closer inspection. A large, blue plastic barrel floated low in the water. It struck the starboard side of the sleek pleasure craft, slowing the object's movement amidst the current to a cartwheeled bobbing.

"When will people learn not to dump their junk in the river?" Kevin tugged the peak of his classic navy maritime cap. "That's so dangerous. Goodness knows what nasties are lurking inside. Mind yourself, Peter."

He lifted a boat hook over the side to direct the jetsam toward shore, where a pair of like-minded boatmen sitting on the deck of their moored barge had also noticed the object.

"Can you lend a hand?" Kevin called.

The two tanned, retired fellows gave him a thumbs up. "Will do," one said while the other reached over with a second hook to take delivery.

"I've no idea what's inside," Kevin added.

"Someone found an abandoned snake in a plastic box last week," the man with the hook replied. "An unwanted, exotic pet. A bloomin' great python, too. The RSPCA took it away."

Kevin shook his head in despair. "Well, you might

squeeze a modest anaconda inside that, so you'd best watch out."

The other man grabbed a broom and helped his companion steer the barrel to the water's edge of the northern bank. They waved Kevin off and Windsor Dream motored away on a westerly course.

Back on shore, one of the impromptu salvagers retrieved a screwdriver from their barge toolbox. He jemmied free a steel ring securing its black plastic lid in place. The top popped off to reveal compacted wet earth. A rancid stench hit both men in a nauseating wave.

"There's got to be more than dirt in there," said the man with the screwdriver. He scooped some earth clear with one hand, depositing it on the bank next to the barrel.

"Oh, Jesus. No." The other pulled back. Teak hair strands emerged, coating the decomposing head of a deceased woman and young child.

"Mother of God." His companion dropped the screwdriver with a clatter on the riverside path.

10

Left Hanging

RETTON HOUSE - NOVEMBER 2019.

Felicity Crane flicked through the morning paper at breakfast, while Bertram spread strawberry jam onto half a croissant.

"Whatever article you're reading, it must be a cracker. I know it's not the FT, but let me know so I can take a look." Bertram flicked flakes of paper-thin pastry between the thumb and forefinger of one hand.

"Pardon?" Felicity lifted her nose out of the broadsheet, face pained.

Bertram examined her expression. "On second thoughts, I'll pass. What is it, Darling?"

"Boaters on the Thames down at Eton pulled a plastic barrel from the river, yesterday. It was packed with earth, plus the body of a young woman and child."

Bertram stopped chewing and swallowed with a loud gulp. "Oh, my goodness."

Felicity rubbed two fingers down one cheek. "It's so close to what Gillian described from her episode at the pharmacy."

"After revelations over that woman's death from High Wycombe, the coincidences are stacking up. Does the article state whether police believe the incidents are linked?"

"No. Their identities haven't been disclosed, if they know them."

Bertram folded his hands. "Eton. That's a stretch downriver, but the barrel could have drifted for miles. Berkshire is only the next county."

"Wouldn't it sink with two bodies inside?"

Bertram weighed up her question. "I'm no flotation expert. If it wasn't weighted down with extra ballast and the bodies gave off decomposition gases, that might provide sufficient buoyancy. A lot depends on its density differential against the water, I imagine. I doubt their plastic tomb broke much above the surface. Either way, it was discovered, which is a small mercy for someone. That pair must have people missing them."

Felicity thumbed the article. "Who would do such a thing?"

"Who knows? A jealous or spurned partner?"

"But to bury a woman and child in earth, then dump them in the river. What kind of dispute did they have?"

Bertram stroked his chin. "I'm not suggesting the aggressor is playing with a full deck. No sane person could rationalise doing that to another human being."

"What will happen when Gillian sees it?"

"That's if she bothers. Gillian isn't a big fan of the

papers. Have you spoken with her this morning?"

"No. She was so tired when we brought her home from Aylesbury last night. I thought I'd let her sleep in."

"Hospitals aren't the most restful places," Bertram replied.

"Do you think I should remove the article?"

"What good would it do? We're trying to have her open up to us, Flick. If we cover this over, Pixie will feel betrayed when she hears the news. Something this major will be on TV or the Internet, without question. The last thing we need is our daughter shutting down and bottling more stuff up."

"I wish she'd accepted our offer to get married at Retton. That way she would have already been here when Brent abandoned her. Gillian could have stayed home. Then the suicide attempt... None of this would have happened."

"We can't say that for certain. Whatever these visions are, they appear tied to her present mental and emotional state. That or something weird that happened when she tumbled off her kitchen table in Alresford."

A fresh voice chimed in from the conservatory archway. "Are you holding a council of war to count my marbles?"

"Good morning, Pixie. How are you feeling today?" Bertram asked.

Gillian shrugged. "As well as expected for a twenty-seven-year-old woman who shat herself in public yesterday."

Felicity flinched. "That's a rather indelicate and unladylike way of putting it, Gillian."

"Sorry, Mum. A twenty-seven-year-old woman who poo'd her panties in public."

Bertram chuckled at Gillian's obvious attempt to disarm an atmosphere of anxiety with humour. "There's no easy way to describe it, is there?"

Gillian entered and sat down at the table. "What was that article I heard you discussing?"

Felicity and Bertram exchanged harried glances. "Just something in the paper," Felicity replied. She lifted the broad sheet between whitening hands.

Gillian watched her. "But disturbing enough to make you wring the life out of it?"

Felicity eased her grip.

Gillian didn't take her eyes off her mother's uncomfortable face. "They've found them, haven't they? They've found the woman and child, stuffed into a container full of earth?"

Felicity put the paper down again to conceal a nervous tremble in her arms.

It was Bertram who answered the question. "That's right, Pixie. They pulled a plastic barrel with both inside, out of the Thames at Eton. I suppose we'll learn more on the evening news, later."

Gillian lifted her face to the sky. Autumn sun shimmered through their high conservatory roof. "How can this be possible? Why me? Why have I shared these women's final moments? It's not like I'm in a position to help. Both experiences happened at the moment of death. There's nothing useful I can do, other than suffer their fear, pain and anguish."

"Would you like me to speak with Maurice Gange? He might recommend someone for you to see." Bertram said.

"A psychiatrist?" Gillian raised an eyebrow. "We're back to my opening statement about you counting my marbles."

"Nobody thinks you're mad, Gillian." Felicity found her voice again; stern, but sympathetic.

"I know, Mum. Sorry, Daddy. No, I want to wait awhile. The last thing I need is to become a guinea pig for someone's latest psychology paper. I couldn't handle all those questions about my childhood and whether every object I look at reminds me of a penis."

Bertram almost choked on his morning coffee. "Not a fan of Freud?" He wiped away a smile.

Felicity shook her head. "She's *your* daughter, Bertram. No question."

Gillian helped herself to a brioche from a basket of pastries. "Don't sell yourself short, Mum. There's plenty of Felicity in here, too."

Felicity watched her eat. "I'm glad you've more of an appetite and are well enough to joke."

"What else can I do? I doubt anyone with a PhD and a dick fixation can wave a magic wand to make all this go away. What I need is space. No more visions would be nice, but I've no control over that."

Felicity turned to a light-hearted letters page in the newspaper. Her taut facial muscles resumed their normal, peaceful expression. "Are you going riding today?"

"I've no plans to. The first order of business is a trip back to the pharmacy with some flowers, like I mentioned yesterday."

Bertram hummed in approval. "Old Joe will hook you up with something nice." His tone grew stern. "Are you sure you'll be all right, so soon after your ordeal?"

"The sooner the better. I need to confront this, not run from it. Though if I start to wobble again, I'll run outside and poo in the High Street."

Felicity rolled her eyes.

Gillian grinned. "Sorry, Mum."

Bertram finished his coffee. "That's a courageous choice. The pharmacy visit, I mean; not defecating in the village's primary thoroughfare. Be careful, Pixie. Now, if you'll excuse me, I've a meeting at the firm today." He got up, kissed his wife and daughter on the cheek, then left.

"Good morning, Joe. I wonder if you've several blooms I could tie up with a ribbon for someone?" Gillian entered one greenhouse as Old Joe finished stacking earthenware plant pots. Her eyes danced across the plain, empty interior. "Didn't we have grapes growing in here, once?"

"Not in my lifetime, Miss. But I found an old gardener's journal with references to growing grapes here. It's got to be a century or more old. You must have dreamt it."

A tingle of recognition fluttered in Gillian's stomach. The grapes she remembered came not from her own experience of the greenhouse; they arose from her dream about Avril and Ted's midnight trysts. Gillian realised she was standing on the spot where the couple made love for the first time. *What was Ted's decision over Avril's suggestion of marriage? He didn't sound keen to commit. I know what that's like, even at the eleventh hour. Or was it all a simple fantasy my mind conjured? A fiction fed by Katie's stories, my experience of seeing Avril's ghost in the garden, and that distressing encounter with Gareth?*

"Are you all right, Miss?" Joe leaned closer.

"Sorry, Joe. I'm a tad distracted. I embarrassed myself in a shop yesterday. That's why I want the flowers: an apology for the owner."

"Crikey. I'd better not ask what you did." Joe blinked.

No shit. Gillian smiled at the irony of her mental phrase. "Good decision."

"If you'd prefer something living as opposed to cut flowers, I can pot you up a few more o' them Scented Pinks?"

"Thanks, Joe. That will be grand."

"Wait five minutes. I've an old trug lying around here somewhere. I'll give it a wipe over and put the potted plants inside. You could tie a ribbon on the handle, if you fancied it."

Gillian smirked. "You're a romantic, aren't you? There must have been some broken female hearts over the years, trampled underfoot by your restless, muddy wellies."

Joe snorted and flushed. "Poppycock. I never was a ladies' man. Ah, here we go." Joe retrieved the trug from a dirty wooden crate. He rinsed a rag from a standpipe, wrung it out and wiped the smart, rustic receptacle free of dust and grime. "There. She's coming up a treat. Let me fetch your blooms."

Gillian watched him tramp outside from her spot within the warm confines of that glass-heavy interior. She spoke under her breath. "Mother Nature was always your mistress, Joe. And what an attentive lover she found in you."

It was early afternoon when Gillian reached the High Street pharmacy in Great Missenden again. For a moment her head became hot. She wondered if her father had been right. But the effects of a mild panic attack soon passed, and she caught the female pharmacist's eye.

The pharmacist pressed flat hands against her counter top. "Hello there. Oh, I'm so glad you're up and well."

"Thank you." Gillian eyed the stiff wooden chair, now cleaned to perfection with no hint of the state she'd left it in the day before. "I brought this for you. An apology for what happened, and a thank you for how you responded." Gillian placed the trug, sporting a fine pink ribbon and containing four small potted flowers, onto the counter.

"How lovely. You shouldn't have done that." The pharmacist's face lit up. "Gosh. At first I thought you were an asthma sufferer. It plagued my sister, growing up. But I've never witnessed anyone dissociate during an episode, the way you did yesterday. Zoned out. Here in body alone, if you'll excuse the term."

Gillian grimaced. "If the label fits... My shortness of breath wasn't asthma. Stoke Mandeville released me last night. I've been having stress-induced issues following an earlier stay in hospital. The err... personal accident was a new one on me. I'm glad your chair is okay. It was so embarrassing. Sorry."

"The chair cleaned up fine. Don't give it another thought." She sniffed the flowers. "These are wonderful blooms. Such a sweet fragrance."

"Our head gardener is a certifiable genius. His fingers aren't literally green, but they may as well be."

"Joe Taylor?"

"That's right. You know him?"

"He's a lovely old boy. Comes in here for odds and ends, now and again. They don't grow them like that anymore."

Gillian licked her lips. "That's the truth. He's a character. Hardworking and faithful as the day is long." She nodded at the grey November sky outside. "If you discount shorter days like this one, that is."

The pharmacist lifted the trug and set it down behind the counter. "Thank you for my present. It was most kind."

"How was your meeting, Daddy?" Gillian entered the living room as her father switched on the TV.

"Long, dull and pointless. I must have a quiet, friendly word with Jason Beale about not trying to impress me through corporate lingo and irrelevant meet-ups."

"Is he one of your new hires?"

Bertram stretched. "He is. Nice lad. Eager to please in a rigid, 'by the book' sort of way."

Gillian took her usual place on the opposite sofa, making a fuss of Mace's ears as he padded over to greet her. She pressed their noses together and spoke to the dog as she looked into his enormous eyes. "Jason has yet to realise Daddy is a maverick."

Bertram cracked a lopsided smile. "How did the pharmacist like your flowers?"

"She loved them. Joe pulled a rabbit out of the hat, as always. Damage control sorted. You can buy aspirin and sun cream at the pharmacy, without fear of violent reprisals."

Bertram watched her kiss Mace. "It's so good to have you home, Pixie. You must be tired of hearing it."

Gillian relaxed into her sofa cushion while the dog retreated to his beloved fireside. "Not tired, Daddy. Thankful."

The evening news came on.

Felicity joined them in time to catch the names Claire and Tony Walker attributed to the Thames barrel victims.

Gillian rubbed her upper arms. "She was from Marlow, then. I'm amazed not to hear the media make a connection with Tara Osmotherley yet. They released her boss without charge, so I presume he had an alibi."

Felicity sat. "Did you witness anything yesterday in common with those first scenes on Halloween?"

Gillian stared at an on-screen photograph of little Tony Walker. The sight of his face amplified her gooseflesh. "No. I didn't notice that grotty old house, nor the creepy guy with staring eyes. Nothing but that terrified dead boy and the barrel interior, filling with earth. I can still smell it, if I close my eyes."

Bertram muted a follow-on news story about unemployment figures. "If these visions are accurate and occur at the moment of the victim's death, Claire Walker couldn't have been in the river long. A few hours, if they fished the barrel out at Eton."

Felicity sat forward on her cushion. "Aren't there locks and other obstructions between Marlow and Eton? Could an object that size and weight travel such a distance in that time frame? Perhaps Gillian is experiencing echoes of recent, past events? That bargeman they interviewed said he thought the bodies were decomposing."

Bertram cleared his throat. "We're assuming because the victims came from Marlow, that they were put in the river there. Goodness, that barrel may have been dumped in the Thames a mile upstream from Eton. As to the smell, who knows what else their killer put inside? Gillian claimed her involuntary bodily functions were an echo of Claire's. Bottled and shaken up, the stench when opened would be far from pleasant."

Gillian got up. "Thanks for doing this, you two."

"Doing what, Pixie?" Bertram asked.

"For humouring me. Going along with your nutty daughter's weird visions."

Felicity watched her. "The boy in that picture was definitely the dead face you saw?"

Gillian nodded. "Unless my mind is so fried, it's mixing stuff up and filling in the blanks wherever it can. The thing is, this feels solid. I'm going to freshen up before dinner."

As Gillian reached the landing, a flash of movement darted past the corner of her eye. It ran towards the guest wing at the back of the house. She slowed her pace and moved with uncomfortable steps down the rear corridor. Gerard and Katie were setting the table for dinner. She could still hear them. None of the other staff would come upstairs.

A door clicked shut on one of the guest rooms. Gillian swallowed and forced herself to make a tentative approach. The brass doorknob chilled her fingers; ice cold to the touch as she twisted it. A smart, wood-panelled door, like so many others in the elegant property, glided open to reveal an empty bedroom overlooking the rear gardens and greenhouses.

"Hello?" Gillian entered the room. An en-suite bathroom door banged to, as though kicked by an angry foot. Gillian jumped. She reached the bathroom and pushed through with a lurch, hoping to catch the intruder unawares. The overhead light clicked on without issue when she tugged a dangling cord. All remained empty and still, bar an intermittent dripping from a mixer tap over the bath. Gillian released a sigh, uncertain whether to feel relieved or agitated by this outcome. *Could it be Gareth again?* Her question received an immediate answer when she tugged the light off and re-entered the bedroom. The boy stood staring at her with a curious mix of fear and anger. He whirled about. Gillian's heart skipped a beat. The rear portion of his skull had been stoved in by a blow of significant force. She'd not noticed before, having only met him once, face to face.

Gareth ran into the corridor and vanished.

Gillian caught her breath. "Of all the times to be hit with supernatural intrusions; ghostly sightings and terminal visions through murder victims' eyes. Like I need another challenge while putting my life back together." She let herself out of the guest room and returned to her own.

*   *   *

ASHBURNHAM - AUGUST 1988.

"Tornado is going to fly. Do you think he can grow wings like Pegasus?" Sally leaned out of a rear upstairs window. The raised sash above mingled its layer of grime with the top pane to present a cloudy combination, impossible to see through. In one gleeful hand Sally waved a black wooden toy horse, the length of a child's forearm.

"Give it back. I want my horse," Banjo shouted between frantic attempts to seize his most beloved plaything. "Give me Tornado."

Sally adopted the air of a sensible adult, trying to elicit manners from their boisterous offspring. "What do you say?"

Banjo whined. "Give it. Give it now, Sally."

"What's the magic word?"

Banjo fumed. "Abracadabra."

Sally stood on tiptoe and held the horse out of his reach. "That's not the magic word, is it?" She chided him and pursed her lips into a triumphant facial expression of superiority.

"I'll kick you." Banjo stomped his foot.

"Good luck explaining the bruises to Mum. She'll lock you down in the cellar again." Sally tucked the toy horse behind her back and jammed her face straight into that of her younger sibling. "Would you like that? Locked in the cramped, dark cellar with the mice, cobwebs and spiders." Sally impersonated the twanging noise her brother made with his throat whenever he became agitated or overwhelmed. She followed it with a rousing rendition of 'Camptown Races,' in perfect tune. "Oh, the long-tailed filly and the big black horse. Doo-da, doo-da. Come to a mud hole, and they all cut across. Oh, de doo-da day." She skipped around the cluttered, dusty room like a child half her age, waving the horse in time with her singing.

Banjo's anger boiled over. He charged Sally and pushed her into the wall. Sally screamed as her ankle twisted. She stumbled against crumbling plaster. Tornado made first contact, one foreleg snapping off like a rotten twig.

Banjo howled. "No! You broke Tornado. I'm going to kill you, filthy witch."

Sally read the relentless vengeance in his stare. In

that moment, she felt he'd take terminal action against her in his fury. She hobbled to the window, wincing in pain.

Banjo grabbed her about the waist. The pair hung over the sill, high above their overgrown rear garden, choked with weeds and the encroaching woodland.

Sally stretched her arms as far out as she dared. "If you make me drop him, I'll throw your beloved horse so hard he'll break into tiny fragments."

Tears welled in Banjo's eyes. He gazed with helpless grief at the three-legged stallion dangling from Sally's tenacious fingers. If she let go, it was all over. He released his sister and pulled back inside.

Sally seized an opportune moment to lob the toy onto the roof above. It slid down loose slates to rest in black metal guttering out of sight above them.

"No. No, Tornado." Banjo punched Sally in the stomach.

Sally doubled-over, winded.

Banjo climbed onto the sill, hoping to find one of Tornado's remaining limbs dangling over the edge, close enough to grab.

Sally shoved him in the back. Banjo toppled over the edge. One hand reached behind to grip the sill with clawing fingers. He swung from side to side and threw his spare hand up to gain a second hold. Gravity pulled at his torso, threatening to drag him down and break both legs on the ground far below. One of his dangling feet tapped against glass. *The kitchen window is underneath. Can I swing through to safety?*

Sally limped to the landing, a rasped call arising

from winded lungs. "Mum? Mum, Banjo punched me in the stomach and jumped out the window."

Enid's footsteps ascended the staircase. Even at this range, Banjo could feel her rage approaching. Any minute now his aching fingers would lose purchase. With what strength that remained, he swung like a trapeze artist and let go. Both feet shattered the kitchen window into jagged shards. Broken glass accompanied his drop onto the sink and draining board. His legs folded, and he tumbled headlong into the kitchen floor tiles. Lacerations from the breakage streaked his bare arms with fine stripes of swelling blood.

Enid stormed back downstairs. Her wide, panda-like eyes sunk into that fiery frizz of thick, electrified hair, filled Banjo's vision. He didn't have time to pick himself off the floor before she hauled him up. Sharp fingernails pressed into the soft, young flesh of his tender shoulders.

"What do you think you're playing at? How dare you punch your sister in the stomach." Enid shook him like a stubborn bottle of ketchup that won't flow.

Fear of his mother evaporated in that instant. Banjo clenched his teeth, then shouted back at her. "Sally broke Tornado. She threw him up on the roof. I hate her. I wish I'd killed that fucking demon."

Enid's insane eyes flared at the profanity and insolence spewing from her eleven-year-old child. She slapped his face first one way and then the other. "Don't you ever speak to me like that again." She pressed one hand on the crown of his head and yanked it around to address the shattered window. "Look at that. See what you've done. How am I going to replace it? Do you think we're made of money? Ever since your father's company folded after his accident, we've precious little to live on."

Banjo twisted his face against the pressure of her hand to make defiant eye contact. "After you pushed him down the stairs, you mean."

Enid roared. She swiped a wooden rolling pin from the table and laid into Banjo with it. Wallop after wallop landed on his limbs with bone crunching force. "I'll teach you a new tune, Banjo."

Banjo curled into a ball and cried. "My name isn't Banjo, it's Simon."

Sally stood in the kitchen doorway, face blending shades from wonder to intrigue and horror. At last she stepped forward and cried out. "Stop, Mum. You'll kill him."

Enid delivered another round of beatings, then halted to catch her breath. Her big-boned torso heaved as she plonked herself down into a wooden kitchen chair to recover.

Sally placed a comforting arm across her shoulders. "He's learnt his lesson, Mum."

Enid growled under her breath. "Time will tell." She patted Sally's reassuring fingers. "Why can't he behave more like his sister? What happened upstairs, child? Was he very cruel to you?"

Sally regarded her whimpering brother, scrunched into a rigid ball on the kitchen floor. "He stole my toy horse and threatened to drop it out of the window. We got in a scuffle and he smashed one of its legs against the wall. It was while I was trying to take Tornado back that he punched me."

On the floor, Banjo's throat twanged. "Liar," he whispered, but didn't dare say anything further for fear of another beating. *That's not how I remember it. Tornado is my horse. Sally took it, not the other way around. Sally took it.* Confusion swamped his brain. Maybe on account of the glass injury and shock from such vicious corporal punishment, but Banjo now doubted his own recollection of events. He shook his head to dismiss the notion.

Enid glanced from the boy back to her daughter. "What happened next?"

Sally nudged a shard of broken glass laying on the floor with the toe of her shoe. "Banjo tried to throw Tornado from the window again. When I resisted, he threatened to shatter him. I pulled away, and he tossed my horse onto the roof. That's when he overbalanced and fell out."

Banjo heard every word and lurched into a jerking fit.

Enid pushed herself out of the chair. "He's starting that again. A few hours in the cellar to reflect on his behaviour should cool him off." She grabbed Banjo by his T-shirt collar and dragged him along the hallway towards the cellar door. Banjo's throat twanged, but he didn't resist.

Back in the kitchen, Sally heard her brother's body collide with each step on the way down into darkness and decay. Enid left him alone and bolted the cellar door shut.

Scurrying rodent feet hurried past Banjo's head in that oppressive, windowless space. The light switch for its two hanging bulbs lay outside, above in the ground floor hallway, beyond the bolted door and his desperate reach. All the boy could do was lay there in pitch black quiet, kept company by unmentionable scurrying creatures. All of them made his skin crawl. His legs, jarred from the kitchen sink impact, ached with a dull warmth. But it was his arms which pained Banjo most. Raised to ward off merciless blows from his mother's rolling pin, they'd suffered the brunt of her physical assault. Both limbs burned with sharp fire. He flinched upon touching them.

"One day, Mother. One day, Sally. I'll return your wickedness in spades." He spat into oblivion, then collapsed in a coughing fit from the dust-filled air.

11

Falling Headlong

CHESHAM - NOVEMBER 2019.

A late twenties legal executive on the pretty end of the nerd spectrum, Amy Yates' blue-framed glasses dominated a petite head framed by straight, auburn hair stretching to the top of her modest chest. Slender and fit - although not toned - she epitomised a grammar school girl who had done well for herself without flourishing in the affective or interpersonal aspects of life. Medium height, medium attractiveness; everything about Amy suggested the acceptable, mediocre and unremarkable. Deep inside, she yearned for more and ached from pangs of loneliness. Yet she couldn't bring herself to engage with the singles scene. Sharing her life and home with another sent chills down her spine, even as she craved love and connection. This desire led to ongoing bouts of depression.

A heartless, sluggish morning in the office transitioned into a bout of crying in the ladies' room. It was there her boss, Yasmin Berry, found her curled up in a stall.

"Sit down, Amy." Yasmin closed the door of her private office. She wheeled her own high-backed leather chair around the desk to sit beside her meek-faced subordinate. A solicitor of mixed English and Persian heritage, Yasmin always spoke with soft, measured tones. Amy couldn't ever recall a time she'd raised her voice or got angry. Hard work, a fair-minded attitude towards her employees and genuine care for their welfare, commanded respect from the firm's workforce with no need for asserted discipline.

Amy lowered herself into a chair, shoulders hunched over. Neck pain from unregistered tension seeped upward into her skull, inducing a headache. She wiped her nose on a tissue. "I'm sorry, Yasmin. I'm ahead on my work. Don't worry, everything will get done."

Yasmin took her seat. She swept a luxuriant mass of long ebony hair back over her shoulders, regarding Amy with warm brown eyes set in a smooth, olive-skinned face. "I'm not worried about the work, Amy. The quality and volume of your output has never been an issue. I'm concerned about you." She studied Amy's nervous, uncoordinated body language. "This isn't the first time, is it?"

Amy hung her head. "No. I'm sorry."

"Stop apologising. You've nothing to be sorry for." She took a breath. "Can I ask how long you've suffered from depression?"

"About three years."

"You hide it well. I've noticed a wobble in your manner from time to time, but otherwise you present a mask of steady resilience to the office."

Amy sniffed. "You've noticed?" Her faced paled. "That's not good."

Yasmin's brown eyes twinkled. "You don't become partner in a law firm without encountering depression sufferers. I sometimes wonder if I got this post on account of being the least strung out, rather than most qualified."

"But you're so good at your job." Amy moved to the edge of her seat.

"You're a sweet young woman. Can I ask if you're seeing anyone about this or taking medication? You're not required to answer. I want to help you cope and stay well, that's all."

Amy blew her nose. "Thank you. I'm not on anti-depressants. I hate drugs of any kind. When it first happened, I went to my doctor. He suggested regular exercise and staying away from caffeine and alcohol. Also to avoid using food as a coping mechanism."

"You appear in fine physical shape. If you're over-eating, the calories must evaporate."

A nervous smile creased Amy's face. "I'm not one for overeating. The doctor suggested I engage with the world. I volunteer at an old people's home."

"How lovely. I bet they appreciate your company."

Amy fidgeted. "It's hard when the residents pass away. We lost a lady called Mary last week. I shared a special bond with her. She lived her entire life as a spinster, like me."

Yasmin placed a finger across pouting lips, then pulled it down to rest beneath her chin. "There're plenty of years for your relationship situation to change, if you want it to. You're a pretty, successful young woman."

Amy looked doubtful. "Anyway. Mary's death sparked another round of sleepless nights and reopened this empty pit I sometimes feel inside."

"That makes sense. What kind of exercise do you partake in?"

"I enjoy walking in the country. Being out in nature and sunlight helps. That's another difficult thing about this time of year. Grey skies, less sunlight and shorter days don't help."

"Seasonal Affective Disorder? That's common. My own mood dips a little toward the end of October." Yasmin stood up and wheeled her chair back to the business side of her desk. "Right then. That presents us with an initial solution." She glanced out the window at a cloudless sky. "It's lunchtime on a pleasant, late November Thursday. I want you to take the afternoon and tomorrow off. Go for a walk now while the weather is decent, then do something fun to treat yourself tomorrow. Will you do that for me?"

Amy rubbed her legs, still glued to the chair. "I suppose I can submit a leave request. I've a little holiday left, though I wanted to take it over Christmas."

Yasmin held up a hand. "This isn't coming out of your leave quota. A day or two off is within my gift to give as partner, Amy. Try those activities that help you reach equilibrium, then come back on Monday - assuming you're well enough."

Amy wobbled to her feet. "I don't want to burden the firm."

Yasmin moved to the door. "You're not a burden. Stop trying to carry everything yourself. That doesn't help anyone. My door may not always be open, but I'll juggle my schedule as best I can if you need to talk. Please consider that, should you struggle further."

"Thank you, Yasmin."

"You're welcome. Take care." Yasmin let her out.

Amy lived in a modest, two bedroom detached bungalow on Chartridge Lane that once belonged to her grandparents. Its silence often felt deafening when she arrived home from the office. Midway through what should be a normal working day, that sensation amplified.

I'm not a failure. I'm not weak. I'm not a burden on others. Amy forced herself to mentally recite calming statements to ward off the black dog of depression. She knew if she sat down in the kitchen, she'd still be there four hours later wallowing in an empty soup of misery.

"Time for a walk." Amy yanked open a hallway cupboard door. She pulled out her backpack and hiking boots, then changed clothes in the master bedroom.

Twenty minutes later, Amy's mood lifted a notch when her feet pressed into the soft turf of a farmer's field. She followed a footpath across an undulating Buckinghamshire landscape of hedgerows and copses, criss-crossed here and there with country lanes in grey ribbons. Her pace quickened with the uptick in her happiness and energy levels.

At Hyde Heath she pondered whether to call it a day and head back. But now the endorphin release acted like a drug. Medication with nothing but healthy side effects. Amy felt around in her blue waterproof jacket pocket. The cold steel barrel of a torch greeted her fingers. *I'll be okay if it's dark before I get home. Yasmin was right: I need this.* She adjusted the straps of her pack, then set off again in a westerly direction.

Another forty-five minutes found Amy exploring a curious dip in a wooded hill. She smiled to herself at the realisation this cartographic feature would be termed a 'depression.' *That label covers a multitude of sins.* Beyond thick stretches of conifer and between a canopy of mixed, bare, broad-leafed trees, an unnatural outline caught her attention. *Is that a house? Crumbs, it looks like an old villa of some description. What's it doing in the woods?* Amy descended a steep incline above the rear of the property. The habitation's dilapidated appearance reminded her of an Internet video she'd watched of a similar house left abandoned, still furnished and stuffed with its owner's possessions. Nobody knew who the place belonged to, but many walkers explored its unsecured interior. From the damage and graffiti shown in that room by room expose posted on YouTube, it was clear others used the place as everything from a teenage shagging centre to occasional squat and drugs den. Amy wondered if this place, beyond the trees ahead, had endured a similar fate. Once upon a time, caring hands built that structure. What would those artisans and labourers think if they could see it now?

She pushed a snagging branch away from her ankle, then stepped into a grassy area beside a pond. The home's dark silhouette reflected in its still surface, brought into sharp relief by the last orange and pink hues of a dusky sky.

I don't think I'll go poking around in there now. What if the place is haunted? She cringed, then emitted an empty laugh which brought zero relief. An inexplicable wave of fear washed over her. Amy shivered. *That's enough exercise for one day. Time to reverse course and cook myself a warming dinner at the bungalow.* She turned and came face to face with two intense, furious grey eyes.

"What the? No. No!" She backed away, tripped over a fallen decayed log, and then tumbled into a bed of crispy autumn leaves.

A lumbering hulk emerged from the shadows and reached for her.

Amy came to with her back resting against cold slates at a pronounced angle. Stars twinkled in a clear, velvet sky. She tried to move, but found her wrists and ankles secured with knotted nylon cord. Every motion dug those bonds deeper into her burning flesh. She looked around. *I'm on the roof of that house in the woods. How did I get up here?* Dull recollections returned. *The man. The man in the woods. What did he do?* Her head throbbed worse than the stress headache she'd endured at work.

"Payback time, Sally." A balding cranium poked through a patch of missing slates, ten feet away. An angry, beefcake figure clambered out of what must be an attic.

Amy's neck stiffened. "Who are you? Why have you done this?"

The man crawled along the roof line, then bent forward to retrieve a bulky object resting in the gutter. "Look what I've found, Sally." He clutched a lump of rotting wood close to one cheek.

In the intermittent light of a low moon shining through the claws of bare deciduous branches, Amy discerned the shape of a carved horse with three legs. Ragged and covered in moss, the child's toy retained its recognisable outline with a tenuous grip. As her captor squeezed it close, that grip failed. The horse crumbled to flakes of dissolving wood in his hands.

The man howled at the moon like an anguished wolf. "Nooo. Tornado." He held out two handfuls of the figure's remains to Amy in an accusatory gesture. "Look what you've done."

Amy shook her head. "What are you talking about?" Tension wracked her body with a vengeance.

"You threw Tornado onto the roof, then pushed me out the window, Sally." The accusation turned to shouting. Insane as he appeared, this lumbering monster showed no concerns over his voice carrying.

That familiar emptiness opened inside Amy at the agonising realisation any scream she released would go unheeded.

The man pawed at her and raised her bound form to

a standing position. "Now it's your turn to fly, Sally."

Amy turned her head and shrieked straight into his face. "I'm not Sally. My name is Amy Yates. You've got the wrong person."

"Liar. Filthy, deceitful trickster." His words dripped with malice and cruel intent.

Firm hands launched Amy headlong out from the roof edge. In her ultimate moments of mortality, Amy's body nosedived towards the ground.

They say life flashes before wakeful eyes during death's approach. For Amy Yates, time slowed, and those pictures came as she always imagined they would. Images of a happy, sheltered childhood danced before her. Then awkward teenage years, never fitting in or going out. At college she secured good grades by dint of hard work and zero socialising. Then came the death of her cherished grandparents and moving into their home to live an independent but miserable life. In chronological terms, her plummet was over in a heartbeat. By the time her face splattered with a sickening and bloody crack on bitter paving slabs, snapping her neck, Amy realised she didn't care. Was it a product of her depression that meant death presented an equal or happier prospect to life in this world? Her only regret was the pain her parents would suffer once they received the news.

On top of the roof, Banjo leered over the black guttering at Amy's lifeless body with its crimson puddle surrounding her shattered form. He twitched and flopped back against the slates. From the deepest recesses of his throat, a twanging sound thrummed.

*   *   *

RETTON HOUSE - NOVEMBER 2019.

"It's arrived. It's arrived." Bertram closed the front door behind a delivery driver who'd deposited a coffin-sized brown parcel on the hallway floor.

Gillian emerged from the living room with Mace at her heels. She fancied her father almost performed a little jig of excitement around his mysterious box. The spaniel sniffed its edges, then - detecting nothing interesting or delicious - wandered back into the living room.

"What's arrived?" Gillian asked.

"My new telescope." Bertram tugged at some brown parcel tape holding the package together.

Gerard came out of the kitchen clutching a sturdy pair of scissors. "Would these help, Mr Crane?"

"Thanks, Gerard." Bertram took the offered tool and set to work snipping through sticky adhesive bonds.

"What's all the fuss?" Felicity appeared from the conservatory.

"Daddy's got a new telescope. Look at him. You'd think Christmas has come early."

Felicity rolled her eyes. "What, another one? Honestly, Bertram, at this rate Retton will end up a facsimile of the Greenwich Observatory."

Bertram snorted. "Nonsense. You could fit all three of my telescopes inside one of theirs with ample room to spare."

Felicity placed a hand on her left hip. "Dare I ask what function this one performs that its predecessors don't?"

Bertram pointed a finger straight down at the parcel between his legs. "This baby is a Newtonian Reflector with a computerised auto-tracking mount. It can find and follow forty-three-thousand objects in the night sky from an electronic database."

"That's why you've had electricians round to fit external sockets near the attic roof hatch? I thought we were having floodlights installed for when guests come and go at parties."

Bertram scratched his head. "I'll fit those too, if you'd like?"

Felicity bit her lip. "Never mind. Have fun with your new toy." She disappeared down the corridor, shaking her head.

Gillian sidled up to her father. "Can I have a look?"

Delight washed over Bertram's countenance. "Of course you can, Pixie. Would you like to help me set it up? The forecast is for clear skies this evening."

"Okay. Tell me what to do."

Gillian carried a series of counterweights and a remote control device up into the attic.

Bertram placed his Newtonian Reflector beside a motorised tripod Gerard had stood near the roof hatch.

Gillian regarded the many boxes piled up in this rarely visited section of the house. Some still contained childhood toys she couldn't bear to part with. Dark and dusty though the attic was, a powerful sense of home gripped her.

Bertram looked over his shoulder. "Everything all right, Pixie?"

Gillian nodded. "The ghosts of a younger me. Nothing more. Will we need Gerard to help us set up?"

"No, we can manage the last bit between ourselves. Are you sure you'll be warm enough in that jacket?"

Gillian set down the weights and controller, then patted her winter coat. "If I feel cold on the roof, I'll pop down to my room for a jumper and some gloves."

Bertram unbolted the roof hatch and pushed it open. Four steps led out onto a limited flat area towards the rear of the main structure. He poked his head back through. "Pass me the tripod, would you?"

Gillian complied. She positioned herself to be ready for the next item on his list. Across the attic, Gareth's pale form stared out of a dark corner. His shadowy outline lingered for a moment before being swallowed up by the gloom. Gillian took a breath. *How long will all this go on?*

"Telescope next," Bertram called.

Gillian passed the fat, tubular device into his outstretched arms.

"Thank you. If you bring those counterweights and the controller, we'll put it all together."

Gillian stepped onto the roof, lugging the last pieces of her father's new astronomical kit.

"Splendid," Bertram said. "Set them down and pass me the first counterweight. We need to balance the telescope. I've already aligned the tripod with Polaris."

Gillian watched him attach first one weight, then the

other. At last he connected the controller and plugged a power lead into one of a pair of external, shielded electrical sockets near the hatch. "What happens next?"

"We'll get a three star fix, starting with Rigel. That should lock the auto-tracking in."

"There's a bright moon tonight. Can we view its surface?"

"Of course." Bertram busied himself adjusting levers and peering through the eyepiece.

Gillian's blood ran cold even as her head heated. *Oh, Dear God, not again.* She stepped away from her father's telescope for fear of knocking both it and him over the edge. Far below, the immaculate gardens tended by Old Joe and his occasional helpers, blurred into an overgrown mess of weeds and encroaching woodland plants. Vertigo caused her to sway. Rough, cruel hands gripped her shoulders.

Angry male words rasped in a venomous lash. *"Now it's your turn to fly, Sally."*

The intense, grey stare of that man she'd seen in the dirty kitchen on Halloween filled her visual space.

A woman's voice, not her own, bellowed from Gillian's lungs. *"I'm not Sally. My name is Amy Yates. You've got the wrong person."*

The killer spoke again in her ear. *"Liar. Filthy, deceitful trickster."*

An unkempt, overgrown patch of weeds assaulting cracked patio slabs flew up to meet her. Air rushing past felt like water against her pale, tender cheeks.

"Pixie." Bertram grabbed his daughter's legs at the knee as her body careened over the parapet.

A sharp snapping noise inside Gillian's head was followed by impenetrable blackness filling her still-open eyes. That final curtain of mortality dissolved into a dizzying arc of the swaying, tidy rear lawn at Retton House below. Gillian shrieked. She thrust her hands down as if to push the ground away.

Red-faced and puffing, Bertram dragged her body back onto the telescope platform, before collapsing in a sweaty heap.

"Daddy. Daddy, are you all right?" Gillian wiped his sweating brow.

Bertram caught his breath. "You took the words right out of my mouth. Tell me it wasn't another vision?"

Gillian's head sagged. "I wish I could."

Bertram pulled her close against the chill night air. "I thought I'd lost you. Do you want to go inside?"

"No, I'm better this time. No choking or embarrassing accidents."

"Almost something far worse." Bertram shuffled them both closer to the attic hatch. "Can we talk about it?"

"I saw that man again."

"The one from the chocolate incident?"

"Yes. He was holding someone over the edge of a shoddy roof."

"The same house?"

"I can't be sure. It was rundown and tucked away amidst trees or shrubs. This time I heard him speak." Gillian poked a finger in one ear.

"What did he say?" Bertram asked.

"Now it's your turn to fly, Sally."

"That explains your outburst."

"Outburst?"

"Right before you tumbled over the parapet, you shrieked." Bertram massaged his left temple with the free hand. "Uncanny. I swear it wasn't your voice. You said-"

"I'm not Sally. My name is Amy Yates. You've got the wrong person," Gillian interrupted.

"That's it. What happened next?"

"The man spoke again. He said, *'Liar. Filthy, deceitful trickster,'* then pushed her off the roof." Gillian shuddered. "I heard her neck snap when she hit a patio below. It was awful."

Bertram kissed her on the crown. "I wonder who Sally is, or was?"

Gillian moistened her lips. "Could that horrible man be acting out vicarious vengeance with these women? Amy was desperate to let him know he'd made a mistake; that she wasn't the Sally he spoke of. I felt her terror, like the others."

Bertram lifted his face to the stars. "We'll all be watching the news for the name Amy Yates, after tonight."

Later, Gillian sank into bed with Amy's last moments still crying out for attention. She forced herself not to endure another replay. *Yates? Like Ted Yates, the gardener in my dream about Avril. Only a coincidence, I'm sure.* True as her assumption may have been, the surname brought up more pondering over

Avril's ghost and why she still ran through the gardens at Retton. Then there was Gareth, the upset nine-year-old who couldn't accept he was dead. Had his father ever come home from the war? Why was the rear of his skull in such a state when she encountered his restless spirit?

Gillian switched off her bedside lamp and sank into an uneasy slumber.

* * *

CHINNOR QUARRY - NOVEMBER 2019.

A shabby, maroon 1999 model Rover 200, 3 door hatchback ground to a halt along a rough tree-lined track following The Ridgeway near Chinnor in Oxfordshire. Banjo checked his rear-view mirror for signs of walkers fading in and out of the early morning mist. Weird, contaminated aventurine water from the Old Kiln Lakes at the bottom of a sheer drop, presented an other-worldly hue like something from a science fiction drama. But the water didn't interest Banjo. Multiple terraces cut into the limestone face of the disused quarry, provided an adequate drop onto unforgiving rock. Amy Yates hadn't drowned. The calculating killer was smart enough to realise the authorities would smell a rat if she wound up floating. His activities were drawing unwanted attention. Caution was required.

Banjo opened the boot and retrieved her body, wrapped in a black tarpaulin. He lugged his burden to the quarry's edge. Loose runs of limestone tumbled free beneath his feet. He slipped and reached out to grab an exposed tree root for safety. The miniature landslide of pebbles ceased.

Banjo settled onto a level shelf and unwrapped the tarpaulin. Amy's lifeless body meant nothing to him. Already the red/blue discolouration of lividity tinted her skin from pooling blood. He remembered the way pressure on his mother's corpse had produced red marks that wouldn't fade, even in the few hours between her drowning and impromptu burial. Care would be needed not to leave tell-tale marks on this lifeless bag of flesh. He looked into her sunken eyes. *It's not Sally, but it should be. I'll make you pay, Sally. We're not through, yet. I'll find another.* He pulled a penknife from his rear trouser pocket and severed the nylon cords securing Amy's wrists and ankles. In a sick echo of her execution the night before, Banjo lifted Amy's dead weight to mimic an upright position, shoulders held fast in his fat-fingered but cautious grip. "Goodnight, Sally." Pushing a dead body from heights wouldn't elicit the same level of satisfaction as before, yet he expected to derive some pleasure in watching her fall.

Banjo shoved Amy's corpse off the ledge into midair, careful to ensure it would go headlong as she had at the end of her life. He didn't fancy climbing all the way down and hauling her body up for another try. Besides, there could soon be dog walkers and fitness fanatics passing by. Nobody should see or remember either him or his vehicle.

Amy Yates hit the rocky quarry floor with enough force to further shatter her battered head and stain the yellow limestone with crimson spray.

Banjo brushed his plastic glove covered palms together like a contented workman, then stomped up the bank and through the ridge-top tree line to his car.

* * *

HIGH WYCOMBE - DECEMBER 2019.

"If they play Slade one more time, I'm going to scream." DS Jason Hargreaves sat down with a thud in his protesting, blue office desk chair at High Wycombe Police Station. He unclipped a snap-on tie and dumped it next to his in tray, before unbuttoning a constrictive shirt collar.

Christmas tunes blared out of a tinny, treble-heavy radio speaker not much smaller than the device it served. The cheap unit sat atop a bulky white cable conduit screwed to one wall above a line of desks.

DC Frances Kelly clicked through pages of a computer police report. Her tongue protruded through sneering teeth. "You love it really, Jason."

Jason cracked his knuckles. "First of bloody December and all they play are the same tired old Christmas songs."

"This station runs them back-to-back. They started last week." Frances made momentary eye contact. "While you were off gallivanting in Scotland. How was life north of the border?"

Jason opened a three drawer desk pod and pulled out a stained, white china mug. "An absolute treat. I may have over-imbibed on heather ale, but I couldn't care less. A bloomin' decent break. Did anything juicy come in while I was Munro bagging?"

"Not much. A body in the Old Kiln Lakes quarry at Chinnor. A twenty-nine-year-old female. Some jogger called it in."

Jason spooned instant coffee from a personal jar into his cup. He kept his coffee supply locked away for two reasons. First, the standard office blend sucked. Second, if he left it in the office kitchen area, some bugger would help themselves. "Swimmer?"

"No. Her head was splattered across rocks, twenty feet from the water's edge. Preliminaries suggest suicide rather than death by misadventure. She had a history of depression. Her body was scored with ligature marks on the wrists and ankles."

"Self-harm?"

"If I had to guess. She wasn't tied up when we found her. No other indications of assault. The coroner had better be good at jigsaws if he intends to piece her skull back together. We haven't ruled out foul play, but the job aren't initiating a murder enquiry at present. Fancy punishing yourself like that, then going full-bore? Jeez, you should have seen the state of her boss, when I dropped by her office for a chat."

Jason stood up and waved his mug. "Brew?"

"I've still got some tea, thanks." Frances lifted a steaming mug between both hands. "The deceased worked for a law firm in Chesham. Her boss - one of the partners - found her crying in the loo around lunchtime the day before she turned up dead. After sitting her down for a chat, she sent the woman home for the afternoon and following day. Even told her to take a hike - in the literal sense."

Jason flinched. "Ouch. That's going to haunt her."

"Yeah. She had no idea the tragic, depressed creature was going to lob herself off the side of a quarry."

"Her medical history and eleventh hour state of mind seem a likely motive for suicide. Anything from her nearest and dearest?"

"Family Liaison spoke to her parents. They're devastated, of course."

Jason shrugged.

Frances went on. "Miss Lonely Hearts lived in her dead grandparents' bungalow. No friends or romantic interests. She volunteered at an old folks' home for company."

Jason perched on the corner of his desk. "Hers or theirs? How bloody depressing. It sounds like she had a lot going for her, but couldn't see the wood for the trees. Why is it always the quiet ones who receive an extra serving of shit? God, I'm glad I'm a heartless, self-interested bastard."

Slade finished on the radio. They were followed by their obligatory Christmas rivals, *Wizzard*.

Jason groaned. "I could have put money on it. Crap, Frankie. One of these days I'm going to break your sodding radio. Either that or I'll be taking a run up to Chinnor Quarry myself, for a spot of terminal skydiving."

Frances sipped her tea. "Piss off. Anyway, with a bit of luck it'll be *The Pogues and Kirsty MacColl,* next."

Jason laughed and wandered off to find some hot water for his coffee.

12

Rotten to the Core

RETTON HOUSE - DECEMBER 2019.

Gillian reclined on a covered platform atop a ladder in the boughs of a massive Western Red Cedar tree. Joe the head gardener had dated this non-indigenous species of conifer at a century old or more. Fond memories of her father building the 'tree house' came flooding back. It wasn't a house in the truest sense; more a collection of sanded and oiled planks bolted together and covered with a pitched roof of waterproof sheeting to allow rain runoff. But she'd spent many happy hours imagining it as a home all her own, before age and propriety caused those once regular visits to dwindle.

Gillian ran her fingers across a carved wooden sign screwed beside the access ladder. It read *'Pixie's House.' Life was simpler then. Look at me: I set off two years ago to stand on my own feet as an independent woman. Now here I am seeking solace in the tree house like a ten-year-old girl.* She swung her legs over the edge of the platform and allowed them to dangle, then laughed at the juvenile figure she must present to the world.

"Is that you up there, Miss Gillian?" Old Joe's characterful voice called from way below on the dewy, emerald grass.

"I haven't been up here in a while, Joe," she replied.

Joe stepped back far enough to make eye contact from the ground. He lifted his flat cap and scratched his head. "I didn't mention if afore, as I wasn't expectin' to see you up there, but the cedar isn't in a good way."

Gillian's face fell. "No. Is it safe?"

"Can't say for certain, Miss. She seems sturdy enough to the touch. Have you noticed the branches?"

Gillian hadn't, but now she observed one side of the tree's branches had faded to a dull brown. "Do you know what it is?"

"I fear it's Armillaria Root Rot. I had a dig around the root system near its edges. There's White Mycelium underneath. She stands alone in a clear expanse of lawn, so there's little chance of it spreading to other plants through the rhizomorphs. I've let things alone for now."

Gillian climbed down the ladder. "Isn't there a cure?"

Joe averted his eyes to avoid staring at her backside in an affront to the woman's modesty. "Sorry to say there ain't. She'll have to be felled and given up to fire, in time."

Gillian reached the ground. "That's a shame. This portion of the rear garden will seem bare without it."

"True enough, Miss. I'll be sorry to see her come down, myself."

"Will you do something for me, Joe?"

"What's that?"

"Unscrew the tree house sign before I return to Hampshire. I'd like to take it back with me."

"Are you going soon, Miss?"

"Not before New Year, at any rate," Gillian replied.

Joe peered up the ladder. "Why don't I fetch a screwdriver now? Best to strike while the iron is hot, or afore Old Peg topples."

A wry smile teased one corner of Gillian's mouth. "Old Peg?"

Joe flushed. "It's what I've always called her. Silly, I know."

"I think it's sweet. Old Peg." Gillian patted the massive trunk.

"Hold up, Miss, I'll be back with that screwdriver. Do you want me to fetch Gerard? I'm not too steady up ladders these days."

"No, that's okay. I'll do it."

Joe returned three minutes later, brandishing the promised tool. Worry lines creased his forehead. "Are you sure you're all right doing this?"

Gillian took the screwdriver. "I'll be fine. You wait down here and keep watch."

"Okay, Miss. Be careful."

Gillian scaled the ladder without a second thought. The four screws securing her 'Pixie's House' plaque had all rusted. Friction burns from the screwdriver handle stung her fingers with the effort of loosening each corroded thread. At last, tired and with palms dark from pressure, she dropped the screwdriver and wooden sign over the side. They bounced on the lush sward around the tree's decaying roots.

"I'm coming down." Gillian descended the ladder in a flash while Joe turned aside once more. She found him lifting the sign between his rugged fingers. A light of nostalgia glittered in his moist eyes.

"This sign has worn better than its fixings. That's what happens when you use properly seasoned and treated wood." He handed it to her.

"It'll make a fine indoor ornament wherever I end up. A small piece of my old home inside my new one."

"That's a nice touch, Miss Gillian." Joe bent over and collected his screwdriver. "I still remember Mr Crane carving it for you, all those years ago." He rubbed his neck. "I was more spry back then."

Gillian clutched the sign. "You could dance rings around anyone your age, if you wanted to."

Joe beamed. "Not sure I'd go in for dancing, these days. Now if you'll excuse me, I've got to prepare an advert for the local paper."

"Cedar wood for sale?" Gillian teased with an uneasy tone.

Joe snorted. "No, Miss. We're getting a temporary, extra pair of hands until Christmas. There's more manual labour at this time of year, what with leaves and such."

"How about Andy Gingham?"

Joe scratched some white stubble beneath his jawline. "I'd take him in a heartbeat. Splendid chap. The spit of what I was myself at his age."

"But?"

"But he's moved away to Norfolk."

Gillian set off with him towards the greenhouses. "That's sad. He was one of the friendliest seasonal workers I've ever met."

"Aye, he was that. Still, there's always a soul looking for casual work in these parts. Someone will turn up."

Gillian inhaled a deep lungful of crisp, December air. "Let's hope they meet your exacting standards."

Joe paused at one greenhouse door as they prepared to part company. "So long as they can push a wheelbarrow and lug stuff around, they'll do fine. That and keep their paws off my gingernut biscuits."

Gillian wrinkled her nose. "Thanks for helping me retrieve this." She waved the plaque. "Good luck with your advertisement."

"Do you remember this?" Gillian set the tree house sign on the conservatory table beside her father.

He sat back, folded his FT, let it drop and held up the chunk of carved wood. "My goodness. It's weathered well."

"Joe said the cedar tree has a disease."

"That's right. He told me back in spring. Some kind of incurable root infection. A real pity." He rested the plaque on the table again. "So you salvaged a memento before it's gone forever? Good for you."

Felicity entered the conservatory holding a glass of water. "There's nothing in the papers about an Amy Yates again today."

Bertram folded his hands. "Maybe her body hasn't

turned up? If we *are* talking about the same killer, he's already dumped one woman down a sewer and the other in a barrel he chucked in the Thames. She could be anywhere."

Gillian sat down opposite her father. "It's been a fortnight. No murder stories. No missing person's reports. If she was killed but not found, somebody must be looking for her."

Felicity joined them at the table. "Jumping is a common way for people to commit suicide."

Gillian groaned. "But she didn't commit suicide, Mum. She was murdered."

Felicity fixed her daughter with a penetrating stare. "Yes, Darling. I realise that. But do the authorities?"

Bertram hunched over the table. "Flick, you're a star. I never thought of that. Do you have your mobile phone, Gillian?"

Gillian pulled out her smartphone. "What do you want me to do?"

"Bring up an Internet search for Buckinghamshire Council Coroner. If Amy is registered as a suicide, there'll be an inquest scheduled in her name. It's a public record for a public event."

Gillian flicked through her phone, clicked on a search result and scrolled the page. "Here we go: *Forthcoming inquests.* They seem to be held on Tuesdays, Wednesdays, or Thursdays. *10am - David Keegan. Died...* Blah, blah, blah." She froze.

Felicity and Bertram watched her rigid features.

"She's there, isn't she?" Felicity leaned closer.

"Yes. *18th December, Beaconsfield Court. 2pm - Amy*

Marie Yates. Died 21st November 2019 in Chinnor. Home address, Chesham. Aged 29 years."

Bertram shifted in his seat. "Chinnor. Across the boundary in Oxfordshire."

Felicity frowned. "What would you jump from in Chinnor? It's a village."

"The parish church or the quarry," Bertram replied. "My money is on the quarry."

"Why?" Felicity asked.

"Because if what Pixie saw was real, Amy died elsewhere. Unless that house from her vision is in Chinnor, but the murderer doesn't live there. He'd hardly stick around with a dead woman on his doorstep. No, he's dumped her body somewhere convincing to make it appear like a suicide. Can you imagine dragging a corpse up the inside of a church tower unnoticed? I don't think so. It has to be the quarry."

Gillian rested her phone on the table. "Why did I have to endure that episode while we were stargazing? Stuck on a roof, of all places. It couldn't have happened while I was dozing on the sofa, could it? A nice soft drop onto the rug."

"You'd have squashed Mace." Bertram winked. "Coincidence? Or could it be part of this temporary bond you've formed with those unfortunate women? A mysterious, universal plan." He drew breath. "Do you want to attend the inquest?"

"On the 18th December?" Felicity drummed her fingers on the table top. "That's her birthday, Bertram."

"Good heavens, so it is. An old woman of twenty-eight."

Gillian grimaced. "Only a year younger than Amy Yates."

Felicity cleared her throat. "You can go if you wish, Darling. We won't try to stop you. It seems a little odd on your birthday though, don't you think?"

"I needn't attend. What would I do, offer evidence? Evidence of what? The moment I claim to have seen Amy murdered in a waking dream, I'll destroy her agonised family afresh, get held in contempt of court and wind up in a psychiatric ward." She grabbed her phone and stuffed it back in her pocket with an angry thrust. "I've said it before and I'll say it again. That's what's so damned frustrating about this whole debacle: I can't do anything with these encounters other than endure them."

Felicity took a small sip of water. "Your father and I were wondering if it's time to invite your friend Deborah over. We promised she could stay."

Gillian's visage brightened a touch. "She'd be a tonic. If Deborah secures a couple of weeks off work, can she come for my birthday and stay through Christmas?"

"Doesn't she have family to visit?" Bertram asked.

"No. Both her parents passed away five or six months before we met. I suppose I've never mentioned that before." Gillian thought for a moment. "She'll go into a blind panic thinking she's supposed to buy you a present of Tiffany's jewellery or goodness knows what for Christmas, Mum. Deborah believes we're posh."

Felicity smiled. "Tell her a small box of shortbread or

something similar will suffice. I'm happy for her to stay if your father is."

Bertram got up from his seat. "She can remain as long you wish, Pixie."

"What if she eats like a horse?" Gillian unearthed a semblance of her buried, cheeky humour again.

"Then we'll stick her in the stables with the others, like you teased." He picked up his paper and swatted Gillian's shoulder. "I'm taking Troy out on Hack. Have a good day."

Gillian had maintained weekly phone calls with Deborah Rowling ever since her return to Retton House. These were always conducted on Friday evenings, without fail.

Deborah's voice blended delight with a hint of concern over receiving a call from Gillian at work on a Thursday morning. "Hey, Fairy Princess. Is everything all right? God, you must be so sick of everybody asking you that all the time."

"Hi, Deborah. Can you talk, or isn't it a suitable moment?"

"I can talk." Her positive response melted to uncertainty. "What are we talking about?"

"My folks wondered if you'd like to visit for my birthday and stay through Christmas?"

Deborah drew in a sharp, if overacted breath. "At Crane Towers?"

"Knock it off, silly. We're not royalty. Okay, Mum is society, but that's not the same. It doesn't amount to a hill of beans, these days. Would you like to? Can you take the time off?"

"Hell yeah. I didn't have more than a couple of days in summer. No proper holiday this year. I'm owed shed-loads of leave. Where are we at now? The 5th."

Gillian sat on the edge of her bed with an open diary. "If you arrive Monday the 16th - two days before my birthday - and leave on the 2nd of January, you'd be talking twelve or thirteen office days; once they deduct stat days over Christmas and New Year."

"It's doable. I can return to work the following Monday. That's the 6th. I wish you were coming home with me. It's been so lonely bashing around Alresford without you."

"Just you and the vase for company?"

"It looks beautiful, but it's a lousy conversationalist."

Gillian rocked on her mattress at the uplifting emotional wave instigated by Deborah's corny humour. "I'll bet it's a good listener?"

"Cheeky mare." Her tone became serious but gentle. "Have you had any more of those experiences?"

"No. Not since November. We found out this morning that there's an inquest for an Amy Yates, the same day as my birthday."

"Holy crap. They'd have burnt you at the stake for those visions, not so many centuries ago."

"Amy was twenty-nine."

Deborah cleared her throat and spoke in hushed tones to avoid being overheard by her office colleagues. "Was she murdered?"

"There's no public report or story I can find about it. Mum suggested they could have recorded her death as suicide. That's how we came to look up inquests."

"Mummy Crane sounds like something of a sleuth."

"Measured and pragmatic. It's her way."

Mirth rose again in Deborah's voice. "Unlike you. Are you sure you weren't left under the cabbage patch?"

"Ha Ha. Mum is where I get my eye for detail from. The wilder aspects of my character are paternal." Gillian hitched her legs up and lay back with the phone. "I want to go back after New Year, too. A lot depends on whether this bizarre chain of events is still unfolding. Oh Deborah, I hope that killer doesn't hurt anyone else. But I'm worried he will."

"What a bastard. The sicko must have shot his bolt. Hey, that palace of yours isn't haunted, is it?"

Gillian bit her lip. She'd neglected to mention anything about Avril or Gareth in her conversations with Deborah. Her mind raced for an appropriate but truthful answer. One that wouldn't scare her bestie away, considering Deborah was due to stay in the very suite Gillian chased Gareth's ghost into. "Well, if it is, I never met any ghosts during my time growing up here. And Retton isn't a palace, it's a house."

"That's a relief. The ghost thing, I mean. I'm not as brave as you. If I clocked half the shit you've witnessed, I'd poo myself."

"Been there, done that," Gillian groaned.

Deborah half laughed. "Whoops. I almost forgot. Sorry, Hun, I wasn't being funny."

"Forget it. When will you have a definite answer on your leave request from work?"

"Give me ten minutes. If it's a *yay* - and it had better be or my boss can make his own bloody tea from here on out - I'll text you."

"Cool. I'm looking forward to it."

"Ditto. Gotta fly. Speak soon. Bye." Deborah hung up.

Gillian swung off the bed, then positioned her *'Pixie's House'* sign on the dressing table as a temporary measure. *I hope Gareth leaves that alone.*

True to her word, a text message pinged up from Deborah within ten minutes: *'It's a go. See you on the 16th. Tell Jeeves I like lemon in my Earl Grey and I'll need an alarm call at seven each morning.'*

Gillian grinned from ear to ear. She keyed in a sarcastic response to Deborah's generic butler name quip: *'Jeeves told you to DO ONE and bring a bloody alarm clock.'* She put the phone away. *That girl is insufferable, but I love her. I'd better let the household know we're expecting company in a little over a week.*

*   *   *

ASHBURNHAM - AUGUST 1988.

"Have you seen Sally?" Banjo's nervous face poked around the living room door.

Enid slouched in a high-backed chair before the empty fireplace. August was one of only four months where indoor temperatures ran high enough for the fire to remain unlit. Still, she gazed at the cold grate as though it leapt with tongues of orange heat and light.

Rays of late afternoon sun slanted between gaps and poked through holes in the moth-eaten curtains. Enid wasn't fond of sunlight. She kept the drapes pulled in most rooms at Ashburnham – bar her own room after dark - and avoided venturing out of doors on bright days.

"Mum?" Banjo prompted her again.

"I'm not your sister's keeper." Enid didn't look round while she spoke. The twist cap on a green glass bottle of gin came free in her grasp. She lifted it to her lips and took a hearty belt like a desert nomad slaking their thirst at an oasis. Folds of sagging flesh jostled around her throat in time with a noisy series of gulps.

Banjo backed away. If Sally wasn't indoors and he couldn't see her playing in their overgrown garden, you could bet she was up to no good. *What manner of torture has she devised for me this time?* He trudged along the hallway and through the kitchen towards the back door. Fresh panes of glass filled two frames above the sink he'd shattered during his attempt to drop from the upstairs window without breaking his legs. While the attempt itself proved successful, the beating Enid gave him afterwards left the boy wondering if broken legs might have been a preferable alternative. Clean glass looked out of place in such a grotty setting. Enid hadn't bothered to wipe the other windows when the glazier arrived to install new ones. Banjo remembered unspoken disdain written across the workman's phizog while he set about his task. He didn't take a break and fitted the new panes in record time. What snide stories had he told colleagues, friends and family after peeling away down the track to civilisation upon completion of his job?

Banjo stopped by the back door then wet an index finger under the kitchen sink cold tap. He leaned across the draining board to reach some older, dirty panes. A film of grime coated his finger at each stroke. It required several more dunks under the tap before he finished scrawling a message with clean water on the filthy window: *'Sally is a cunt.'*

Banjo laughed to himself. Forbidden profanity felt like striking a blow for rebellion and liberation in his mental prison world. If his mother read that message, more beatings and another spell of incarceration in the cellar would follow. Right now, dry gin was keeping her occupied. He expected that to be the case for the rest of the day. He'd lost count how many times their neglectful mother sent him and Sally to bed without supper. She was always a tough woman, but her harshness amplified after Derek's 'accident.' No way would he have let his children go unnourished.

Banjo shut off the tap and opened the back door. *I'll wipe the message off later, before Mum sobers up. There's time enough for Sally to see it and me to destroy the evidence before she tattles.*

Hearty warmth soaked into his bones as a bumble bee buzzed past on its never-ending quest for pollen.

A sound of dull pottery falling and breaking drew his attention towards a tumbledown outbuilding near the foot of what had once been a rear lawn. Banjo pushed through a bank of invasive ferns and approached the long, stone hut. Assorted miniature squares of glass in its rotting window were interspersed with missing companions. Moss and passing time chased out mortar from between the structure's rough building blocks. Banjo crept up to one windowsill, hoping to catch Sally at some illicit activity he could later accuse her of. *Mother won't believe me, even if it's true. She sides with Sally on every occasion. Why am I always blamed for my sister's wickedness?*

The outbuilding appeared empty, save for a rusty collection of gardening implements, assorted ceramic pots, freestanding shelving and enough cobwebs to spin a fairy gown.

No sign of her. I'd better check to see what caused that noise. He slipped around the side and clicked open a wrought iron Suffolk latch. The door creaked on hinges that hadn't been oiled in living memory. They only used the outbuilding during daytime. Since he'd possessed few power tools and had no use for electricity there, his father never bothered connecting this crumbling storage shack to the supply. You were always at the mercy of ambient light levels or a torch beam when rummaging around inside. Banjo didn't have a torch on him. He paused in the doorway, waiting for his visual purple to adjust and improve detail levels along the shadowy outlines of various objects.

"Sally?" His voice deadened without reflecting; each tone muffled by the obligatory coating of crud that plagued every inch of Ashburnham like a body riddled with cancer. *Why am I surprised there's no reply? Would*

Sally reveal herself if she's up to no good? He pushed further inside the outbuilding.

The door slammed shut with a bang. Dislodged flakes of corrosion fluttered from its noisy hinges. The portal's impact was followed and overtaken in volume by the deafening creak and topple of a floor to ceiling section of shelving, crammed with old pots of paint, varnish and weed killer. Banjo collapsed with the storage unit's bulk pinning his lower body to the uneven, earth dusted floor. He lay face up, choking on clouds of grime particles shaken free by the disturbance's kinetic energy.

Sally leaned over the collapsed shelving to leer into his face. "You look pale, Banjo. You should spend more time outdoors in the sunshine. I read that it's good for you."

Banjo scowled. "Don't call me Banjo." He struggled against the weight, unable to free his legs. "What do you want? Get this thing off me, Sally."

Sally pouted. "I want to help my brother. Your bones could become brittle if they don't receive enough vitamin D from the sun. This shelving might have broken your legs."

Banjo coughed again. "Then get it off me and we'll go outside to play." He realised his helpless predicament, pinned beneath a weight he couldn't shift and at his spiteful sister's mercy.

Sally pulled a gunmetal cigarette lighter from her skirt pocket.

Banjo stared at it. "What are you doing with Dad's old lighter? Does Mum know you've got it? There'll be trouble when she finds out."

Sally shook her head. "She doesn't know. Who's going to tell her, you? Mum will soon be lost in another drunken haze, if she isn't already. That's for the best."

"Why?" Banjo strained to lift his head off the grimy floor.

"Because retrospective sunlight therapy can be painful, or so I've heard." She flicked the flint wheel. A flame sputtered to life atop the lighter. "Some patients are even known to scream. We won't disturb our mother if she's drowning her sorrows in alcohol."

Banjo tried to tug his legs free again, without success.

Sally put her full weight on top of the collapsed shelving.

Banjo cried out. "Sally, you're crushing me."

A maniacal light flickered in Sally's eyes. "That sensation should distract from any negative reactions to your therapy."

"What's this thera-?"

He never finished before Sally ran the lighter beneath his left forearm. The flame licked and singed his soft flesh. Banjo screamed. He threw a thrashing fit until his pinned left wrist sprained and broke free of the crushing furniture. He raised the agonised arm to wrestle against Sally's attempts at burning the opposite one. "I'm going to kill you, Sally." He spat in her face.

Sally pulled back, dropping the lighter. Its still-burning flame caught against a small heap of oily rags dumped in one corner of the building. They ignited with a spontaneous whoosh. Flickering light illuminated the stone shack's interior. Onyx clouds of choking smoke billowed towards the door. A thin trickle of flammable liquid seeping from one of the toppled cannisters caught. Its tiny river of fire snaked back to lick at the rotted shelving timbers.

Sally grabbed an old bucket and ran to the pond. She returned to douse the flames while the fire caused enough structural weakness in the shelving for Banjo to break free. The blaze ended with equal rapidity to its ignition.

Brother and sister staggered from the outbuilding, faces and clothing blackened.

Banjo noticed burn marks on his sister's arms. *Did she have those before the blaze?* Why did his mind get confused about such details?

Sally doubled over to clear her throat. When she lifted her eyes, they fell upon the reverse side of Banjo's kitchen window inscription; its lettering large enough to view from this distance. "That's it, Banjo." Calm determination buttressed the tones of her statement. "I'm going to rouse Mum if I have to slap her back to consciousness." She ran for the house.

Banjo's lungs heaved, fit to burst. He'd missed catching on fire by a whisker and was desperate for revenge. He tugged a crumbling chunk of stone free from one corner of the outbuilding's exterior wall. *We'll see who's unconscious the longest: you or her.* "I said: don't call me Banjo," he shouted, then lobbed the missile after his sister with as much strength as his stronger right arm could muster. It arced through the air. For one brief millisecond of glee, Banjo thought the stone would intercept her flight to the back door. Then the realisation it was heading wide towards the rear windows, hollowed out his aching gut.

Sally stormed into the kitchen as the projectile meant for her smashed the wording *'Sally is a cunt'* into splintered fragments of jagged glass.

Banjo staggered for support against the outbuilding wall. His heart thudded against his chest in a rhythm redolent of an accelerating steam train. Like a convicted murderer of old awaiting his judge to don the black cap and deliver a sentence of death, he wondered how much pain he would feel from the inevitable punishment to follow. Already his body protested. Or did it? Why had pains from that toppled weight and scorched flesh vanished, as though they never existed? Why was Sally hobbling like the one injured and how did she come by those burns? *I've got to stop her before she spins another web of lies to our drunken mother.*

Inside the living room, Sally cried into Enid's chest. Her mother rose, letting the empty green gin bottle topple onto a rug of sufficient pile depth to avert another broken glass item.

Sally blubbed. "He pushed the shelving down on top of me, then burnt me with Dad's old cigarette lighter. Look at my arms."

Enid studied her daughter's charred skin.

Sally went on. "When I tried to break free, Banjo dropped the lighter and almost destroyed the outbuilding. I escaped and fetched water from the pond to extinguish his fire. Then he threw a chunk of rubble at me when I tried to run. It shattered another of the kitchen windows."

Banjo skidded into the living room archway in time for Enid's black-ringed, furious stare to fall upon him like the last judgement from Heaven.

"What has she told you? Sally is a liar." Banjo blurted out an attempt to defend his innocence before their mother passed sentence.

"You mis-er-ab-le lit-tle sh-it." Enid slurred, holding onto Sally as much to prop herself up as offer emotional support. She pressed her nose into Sally's left ear. "Pick up my bot-tle, Sssally."

Sally crouched to retrieve the empty glass container.

Enid swiped the item from her grasp and smashed it against a wooden wing of the high-backed chair. "Sso you like bro-ken glasss, do you, boy?" She waved a vicious looking stump of cruel green shards in Banjo's direction. "Let's sssee how much you like it wh-en I'm finissshed with you." She zigzagged across the living room towards her son in a wobbly charge.

Banjo turned and ran for the garden. His only hope of survival rested in lying low until his mother's rage and drunken state blew over.

13

Ageing Rockers

"Left a bit. A little more. Okay, there we go. Perfect." Emma Clarkson looked every one of her twenty-eight years, if not five more on top. Whether due to the highlighted autumnal browns of her messy curled hairdo, or the elegance of her understated fashion sense, Emma exuded pretty maturity. Her job as a self-employed antique shop owner contributed to the gravitas of her appearance. Yet those who crossed the threshold of her perfectly arranged business establishment, discovered a warm and helpful vendor, quiet of tone and meek of spirit.

On this crisp, frosty morning a fortnight before Christmas, she was hard at work taking delivery of an antique leather sofa. Two red-faced removal men set it down next to one of four single-storey height panel windows surrounding the shop's sturdy oak door on both sides.

'*Clarkson's Antiques*' lay in a former cooper's yard off the High Street in Berkhamsted. This quaint, dead-end commercial area also featured a tiny independent jewellers and low-impact living, pseudo-bohemian (except for its prices) coffee shop cum veg box supplier. Hertfordshire's financially liquid champagne socialists frequented all three.

Emma demonstrated a natural flair when dealing with the chattering classes. As a Buckinghamshire lass from Milton Keynes, her personal provenance didn't quite pass muster around here. Yet she kept her origins out of conversation with picky but flush clientele; focusing instead on their favourite topic: themselves. Emma had a smart enough head on her shoulders to recognise the pretty, historic market town was also home to many ordinary people. She only wished a few more would develop a taste and budget for antiques. Anything to save her from the narcissism of social climbers seeking a talking point curio for next month's dinner party.

"There you go, Emma." The older of the two removal men scribbled a total in blue Biro on a headed invoice pad bearing the logo: 'Oliver's Removals and Deliveries.' He tore off the A5 sheet and handed it across.

"Thanks, Graham. Cash on the barrel all right for you as usual?" Emma read the total and walked towards a smart desk piled high with paperwork and antique price guide volumes.

"Cash will work a treat," Graham Oliver replied. "I see you're getting ready for Christmas." He jerked his nose towards a sturdy cardboard box of holly and other seasonal greenery resting on the floor beside a free-standing lamp.

"A touch here and there. Yuletide decorations at the shop can prove stressful, given the particular outlook of my regular customers."

Graham frowned.

Emma opened a steel cash box and sifted through a pile of Twenty-Pound notes. She recognised the confusion on his weathered face. "If I put up anything some construe as tacky or not according to their taste, I could lose business. Reputation is a big factor in my line."

"You've no battery operated singing Santa in there, then? One that pulls its trousers down and moons when it detects your body heat?" Graham winked.

Emma bit her lip to stifle a smile. "Do they sell those? Something to buy and put away for if I win the lottery and don't need an income from my shop anymore."

The other removal man, a lad around nineteen, called from the doorway. "Do you want me to buy us a couple of coffees, Uncle Graham?"

"Not from that place, Jimmy," Graham barked at him.

Emma counted the required amount of cash into Graham's palm. "*Uncle* Graham?"

"Jimmy is my nephew. Stan, my usual guy, put his back out. My sister's boy has been sitting on his arse since leaving school. She was delighted to disentangle him from his games console when I phoned her to see if he could help."

"You don't rate Janice's coffee?" Emma jiggled a disposable takeaway cup of steamy, sweet-smelling brown liquid. It bore a label from the neighbouring coffee shop: '*Arabica*.' "This new Christmas Pudding Latte isn't half bad."

Graham tucked the cash away and pulled out his Biro. "I don't want an ethically sourced blend of arty farty beans, roasted in a handmade drum with wafts of cinnamon and chocolate, then brewed with spring water drawn from the Atlas Mountains and sweetened by Moroccan goat's milk. All that for £5.95. It wouldn't surprise me if that woman knew the name of the chuffin' goat it came from." He scribbled '*Paid in full with thanks*' across the invoice he'd given Emma, then initialled it. "Nope. Give me a plain old cup of Joe any day of the week, thanks."

Emma couldn't hold in the laughter this time. "I love that. In my defence, Janice offers me a regular coffee discount. But I'm curious about the goat name thing, now." She pierced the invoice on a spike, upon which a half dozen others were impaled. "Thanks for the delivery *and* a giggle, Graham."

"See you again soon." Graham stomped off and ushered Jimmy out of the door.

Once her movers had left, Emma spied a large-framed man who'd wandered into her shop unnoticed. He stood transfixed by a modest but well-polished rocking chair, fashioned from dark wood with a reddish hue. Emma sized him up. His clothing was poor and unkempt. A sheen reflecting mini halogen spotlights showed him to be balding on top. Would a full head of hair appear as dishevelled as the rest of him, if it still grew? *Well, you're a big boy, aren't you?* Emma waited a few seconds more before initiating a cautious approach. *Does this guy have any money, or is he another vagrant drifting from shop to shop in search of respite from declining winter temperatures outside?* Experience had taught her to study a potential customer's appearance, though not write anyone off based upon it. During her second year of trading, a far scruffier individual popped in and ended up buying a £12,000 dining suite. He was a minted and retired musician, now living as a gentleman farmer. That tramp-like millionaire filled his days producing reusable alpaca fleece tampons, or some other pointless product most people would never consider.

"Can I help you?" Emma leaned round to make eye contact with the stocky beast.

"I like this chair." The man's voice sounded far away. He moved his head to avoid her questioning eyes and not miss a moment of surveying the rocker.

Emma gave him a little more space. "You're welcome to try it out, if you'd like."

The man eased himself into the seat without another word. Corded and tense though his physical outline and personal demeanour appeared, he tilted the rocking chair back and forth in a series of gentle motions, eyes shut tight in apparent ecstasy.

Does he know the alpaca guy? This bloke looks half baked. Emma sniffed but detected no obvious drug aromas. "It's a good fit. How are you finding the chair for comfort?"

"Can I pay cash?" Hard grey eyes snapped open to

watch her while he continued to rock.

"If you'd like." Emma swallowed. *Straight down to business. Fair enough. I'd better check any notes this guy passes me for funny money.* "Would you like me to hold it for you?"

"No, I'll pay now. Do you deliver? This chair won't fit in my car."

Emma collected a pad and pen from her desk. "Certainly. I can arrange that. There's a firm I use for larger items, but I do some medium-sized evening deliveries myself. The rocker fits in my van. I know because I purchased it at auction."

The man rocked harder. "Perfect." He looked around the shop. "You have an eye for presentation. If you deliver the chair, you might help me pick the correct spot for it."

Emma didn't respond straight away. *Pick the correct spot for it? How big is this guy's place? Is he another rich eccentric? Easy Emma, this gentle giant looks like a middle-aged singleton. God, what's with his eyes? If he's peeking for a poke, you'd best keep your wits about you.* "I'll need a name, address, and telephone number." Her business head took charge.

"My house is called Ashburnham. It's out of the way with no formal address. They deliver our post to a P.O Box."

Emma raised her pen. *Our post? That's a positive sign. Time to go digging.* "How does your wife enjoy life in the sticks?"

"I'm not married. I was referring to my mother."

Emma's shoulder muscles eased. The action

surprised her, since she hadn't noticed them tense up. *His mother? Bless. Look at him rock. He's a big softy. Some ageing, shy chap who still lives with his mum.* "I'll get you to jot me down a set of route instructions in a minute, if you could. What about that name and telephone number?"

The man ceased rocking. A shadow of controlled anger flitted across his visage for a split second. "People call me Banjo. We're not on the telephone."

Emma clicked her retractable pen nib three times. *Banjo? He could be a musician. Some progressive folk/rock type made good.* "What about a mobile?"

"I don't have one."

"E-mail?"

"No," Banjo lied, all the while visualising the laptop computer he used as a portal to connect with the outside world.

Emma thumbed the notepad. *Who doesn't have either a landline, mobile phone or e-mail address? Okay, my mum doesn't have the last two, but still...* She handed him the pad and pen. "Be as specific as you can with those instructions. If I've no way to contact you, I can't afford to get lost."

After the clocks went back in late October, Emma Clarkson enjoyed a brief spell of lighter mornings. An early riser, this suited her industrious nature. Its downside always balanced out with evening deliveries taking place after dark. On regular residential streets, this didn't cause her a second thought. But bumping her white Ford Transit van along the woodland track to Ashburnham was another matter. The vehicle's suspension groaned as her left, nearside front wheel sank into and then bounced out of a rut.

Thank goodness I secured that rocking chair with straps in the rear. This Banjo character would receive a pile of well-polished firewood, otherwise. The van lurched again. *I don't mind a ten mile delivery. It's the last three-quarters of a mile that's caning the Transit. I hope this doesn't invalidate my lease agreement.* The van's headlights reflected off dented, metallic maroon paint of a decrepit Rover parked in tall grass outside an overgrown, dilapidated Victorian villa. "Fuck." The sight of Ashburnham's dark, oppressive outline against a clear, starry sky vocalised her mental dialogue for an instant. *His mother must be in her late sixties, at least. She lives in a draughty, damp hole like that? Is the woman bullet proof? My mum's arthritis plays up if there's so much as a thunderstorm nearby, and she owns a cosy, centrally heated semi. Man oh man, look at that roof.* Emma rolled the van to a halt and pulled up the handbrake. She scrunched Banjo's handwritten instructions into a ball and stuffed them in a rubbish container secured near the driver's footwell. *This guy had better be home. I'm not hanging around in this place alone at night.* She opened her door and slipped down into lush, wet grass, sparkling with the first signs of descending frost.

"Hello, Sally." Dim light silhouetted a familiar outline standing in Ashburnham's open doorway.

"My name is Emma. Emma Clarkson. You weren't

kidding about this place being out of the way. I'm glad it isn't raining or my van would sink on that track of yours." Emma rounded the front of her commercial vehicle.

The shadowy figure remained silent.

Emma stiffened. "Is your mother home?" *I hope this weirdo isn't flying solo tonight. He gives me the creeps.*

"Would you like to see her?"

An uncomfortable knot formed in Emma's stomach at his response. Its tone suggested a hint of mockery. "That would be polite. I'm sure she'll want to try the chair and have a say in where we place it."

"Follow me." The silhouette turned.

Emma followed him beside a dusty staircase, past walls of peeling paper, paint and crumbling plaster exposing wooden laths. A chill wind circled down into the ground floor hallway from an attic far above. *How can anyone live like this? Small wonder he looks such a mess.*

They passed through a high-ceilinged kitchen whose fixtures and fittings - like the rest of Ashburnham - were lost somewhere in time.

Banjo tugged open the rear door.

Emma frowned. "Is your mother outside?" She accompanied him into what had once been a garden, now invaded by woodland. A shabby outbuilding lay at one end, followed by a pond and a patch of ash trees beyond it. "Is your mother walking in the garden?" Emma almost choked on that last word. "I don't see her."

"There." Banjo pointed to a rose bush close by. He

stepped back, breathing laboured like a panting dog.

"Where? All I can see is a plant."

"She's tucked up warm and dry beneath it."

Emma froze. She'd had enough and wanted to cry out for someone - anyone. She didn't have time to pivot before something firm struck the back of her head.

A blowtorch roared to life. Its blue jet of noisy flame glittered in Banjo's gleeful eyes.

Emma shook her head. Plastic cable ties secured her feet and wrists in a horizontal spreadeagled shape. Each bit into its respective limb then looped through iron rings bolted into the walls. She guessed they were inside that outbuilding she'd seen before Banjo struck her. Emma fought to quell the tremor in her voice. "What do you want?"

"It's time for your sunshine therapy, Sally. A lack of sunlight isn't good. Your bones could become brittle."

"My name isn't Sally, Banjo. I told you."

Apoplectic, her captor shrieked a hissing rebuke. "Don't call me Banjo." His head twitched and an odd thrumming gurgled from his throat.

The blowtorch flame came down upon the middle of Emma's left arm. She screamed in relentless agony, almost passing out from the pain while her flesh singed and blackened.

"How is your therapy helping, Sally?" Banjo laughed in wide-eyed delight. He moved the blowtorch steadily across each limb. After a few minutes of ear-splitting outbursts, the screaming stopped and Emma

Clarkson's glazed, lifeless eyes stared at the outbuilding's cobweb decorated ceiling. Her ultimate expression of terror remained until it too was blackened beyond recognition by flame to expose the skull beneath. Burning up this Sally surrogate wouldn't be as much fun with her life extinguished, yet Banjo planned to leave no fragment of flesh uncharred. Even the fetid stench of his captive human barbecue couldn't detract from the thrilling release of paying Sally back for her misdeeds. Banjo felt a wet sensation. He stepped back to discover a dark patch spreading across his trouser crotch. His joy had run full to overflowing from a neglected sexual organ he never understood. Banjo closed off the blowtorch valve and stomped back to the house for a change of clothing.

* * *

RETTON HOUSE - DECEMBER 2019.

"Will we be decorating the house for Christmas, right after my birthday?" Gillian knelt by the living room fender and stroked Mace's ears.

Felicity took a seat on one sofa. "Your birthday is on a Wednesday. I thought we'd start on the Friday."

"The twentieth? That's ample time. Has Daddy arranged the hallway tree?"

"Daddy has." Bertram entered the room, rubbing his hands together. "There's a rare frost coming down outside tonight. Throw another log on the fire, would you, Pixie?"

Gillian tugged an ash off-cut from a log basket and plonked it atop a sparking pile of glowing embers.

Mace yawned, then rested his face back on the rug. The whites of his eyes rolled up to watch Gillian in the perfect picture of an adorable pooch.

The log shifted and threatened to roll out. Gillian grabbed a poker and tongs. She leaned over to reposition it. Heat from fresh tongues of flame crept up the off-cut's sides, yet the pain that shot through her arms burned with disproportionate, scorching fury.

Fierce eyes sunk into that monstrous balding head appeared before her face. Its furious owner shrieked with deafening rage. *"Don't call me Banjo."*

Gillian dropped the brass fireplace implements with a clatter and screamed.

"Bertram." The cry was still on Felicity's lips when her husband lunged to grab Gillian around the waist. He fought against her frantic arms, while Mace stood and barked in a furious, rapid-fire series of gunshot-style reports.

Bertram toppled backwards, pulling Gillian's singed fingers away from the building fire.

Gillian wailed and fitted like an extreme cramp sufferer, unable to move their body in such a way as to lessen its agony.

Gerard appeared in the living room doorway. "Shall I call an ambulance, Mr Crane?"

Bertram wrestled to hold Gillian still on the rug.

Felicity shook her head, eyes watering. "I don't think that'll be necessary at the moment, Gerard. Thank you. Gillian is suffering another of her difficult episodes."

"Should I fetch her some water?" Gerard pressed his hands together in helpless discomfort.

"If you would," Felicity replied. "Please ask Jenny to put the kettle on. We may all require a warm drink, once this subsides."

"Very good, Mrs Crane." Gerard hurried away down the corridor.

Gillian went limp in Bertram's grasp, eyes shut fast. He leaned over her face. "Pixie?"

"Is she breathing?" Felicity asked.

"Yes. I can feel her breath and pulse." He touched her forehead. "She's burning up."

Mace whimpered and licked Gillian's face. His wet tongue caused her to splutter back to consciousness.

She shot up with a start in Bertram's restraining arms.

"Easy." Bertram held her firm. "Let's lay you up on the sofa for a minute." He lifted his daughter while Felicity gathered two cushions to form a makeshift pillow.

Silent tears streamed down Gillian's face as she lay back, head pressed into the cushions. "He's killed another one."

Felicity knelt beside her husband and smoothed the lava blonde hair from Gillian's forehead. "Shh. Easy. Gosh, you're hot."

Gillian's brow creased. "Not as hot as his latest victim. He burned her flesh off with a blowtorch while she was restrained."

Felicity's mouth hung open.

"You had a fair go at your own," Bertram shot a

sideways glance to make sure the burning log remained in a safe position, without danger of tumbling onto the rug. "Did you see him? The same man?"

Gillian swallowed hard and nodded. "Right before the pain started. He yelled, *'Don't call me Banjo.'* Goodness knows what that was all about. Then he took a blowtorch to her."

Felicity touched the base of her neck. "God help the poor woman. Why is he doing this?"

Gillian sat up as Gerard returned with a glass of water. "All I know is, he's always angry. I'm still convinced he's enacting a twisted revenge on others, because he can't find the actual person responsible."

"If they even exist, or ever did. They may be nothing more than the product of a diseased mind." Bertram ran a hand through his hair. "This man is way beyond help or redemption, if you ask me. It's a shame he didn't give you a name other than Banjo to go on. Where do we, or the police start?"

Gillian sipped some water. "Once again, I can't report this."

"Did you get a sense of location? Was it that house?" Bertram sat on the opposite sofa.

"I'm not sure. It looked like a dirty shed or outbuilding. Narrow. The woman was strapped to rings on two inside walls. I remember cobwebs coating a dishevelled roof above. They were the last thing she ever saw." Gillian clutched fingers around her right eye. "Her screams are still bouncing around in my head, like before."

Felicity sighed. "You don't need this right now."

"Or ever," Gillian added. "But there it is. What can I do to escape? I don't want drugs. They wouldn't make a difference to whatever is causing this. Someone needs to find and stop that monster. Nobody is safe. He isn't finished yet; I know he isn't. His anger was too fresh and keen. God help us all, there's more to come. I'm sure there's more to come."

* * *

ASHBURNHAM - DECEMBER 2019.

An Advent bonfire on a cold winter's morning wouldn't arouse suspicion to the casual passer-by. Not that Ashburnham experienced such visitors, with the tragic exception of the late Amy Yates during her battle with depression.

Banjo nursed a pile of seasoned wood. It stirred from a smoking heap to a glowing conflagration in a bare patch of grass twenty feet clear of the rear outbuilding. Beside him on crisp, white frosty grass lay a brown sack. He reached inside and pulled out the damp, bloody remains of a human femur to chuck into the fire. A crow cawed from one of the bare treetops, welcoming a dim, orange dawn.

Flames licked the bones dry and consumed dripping strands of gore. A wall of heat moved outward from the blaze.

Banjo left his fire and tramped over to the kitchen. He returned clutching a bag of sausages and a toasting fork. *Such a shame not to take advantage of this burning fuel. 'Waste not, want not,' our father used to say.* He stuck a sausage onto the toasting fork tines and inhaled its meaty aroma. *Mmm, pork and apple. My favourite. It's a far better smell than stinky Sally and her sizzling body.* He yanked a semi-skeletal foot from the bag with his free hand, tossed it onto the bonfire and held out the toasting fork with the other. It had taken time to saw up Emma Clarkson's remains into convenient pieces on the outbuilding workbench. He'd started before daybreak, after a peaceful night in the company of dreams filled by the thrilling, imaginary agonised wails of his burning sister.

Fat dripped from Banjo's suspended sausage, to fizz against the blackening bones of Emma's left foot in the flames beneath. Banjo rotated the fork to ensure even cooking, then added fragments of broken ribcage to his fire from the sack. He perched on an upturned sawn log; the picture of some woodland charcoal burner preparing breakfast as though it were the most natural thing in the world. Once the meat browned, he tested it with the tip of one finger. "Ouch, that's hot." The irony of his statement, considering what he'd put Emma Clarkson through, sailed away unnoticed with billowing columns of smoke from the bonfire. Banjo blew on the sausage, then pulled it free with delicate fingers. He took a bite and kept his mouth open for extra cooling air to ward off a burnt tongue. Steam blew from his slurping maw. *Oh, that tastes fine.* He continued to munch his way through the sausage. Its warmth overcame a chill in his stomach from the brisk winter morning. He put down the toasting fork and lifted Emma's skull from the sack, holding it at eye level as though it were Yorick from '*Hamlet.*' Blistering those now-melted staring eyeballs to nothing with the blowtorch proved a special delight. He could visualise Sally's haughty expression while erasing it forever with his powerful blue flame.

"You won't tell Mum now, will you?" he muttered, before twisting the skull left and right, mimicking a head shake in response. Banjo tossed it onto the pile of crackling logs and human remains, as though it were yesterday's rubbish. He picked up his toasting fork from beside the upended log and impaled another sausage for barbecuing.

By mid-afternoon the fire had cooled to ash and Emma Clarkson's baked bones turned fragile. Banjo shovelled the combined mixture back into his sack. He knotted the top, slung it over one shoulder and disappeared inside the outbuilding.

"Your bones could go brittle, Sally." Weighty mallet in one firm grip, he hammered the sack's contents into pulverised powder through its material. Stroke after stroke shadowed through the semi broken window, casting long, dark movements across the garden's unkempt greenery.

Banjo stepped into the fading light and inhaled fresh air. He wiped sweat from his brow, then returned to fetch the sack of friable remnants. He upended it into a rusty oil drum and retrieved a heavy, sealed plastic container from inside. The lid came off long enough to shovel three scoops of quicklime onto the powdery remains. He placed the tub back inside, before lugging a familiar old bucket down to the pond. A slosh of water into the drum started a thermo-chemical reaction, producing clouds of scalding vapour.

Banjo stepped clear, careful not to inhale the spiteful fumes. *I'll leave that until the morning. I could scatter what's left on the rosebush. Mum always took Sally's side. Now she can feed on her burnt and powdered remains.* An objecting voice stabbed into his skull. *But that isn't Sally, it's someone else.* Banjo grunted at the unwanted mental intrusion. *More of Sally's lies, trying to confuse and dull the mind.* He shouted a vaporous breath across the misty garden. "It won't work, Sally. I'm wise to your tricks by now."

Banjo rocked in the beautiful antique chair, which he'd fetched from Emma's van and placed before the living room fireplace. At present its polished, dust-free finish set it at odds with such shabby surroundings. All that would change with time and wear. The writhing dance of flickering flames in the grate cast ominous shadows of the stocky, rocking figure across tarnished wall surfaces. *Soon it will be dark enough to dispose of the van. How far should I travel? I must find my way back on foot. But then, I always do. Like that time I returned from spending years away. That time after Sally's fakery took me from home and broke my heart. How like her not to be here once I got back.* He rocked on.

The white Transit turned off a single track lane,

ascending to a sloped woodland copse above Bellingdon. A dirty smile chased Banjo's lips when he read the sign for '*Braziers End*.' A fitting location to create a four-wheeled brazier. He hopped out of the van and ambled around to open the rear doors. There lay a green plastic petrol cannister he normally kept in the Rover.

Pungent fuel aromas accompanied his sloshing motions, as Banjo took care not to get any flammable liquid on himself. *There's enough left for a liquid fuse.* He backed up, leading a short trickle away from the concealed commercial vehicle. He walked ten paces to set the recapped cannister aside, then pulled an oily rag from his jacket pocket. The flint flared on his father's old cigarette lighter and the rag caught. He tossed the burning fabric at the base of his liquid trail. Its petrol ignited and raced in a blinding flash towards the van.

Banjo grabbed the empty fuel cannister and hurried away downhill without looking back. An explosion lit up the night sky with an amber glow from flames licking at nearby trees in the copse.

At Pednor, a passing motorist flashed his headlights and slowed to a whining halt. Banjo was about to cross the road and connect with another public footpath leading southwest.

"Run out of petrol?" A clipped, articulate voice emerged from the lowered driver's window of a Seven Series BMW.

Banjo lifted the empty cannister with one limp hand

and shrugged.

The driver jerked a thumb at his spare front seat. "Hop in. I've got to fuel up, myself. I can take you as far as the nearest service station."

Banjo opened the passenger door to join his unexpected chauffeur for a lift. His empty cannister required a re-fill, and he knew the service station to which the driver referred. Not far out of the way. This provided another alibi and sped him further from that blazing van. It would have attracted significant attention by now, despite the rural location.

The driver raised his window again and pulled away into the night.

Banjo gave a thumbs up as the BMW owner's vehicle left him behind on the service station forecourt. He'd let the motorist fill-up first, before taking his time at a pump.

Inside the kiosk, his eyes fell upon a rack of newspapers. He picked up the Amersham and Chesham edition of '*Bucks Free Press.*' It ran with a headline about compulsory purchase orders for housing in the region under HS2 and their resulting protests. Outside the service station, a police car tore past the forecourt with lights flashing but no siren.

A Pakistani shop assistant sitting behind the till cleared his throat. "Five litres of unleaded. That's £6.90."

Banjo yanked a worn, brown leather wallet from a pocket of his torn jacket. "I'll take a newspaper, too."

14

Inseparable Souls

RETTON HOUSE - DECEMBER 2019.

"Oh my Lord, look at this," Deborah Rowling spoke to herself as the elegant Georgian outline of Retton House appeared. She cruised towards the end of a sweeping, private tarmac drive skirted by trees and topiary hedges. Her freshly washed and waxed red Honda Civic lost some of the proud lustre it took on in her mind's eye, after she'd valeted it for her Christmas getaway from Alresford to Great Missenden. *I don't want to guess what a place like that costs. In Buckinghamshire, too.* She eased her right foot off the accelerator pedal of her ageing but trustworthy motor. *Thank goodness I've met Gillian's parents and they're friendly. I'd be bricking myself about this, otherwise.*

The Honda coasted to a quiet halt outside a tall, arched door the colour of faded peaches. It swung open as Deborah applied the brakes.

A frantic, barking Blenheim Cavalier King Charles

Spaniel darted between Gillian's legs. He ran round and leapt against the driver's side door of the Honda, tail wagging so fast as to appear invisible.

Deborah clicked her seatbelt release button and eased the door open enough to slide a leg out. The dog's wet nose was already sniffing one calf muscle before the other joined it. Deborah lowered to her haunches and ruffled the animal's ears. Mace's tongue lolled out, and he buried his head in her chest, eliciting a giggle from the new arrival.

"If he gets annoying, push him aside. Mace can be a handful, but he's a good-tempered dog." Gillian reached the car.

Deborah rolled the animal over and tickled his tummy. "Oh, he's adorable. Aren't you a handsome boy, Mace? Yes you are." She continued to make a fuss of the delighted pooch.

Gillian folded her arms across her chest. "You've a friend for life, now."

Deborah stood while the dog leapt around her legs. She fixed soft eyes on Gillian. "How are you, Fairy Princess?"

Gillian blinked back a tear. "Better now you're here."

Another second of waiting would prove unbearable, had the two friends not embraced. Both women sniffed.

Deborah pulled back. "I promised myself I wouldn't cry when I saw you. Now look at me. I'm a mess."

Gillian wiped one eye with a slender middle finger. "That makes two of us. I watched you approach from a landing window."

Deborah looked from the impressive house back across its open acreage. "Crumbs, I'm not surprised. Talk about advanced warning. If the postman was a looker, you'd have time to brush your hair and shine your shoes before he reached the front door."

Gillian's shoulders twitched in a display of mirth. "That's my bestie. Now I know Deborah has arrived."

Deborah lifted Gillian's fingers into the sunlight for an inspection. "You didn't burn them too badly."

"No. Of all the weird episodes I've experienced, that most recent one wasn't so traumatic in physical terms. I wish I could say the same about its emotional impact. Okay, I wasn't hurt on the roof when 'Banjo' pushed Amy Yates to her death. But I'd have toppled to my own, had my father not been present."

Deborah let her hand drop. "We're calling this thug by that unwanted nickname he rebuked the burning victim over now, are we?"

"In lieu of something more concrete," Gillian replied.

"Burned with a blowtorch." Deborah shook her head. "Anything on the news?"

"Not yet. It only happened towards the end of last week. Who knows what he's done with the body, this time."

"You said on the phone Friday, that you're convinced he hasn't finished." Deborah patted Mace to calm his rising excitement levels and pestering insistence for attention.

"No. He still isn't satisfied. Don't ask me how I know. A feeling, I suppose." Gillian squinted into the firmament. "That day I almost killed myself in

Alresford, I heard Andrew and Coralie remark that I had *'dead eyes.'* At the time they were referring to my inner devastation over Brent's betrayal, reflected at the world. Now the term has a new connotation."

"Because you see through the eyes of the dead during their passing?"

"Exactly. See, feel, hear, taste, smell. All senses are firing, in reality. But other sensory feedback would be unintelligible, minus the visual aspect tying it all together."

Deborah closed her driver's door. "Let's hope your birthday and Christmas upstage the monopoly these experiences have on your attention. I'm super excited about Wednesday. You're going to love the present I've brought you."

Gillian smiled. "Having you here is present enough. But, I'm sure it'll be great."

Deborah raised the car's boot lid. "It isn't Alresford RFC. I couldn't fit all the boys in my suitcase, and I thought they'd eat your parents out of house and home. Though, I'd say you've room to put them up."

Gillian pulled Mace back from climbing into the boot. "Cheeky woman."

Gerard crossed the threshold with his hands raised against the blinding, low sunlight. "I'll fetch those for you, Miss. If there's anything you don't require moving to the guest suite at present, please let me know."

Deborah gawped.

Gillian prodded her with a stiff finger. "Gerard, meet Deborah Rowling. Deborah, this is Gerard. He and his wife, Katie, take care of cleaning, property maintenance and a million other things."

Gerard grabbed the handle of Deborah's largest case, then realised he'd underestimated the effort required. "Pleased to make your acquaintance, Miss Rowling."

Deborah blinked. "Likewise, I'm sure." She watched him haul her case into the hallway before turning to Gillian. "How cool is that? How many like him do you have?"

"Five. Gerard and Katie are part of the main household. Jenny runs and/or helps Mum in the kitchen. Lorcan is our lively, Irish stable manager. Joe, or 'Old Joe' as he's sometimes called, maintains the grounds with occasional extra help."

"Old Joe?"

"He's seventy-three. Though, I wouldn't challenge him to a race. Don't let his years or looks fool you. If I've half that energy when I'm his age, I'll count myself lucky."

Felicity and Bertram appeared on the doorstep.

"Welcome to Retton, Deborah." Felicity stepped down and extended a hand.

Deborah shook it. "Thank you for having me, Mrs Crane. You too, Mr Crane."

Bertram rocked on his heels. "Think nothing of it. Pixie has been so excited about your arrival, it's done her a power of good. We couldn't be happier that you've come."

Mace jumped up and placed his forepaws against Deborah's upper legs.

Gillian smirked. "I'd call that a universal welcome.

You've done it now. He'll never let you go home at this rate."

Gerard returned to retrieve the rest of Deborah's luggage.

Deborah intercepted him. "Please take extra care with the brown box, it's fragile."

"Very good, Miss." Gerard handled it like a ticking bomb.

Deborah closed the boot. "That's your birthday present, Gillian." She glanced around for signs of other vehicles. "I'm guessing you don't want me to leave my Civic stuck outside your doorstep."

Gillian opened the car's passenger door. "I'll accompany you to the garage block."

Deborah jumped inside, then started the engine. "The garage block? Dare I ask how many cars you own?"

Gillian clicked her seatbelt home. "Three. We've one each. It's a five bay garage, so you can tuck your Honda beside my Nissan. You'll find assorted staff vehicles parked nearby, too."

The car cruised around the right-hand side of the house.

Deborah motioned to a rectangular building behind the primary structure. "What's that?"

"Staff apartments. Behind them are the stable block and garaging."

Deborah followed the driveway. "Is that the stable block you threatened I'd be sleeping in?"

Gillian snorted. "Katie has the guest suite prepared. It's on the same floor as my room, but at the rear overlooking our greenhouses and Old Peg."

"Old Peg? Is she another servant you omitted to mention?"

"No. Old Peg is what Joe the gardener calls that humongous Western Red Cedar." Gillian pointed out of her window.

"Wow, what a beauty. Is that a tree house?"

Gillian flushed. "Mine. Old Peg contracted a root infection earlier in the year. She's got to come down soon. You'll be the last guest to enjoy that view from your room."

"I must take a picture with my phone. Hello, who's this?"

A broad-shouldered man capped with curly hair, tightened nuts on the rear, nearside wheel of a blue Vauxhall Astra.

"Lorcan Donnelly, the stable manager," Gillian replied. "There's my Qashqai. You can park alongside."

Deborah manoeuvred her car into a satisfactory position and the women decamped.

Christmas music blared from the Astra's stereo. It faded into time pips, followed by a dramatic news jingle.

"Flat tyre, Lorcan?" Gillian asked above the din.

"I picked up a nail at the supermarket, so I did. Another hand going into my pocket at Christmastime, once I've had it repaired." He straightened and kicked the rear wheel. "The tread on this spare is diminishing faster than my bank balance. I hope I don't get pulled over by the rozzers before the original is refitted." His eyes glittered at Deborah. "And who, may I ask, is this lovely young lady?"

Gillian motioned between them. "Lorcan, Deborah. Deborah, Lorcan."

Lorcan wiped his palms on a rag and extended a brawny hand in greeting. "Right glad I am to meet ya, Deborah. That's a fine name."

Deborah pursed her lips and accepted his firm grip with unyielding reciprocal pressure of her own. "I'm pleased to hear it. It's the only one I have."

Lorcan let go and dragged two fingers across his mouth to downplay amusement at her robust confidence. "And how long will we be having the pleasure of your company? If you don't mind me asking?"

"I'm here for Christmas. Gillian…"

Deborah's flirtatious exchange continued, but Gillian tuned it out. Her attention latched onto a male radio newscaster's voice emanating from the Astra. "*Twenty-eight-year-old Emma Clarkson hasn't been seen since Thursday evening. The owner of 'Clarkson's Antiques' in Berkhamsted, Miss Clarkson's shop remained shut throughout what should have been a busy weekend of trading. After concerned locals and her family contacted the police on Sunday, Hertfordshire Constabulary launched a missing person's enquiry. Information received from Thames Valley Police indicates a van leased to the antique dealer was discovered burnt out near Bellingdon in Buckinghamshire, on Friday night. Following the abduction and murder of Tara Osmotherley and Claire and Tony Walker, Thames Valley aren't ruling out a potential fourth victim in what*" *appears to be the work of the same killer."*

"Make that a fifth victim, if you count Amy Yates," Gillian muttered.

"What's that, Gillian?" Lorcan lifted his nose at her.

Deborah's playful manner evaporated the moment she clocked Gillian's face. "What is it?"

Gillian shuffled her feet while Lorcan reached in and turned his stereo down. "On the news a moment ago. Emma Clarkson, an antique dealer from Berkhamsted. She hasn't been seen since Thursday. Her van was found burnt out, not ten miles from here on Friday evening."

Deborah gulped. "Do you think she's the one?"

"If the police are making connections with two other women and a child who were murdered, it's a reasonable assumption."

Lorcan crossed himself. "Jesus, Mary and Joseph have mercy. Sure and I'd like to drag that bastard round the back of the stables to explain a few things with my fists."

Gillian frowned. "Join the queue."

"Open it, open it, open it." Deborah bounced on the edge of a living room sofa cushion.

Gillian sat beside her, clutching the brown cardboard box Deborah had indicated as fragile to Gerard, two days earlier. Now, metallic green wrapping paper and a pink bow concealed its otherwise dull packaging.

Gillian untied the bow. "You're more excited than I am. That doesn't mean I don't love it, by the way."

Deborah swirled an index finger across the paper. "The colour matches your eyes."

Felicity and Bertram sat opposite, amused by the exchange. An array of birthday cards adorned the elegant mantelpiece.

Mace padded over to sit beside Gillian and observe the unwrapping.

Gillian wound the ribbon around her wrist, then set it on a compact, circular side table.

Deborah sucked her teeth. "Knowing you, that ribbon will appear on some jaw-dropping jewellery packaging people gladly pay through the nose for."

Gillian slid a thumbnail along a taped join. She was enjoying making Deborah suffer by dragging out the suspense.

Deborah poked her best friend's shoulder. "You're such a tease. Oh Gillian, behave and open the jolly present already."

Gillian pulled the paper apart and untucked folded cardboard box flaps. She rested the parcel on the floor between her feet to yank out scrunched, brown paper cushioning.

Mace poked his nose inside the lid.

Gillian nudged his face aside. "There's nothing to eat, chew, or wrestle with in there, Mace. Not if I know Deborah." She leaned her head against Deborah's shoulder in playful mockery. "Of course, when it's your birthday I could tie a bow on Lorcan and give him to you. Then you can do all the eating, chewing and wrestling you please."

Deborah's cheeks turned crimson. "Don't you think I

wouldn't, either. He's a dish."

Gillian regarded her parents while extracting more safety packaging from the parcel. "Deborah has taken a shine to our stable manager."

Bertram raised a cup of tea in salute. "Excellent choice. He's a capital fellow."

Deborah stuck her tongue through bared teeth at Gillian. "Daddy Crane rocks."

Gillian's laughing eyes widened and her jaw dropped. "Oh, Deborah. However did you manage it?" She lifted a beautiful, bone china cup and saucer of identical design to the treasured teapot she'd bought the day the friends met.

Deborah clapped her hands together. "There's more. There's more." She watched Gillian unwrap three additional cups and saucers, plus a sugar bowl and miniature milk jug. "I got the contact details for the guy who made your teapot from the venue on West Street where they hold Alresford Craft Show. When I met him, he remembered the piece and had kept the design on record. So, I commissioned him to produce a tea service according to the same pattern."

Gillian wrapped both arms around Deborah's shoulders and pulled her close for a warm hug. "Thank you. This means the world to me."

Deborah released a satisfied sigh. "It's not entirely selfless. Now I won't have to drink out of a chipped mug when you invite me up to the flat for a cuppa." She cleared her throat to add a clarification. "Or wherever you go."

Gillian eased back and pinched her leg. "The flat, I

hope. And when have I ever served you tea in a chipped mug? Anyway, I spoke with Andrew and Coralie on the phone last week, to wish them a Merry Christmas. They're hoping I'll come back. My garret is still unoccupied."

Deborah nodded. "I drop by the gallery when I can. They miss you. No surprise there."

The whirring of an electric hedge trimmer carried from outside the bay window.

Felicity rose to peer through the glass. "Joe is hard at work as ever. He's such a dynamo."

"Only death will slow him down. But it'll have to catch him first," Bertram added. "He's happy as Larry this morning. The casual temp starts today."

Gillian re-wrapped her china to keep it safe. "His newspaper ad worked, then? Who did you interview?"

"I didn't."

Gillian folded the box flaps shut. "Are you slacking, Daddy?"

"No, Pixie. I haven't had time. The chap dropped by yesterday. He'd read the advertisement. Joe invited him in for a natter. He was happy with the guy's ability to fetch and carry, so hired him on the spot."

"That's a relief." Gillian eyed a small pile of parcels sat on the low coffee table between them. "What's next?"

Gillian rose from her dressing table on Friday morning, after a knock disturbed the last moments of personal grooming.

Deborah waited on the landing, dressed and ready to go for the day.

"You're an early riser." Gillian beckoned her inside and shut the door.

"I don't want to miss a moment of this." Deborah pointed to the weathered wooden sign resting on Gillian's dressing table. *"Pixie's House.* I love it. Did your dad make that?"

"He did. It was screwed to my tree house. I'm taking it back to Alresford with me whenever I return."

Deborah wandered over to the window. "You were right about the view from my room. That cedar is gorgeous. Pity your bedroom faces to the side. It's a shame the tree has to come down."

"I know." Gillian finished fixing her hair. "Are you comfortable at the rear of the house?"

"Is the Pope Catholic?"

"I assume so. Lorcan is," Gillian winked.

"Oh stop teasing me about him, you minx. The room is grand. There must be a draught, though. I often find the bathroom door wide open by morning. I always close it before turning in."

Gillian almost choked on a bubble rising in her throat. "High ceilings. Enormous windows." She attempted to nip an awkward conversational topic in the bud, hoping all the while Gareth wouldn't do anything more overt, if he *was* responsible.

Deborah tapped the base of Gillian's packed removal boxes with a gentle foot. "Have you made any more jewellery? Business must be suffering."

"No. I stuck a notice on the website telling customers

I would ship any existing stock ordered, but that no new products will be available before 2020. Most of my regular clientele have been understanding about it." She gestured around the room. "You've seen my family home. There's no danger of me going broke or hungry, though I hate sponging off my folks."

"So what's on the agenda, today?"

"Christmas decorating. And believe me, done right, it's quite a marathon at Retton House. Mum has exquisite aesthetic appetites."

"That's where you get it from. I love hanging baubles and tinsel on trees."

Gillian wrinkled her elfin nose. "Keep that nugget to yourself. The tree Daddy has felled and erected in the hallway, is always two storeys high. It stands in the gap our sweeping staircase wraps around, up to the landing outside my room." Gillian jerked a thumb at her door. "Gerard and Katie have to clamber all over it with tall ladders. It's not a job for the fainthearted."

Deborah grinned from ear to ear. "Epic."

*   *   *

ASHBURNHAM - SEPTEMBER 1988.

"I'm going to kill you." Sally raised a gleaming chef's knife above her head as she charged through the hallway.

Banjo twisted on the spot in the space between the front door and main staircase. He launched himself forward before Sally's advance could cut off any route of escape to the floors above.

Sally shrieked and stomped up the stairs in pursuit. Early autumnal shafts of sunlight pierced random chinks in Ashburnham's armour to project the raised, knife-clutching hand against the staircase wall.

Banjo ran into his mother's room and slammed the door.

Sally hammered on it with a balled fist. "You won't get away from me. I'm going to cut you. Cut you into a thousand pieces."

Banjo set his shoulder against the wooden obstruction and banged it shut as Sally attempted to breach. *Where does Mum keep the key? Her door locks. Mum and Dad often used to lock their door at night.* His eyes fell upon a rectangular nightstand beside the bed. Rings from water damage caused by overnight drinks stained its faded surface. *It's in the top drawer. I know it is.* If he ran for the nightstand, Sally would be on him before he ever made it back.

Sally threw her weight against the door, causing it to shudder. The force of impact knocked Banjo sideways. Sally's foot poked through and wedged in the frame before Banjo could retaliate. He kicked her shins and put both hands into a focused shove against the dull brass doorknob.

Sally screamed, unable to free her pinned and bruised ankle. "You're going to bleed, Banjo. Wait until Mum comes home to find you've slashed yourself to death. Bloodied and cold on her own bedsheets."

Banjo rammed a hand deep into his trouser pocket. Smooth steel pressed against his questing fingers. He pulled out his father's old cigarette lighter. *How did I get this? Sally must have planted it in my trousers after she accused me of burning her. Well, she'll get a taste of her own medicine, now.* He swiped the flint to produce a flame, then slipped down with his weight and one hand thrust against the almost closed portal.

Sally screamed again. Exposed flesh above her short, white socks blistered and blackened. She pulled with adrenaline-fuelled agony lending strength to her slight, fourteen-year-old body. The foot squeezed clear, and she toppled onto the landing floor.

Banjo slammed the door and darted towards the nightstand. He yanked the first drawer open to reveal a broken old watch and half-empty gin bottle. His pulse quickened. Sally would recover in seconds. He opened the second drawer. A blue cardboard box of something he'd never seen called 'Durex' lay beside a pack of AA batteries and compact torch. Still no sign of a key.

"Mum doesn't keep the key in there. It's in her wardrobe." Sally's calm but menacing voice cut through the rush of blood pumping in Banjo's ears.

He turned to face her.

Sally hobbled into the room, lifting the broad kitchen blade above her head once more. "It's time to bleed, Little Brother."

Banjo gritted his teeth and hurled himself at Sally. The pair tumbled into the upstairs hallway. Cruel lacerations dug into legs and arms, blood smearing between clothes pressed together in the furious scuffle.

Outside, the tinny, asthmatic rattle of an air-cooled boxer engine disturbed the entwined siblings. A resounding backfire from the rusting exhaust of Enid's pale blue, 1971 VW Beetle halted the frantic struggle.

Sally pushed away from her brother and ran for the staircase. She pivoted around the newel post like a slingshot and lost her footing on the top step.

Banjo grabbed the chef's knife. He reached the head of the stairs in time to watch Sally crash headlong into a whirling mass of arms and legs. Her shrieking body halted upon hitting the hallway as Enid opened the front door. The wild-eyed woman's gaze moved from the sobbing form of her motionless daughter up to the boy wielding a glittering blade on the landing above.

Banjo let the knife fall with a clatter. It cartwheeled down the staircase to land handle up, tip wedged between hallway floorboards alongside Sally.

Enid dropped two bags of shopping, ready to blow her top. "What have you done to your sister?"

Banjo grabbed the banister for support. "Sally stabbed me. She was going to cut me to death. See." He raised one arm, then blinked. No blood or injury of any kind disturbed the smooth, perfect skin. He checked the other with similar results.

Sally lifted her head. She clutched a motionless arm broken during her fall. Fresh, seeping blood coated both it and the other supporting limb. "It hurts so much, Mum," she gasped between copious tears.

Enid reached down and plucked the chef's knife from its resting spot.

Banjo fled back to his parents' room. His head throbbed with fear, grief and confusion. *Is Mum going to kill me now? Why wouldn't she? She always takes Sally's side.* He rifled through the wardrobe to discover the room key hanging from a loop beside his father's old work trousers. Banjo locked the door and scrunched himself into a ball beneath the window.

Enid's heavy footsteps thudded on the staircase. The bedroom's brass doorknob rattled and turned, but the door held fast.

Banjo waited on tenterhooks for an angry rebuke that never came. Instead, Enid returned to Sally in the hallway. Fading sounds of the pair moving out through the front door were followed by the starter motor and another backfire from the VW. Its asthmatic revs blended into Ashburnham's signature nature sounds as it drove away. Banjo released a heavy breath and dribbled.

* * *

RETTON HOUSE - DECEMBER 2019.

Gillian tossed and turned during the late night watches. Fleeting images of Retton's past surfaced. Each pulsed with equal intensity but less coherence than her initial replay of Avril's nighttime liaisons with Ted Yates.

Avril darted between bushes in the garden, wearing a nightdress like before. She nipped inside the greenhouse that doubled as a nocturnal love shack for the passionate pair.

The scene faded and switched to Gareth Morrison watching her run past from his bedroom window. He pressed his nose against the glass, then hurried away to grab a warm jumper. Gareth crept down the main staircase, unsure whether any household staff were still up and could be alerted to his movements. He found the main house empty and snuck into the conservatory. He adjusted the jumper to ensure maximum coverage, then let himself out onto an open expanse of plain lawn.

At the greenhouse, Avril backed away from Ted. "But why won't you marry me? Ted, I'm carrying our baby."

Ted folded his arms. "It's not my baby. Can you prove it?"

Avril's jaw clicked. "I'm going to tell James Farrell."

Ted sneered. "What has the head butler to do with me? Tell him. He'll sack you; see if he doesn't."

"He knows I'm not a liar. Wait until I show him my diary. I've recorded all our meetings in detail, from the first moment I thought you loved me." She stuck a defiant nose in the air, but wanted to curl into a ball and weep. Her voice stammered. "James Farrell will recognise the truth when he reads it. Then you'll have to make an honest woman of me, or we'll see who loses their position." Those words agonised her to utter. She loved Ted. How was it he'd only been using her?

"Why you scheming little slut," Ted fell upon Avril, strong hands clasping her windpipe.

Avril tried to call out, but only a faint croak escaped

the throttling grip, choking breath and life from her body.

Gareth peeked over the brick supporting base beneath glass panes at one end. A flash of sheet lightning pulsed overhead, casting silver highlights across Avril's gasping mouth and swelling eyes. Final spasms of self-preservation dimmed to leave her arms and legs hanging loose in Ted's tensed frame. The gardener looked up as another flash turned night into day for what seemed an eternal second. Lightning traced Gareth's terrified, nine-year-old face. He pushed away from the bricks and ran for the conservatory.

"Damn. They'll hang me for certain if he talks," Ted growled. He grabbed a spade and gave chase.

Gareth made it halfway across the lawn before the flying gardening-implement-turned-projectile collided with his spine and knocked him face down into the dewy grass.

Ted picked up the spade with both hands and held it aloft. It came down upon the rear of the child's skull with a sickening crack, compressing his nose into the lawn as blood splattered Ted's cheeks in the glimmer of further lightning. A soft rumble of distant thunder reverberated across the night sky.

Next morning, Peter Lewin, the head gardener halted beside the kitchen garden carrying a trug of vegetables for the house in the crook of one arm. "You were up early, Ted."

Ted Yates stepped back from patting down earth around the trunk of a cedar sapling. He retrieved a handkerchief from his trouser pocket, then turned aside from his boss to wipe both cheeks clean. "I was worried this here tree would get pot bound. It's strong enough to cope outside, now. The master wanted it positioned dead centre in the rear lawn when it was ready, so I thought I'd plant it."

"Good job. Did you dig down far enough to remove any stones and junk that could interfere with root development?"

"Just like you taught me, Mr Lewin. I dug deep to make sure."

Peter nodded at a wheelbarrow full of earth. "Where did that come from?"

Ted scratched his neck. "I thought I'd better bring some extra earth to replace any voids left by rocks after digging them out. I didn't need it." He avoided making eye contact, lest his lie become clear from an uncomfortable and dishonest expression. His wheelbarrow earth once rested beneath the sapling. Something now displaced both it and several other loads he'd already carted away. Two somethings.

Peter clapped him on the back. "Good thinking. Always best to be prepared. You'll be up for a promotion at this rate." He noticed an agitated figure approach. "Hello, what's wrong with the household this morning?"

James Farrell strode across the lawn, face strained. His characteristic calm and disciplined manner had vanished, replaced by a flap neither man had ever witnessed.

"Whatever is the matter, Mr Farrell?" Peter asked.

Farrell stopped beside them. "The Mistress has come home."

Peter frowned. "Isn't that a good thing?"

"She received a telegram while tending to her sister. The Master was killed in action at Amiens. I went upstairs to fetch young Master Gareth, but nobody can find him anywhere. On top of all that, Avril ran away last night."

"Ran away?" Peter blurted. "That doesn't sound like her. Are you sure?"

James nodded. "All her belongings were gone when we checked the staff quarters. There are rumours she'd been sneaking out at night to meet someone."

"From the village?" Peter asked.

"I don't know. I don't even know if the rumours are true. Either way, she departed without tendering her notice."

"Poor form," Peter replied. "Still, love makes people do silly things. If that's what it was about."

Ted rested his spade atop the earth-laden wheelbarrow. "If you'll excuse me, Sirs, I've a bonfire to manage behind the kitchen garden."

Peter waved him off. "Carry on, Ted."

As he wheeled the dislodged earth away to a smoking pile on which Avril's clothing, diary and other few possessions smoldered, Ted caught Peter singing his praises to the head butler.

Gillian Crane's eyes snapped open. Breath wheezed from her dry throat in a scratchy rasp. *Oh, my God. Ted murdered Avril and Gareth, then buried them in the garden and planted Old Peg on top.*

15

Labourer Lost

Gillian awoke the next morning, still with the visions of Avril and Gareth's deaths fresh in her mind. *Do I relay it all to my family and see if they'll take Old Peg down early? Or, should I avoid sounding like more of a wacko than I already do, and keep quiet? What if they fail to dig out the roots and leave Avril and Gareth's skeletons buried? I can't allow that. I may not understand these episodes and sensitivities, but this time I can at least do something useful with them.*

She showered, dressed and stepped out onto the landing. Gerard and Katie worked hard the day before, decorating the enormous tree whose star-capped peak now poked up through the stairwell. Deborah had even climbed on a step-ladder to titivate lower branches in the downstairs hallway. Ivory LED lights circled the conifer's branches, lost in the welcome splendour of a glorious, sunny late December morning. Gillian clutched the sweeping banister with both hands to lean over the edge and take in the seasonal greenery's magnificence. Its natural scent teased her nostrils to conjure scenes of similar evergreens in years gone by. The ghost of herself as a small child stumbled past, shuffling down the stairs one at a time on her bottom. One tiny hand passed from vertical railing to vertical railing for added safety, while the other held fast to a well-loved plastic doll. Present-day Gillian smiled to herself as the imaginary figure faded. She glanced back towards the landing's rear corridor. *Should I see if Deborah is up? She's always an early riser, but hasn't knocked on my door this morning. I'll bet she's flitting from room to room downstairs, soaking up excitement induced by the wreaths, garlands and table centrepieces.* Tempted though she was to re-create her childhood descent for the joy of nostalgia, Gillian decided against it. *I've done enough odd things since I came home.* Gillian took the steps in stages. Each inspired fleeting memories of different Christmases past and the girl she was during each.

"Good Morning, Pixie. Have you recovered from yesterday?" Bertram Crane looked up from writing last minute Christmas cards at the conservatory table.

"I'm fine. Have you given Gerard and Katie the morning off? They deserve it," Gillian replied.

Felicity entered from the kitchen, adjusting a new table centrepiece of mistletoe and pine cones sprayed with a dusting of fake snow. "We'll be keeping their duties light, today."

Gillian nosed over the decoration. "You've been busy."

Felicity set it down on the table. "I've left room for three tealights in glasses, positioned down the middle. The pale, snowy colouration matches the conservatory interior, wouldn't you say?"

"It's fab, Mum. Have you seen Deborah this morning?"

"Isn't she with you?" Felicity peered round Gillian's shoulder towards the corridor.

"No. I thought she'd be up with the sun as usual, running around enjoying the fruits of Friday's decorative labour."

Bertram sealed a card in its accompanying envelope. "All her hard work yesterday must have taken its toll. She's due a lay-in."

"That's true." Gillian's attention drifted through the conservatory windows towards Old Peg, standing firm in the middle of the rear lawn. She was about to bring up her dream, when a red-faced Joe stomped past the main building, cursing under his breath.

Gillian raised an eyebrow. "What's wrong with him? I can't remember the last time I saw Joe in a bad temper."

Bertram twisted round with a frown. "I don't know." He stood and opened a pair of French doors. Cool air from a melting frost drifted into the conservatory, extinguishing the afore-mentioned tealights Felicity had just ignited. "Joe? What's the matter?" Bertram called.

Joe removed his flat cap and shuffled closer to the open doorway. "Beggin' your pardon, Mr Crane, but my new temp didn't show up for work this morning."

"Do you have a lot scheduled? He knows you work on Saturdays, right?"

"He does that, Sir. I made it plain as day when I

interviewed him. This was supposed to be our final big push before Christmas. Only odds and ends left for the last few days afterwards. We've so much tidying up to do, I asked him to come over for seven. Now it's gone nine and there's no sign of the fellow. He was working late yesterday and left a right mess behind. I even found one of my long ladders dumped beside the conservatory, this morning."

"Was he hedge trimming?"

Joe shook his head. "No. Can't think why he'd need it."

Bertram examined a hangnail on his little finger while he spoke. "Have you tried phoning him?"

"No, Mr Crane. He didn't leave any contact details. No address or phone number. You know we don't push for it with our casual staff. How many down-on-their-luck types have we paid cash-in-hand over the years, without asking questions?"

"Hmm. That presents a problem. Well, he can't live far, unless he's staying at a shelter or some other anonymous address. If you give me his name, I'll ask Pixie to look it up on her phone."

Joe flushed. "I'm sorry to admit this sir, but I don't even have that. When I explained your low key approach, the fellow told me it suited him right well. Said people always called him by his nickname, whether or not he wanted it. Either way, the name had stuck and become habit, so I played along."

Bertram rubbed his arms to ward off the cold. "That's a shame. We've no time to recruit someone else before Christmas. He may turn up late. It could be car trouble, roadworks, you name it."

Joe sighed. "Yes, Mr Crane. Well, I'd best get started. All this work won't do itself."

"Don't overdo it, Joe. I know you're particular, but the garden looks grand. If it's tidying, that can wait a fortnight until we source another helper." He began to close the French doors, then hesitated with a curious glint in his eyes. "What *was* your helper's nickname, Joe? I didn't ask."

Joe pulled his cap back on. "The daftest thing you've ever heard, Sir. Banjo. Like the musical instrument. Heaven knows how he came by it."

Gillian dropped a cup and saucer where she stood frozen in the middle of the conservatory. China shattered on the tiled floor with a sharp tinkle, reverberating off copious glass panes.

Bertram caught his daughter's paling countenance. "Joe, can you describe this fellow?"

Joe shrugged. "Early middle-age. Balding head shaped like a butter bean. Tall, quiet and built like a brick outhouse. I didn't care for his eyes much. Grey and flat they were. But he did what I told him. Worked hard, before today."

Gillian reached Bertram's elbow. "Where did you find the ladder, Joe?"

Joe pointed to a patch of grass thirty yards distant. "Right there, on the lawn beneath the guest suite."

Gillian's feet thundered up the sweeping staircase. So vigorous was her frantic climb, the breeze of her passing set baubles swaying on the massive Christmas tree. She hurried down the landing corridor and turned right towards the rear guest suite.

Gareth's silent ghost stood at the opposite end, soulful eyes fixed upon her. He shook his head in a series of slow movements.

Gillian reached Deborah's door and knocked on it. "Deborah?" No response. She knocked again. "Deborah, are you awake?" She half expected a tired groan to follow from inside, backed up by a sarcastic comment like: '*I am now.*' But it was too much to hope for.

Gillian took a breath. "Deborah, I'm coming in." *I hope she hasn't locked the door.* Gillian grabbed the handle and found to her relief that the barrier swung free. Poking fingers of cold air chilled her bones from an open sash window looking out across the rear garden. A matching chill of fear and dread smote her heart to find the sheets pulled aside and a bedside lamp toppled to the floor, indicating a struggle. "No." The word left Gillian's mouth without force in a pleading tone. She pivoted right to find Gareth had vanished. *What about her bathroom?* Gillian was clutching at straws and she knew it. The en-suite door hung open as Deborah said it often did in the mornings. Gillian stuck her head through to discover the washroom devoid of life. She shook herself free of an energy-stealing malaise. "We've got to call the police." Gillian ran from the room, repeating her realisation in a wavering crescendo. "We've got to call the police."

"So you've no contact details for the labourer at all?" DS Jason Hargreaves scribbled down some lines in his pocket notebook. Joe the gardener stood before him with Bertram Crane, recalling any scraps of information he could summon. Pickings remained slim. DS Hargreaves clenched his teeth. "What about a vehicle? Even if you don't have the registration, a make, model and colour would help. We can run a check for the registered keepers of similar matches."

"Never saw one," Joe replied. "The day he showed up in response to our advert, he walked down the driveway. I don't recall odd cars parked in the staff area I didn't recognise, after he joined us."

"Are there any neighbouring properties?" DS Hargreaves asked.

"Not within walking distance," Bertram folded his arms. "There's no bus service out here, either. I'd suggest a taxi, but if this guy is who we think, would he be dumb enough to leave such an obvious trail to follow?"

"Unlikely. I'll make enquiries with local firms on the off-chance. If he abducted Miss Rowling, he'd hardly use a taxi. He's not likely to have carried her, either, with no other properties in the vicinity."

"Tracks and bridleways crisscross and surround the freehold. Might he have parked a car nearby, out of sight?" Bertram asked.

DS Hargreaves examined Bertram with intense curiosity. "It's a logical suggestion. I would say you missed your calling, Mr Crane, but considering your home that's no personal loss." He waved at the roof. "Even our Chief Constable couldn't afford this, let alone any detective I've ever met."

Across from them, DC Frances Kelly sat at the conservatory table with Felicity and Gillian. She too transcribed pertinent details gleaned from her line of questioning. From the moment Gillian launched into an explanation of her visions and how she came to link the temporary garden labourer's nickname with a wanted serial killer, the pen nib scratched less against paper. DC Kelly appeared to mentally edit everything she heard before recording Gillian's assertions.

"So you claim to have seen this Banjo character force feed Tara Osmotherley chocolate, as though you were the victim yourself?" DC Kelly put down her pen.

"That's correct."

"And where did this happen?"

"In the middle of a dinner party at the house on Halloween."

"Halloween?" DC Kelly raised an eyebrow. "I see."

Felicity frowned. "This isn't a joke, Officer Kelly. Gillian almost choked."

"Was she eating at the time?"

"Well, yes. But that's not the point. She described what she saw, afterwards."

"Did you watch the news about Tara Osmotherley on TV, or read any newspaper articles describing her death?"

Gillian's cheeks rouged. "Not until after the fact."

DC Kelly read back some of her notes in silence. "Then a similar thing happened around the time Claire and Tony Walker were stuffed into a plastic barrel of earth?"

"Yes. I was at the pharmacists in the village with my mother. The pharmacist called an ambulance for me. She'll verify my story."

"No doubt. But she didn't share these visions nor experience any oddities herself?"

Gillian sighed. "No. Other people don't partake in them."

"Miss Crane, I'm afraid I'm compelled to ask this: Have you ever been diagnosed with a mental illness?"

Gillian lowered her head. "Not formally."

"Are you on medication or have you ever experimented with recreational drugs? It's okay, you won't get in trouble about it now."

"No."

"How long have you had these, err… supernatural or psychic experiences?"

"Ever since I came home from Hampshire in October."

"You've moved back in with your parents?" Her tone suggested no hint of mockery, but its probing proximity to Gillian's still raw pain over Brent's betrayal stung.

"For now. I'm hoping to return to Hampshire in the New Year."

Felicity read her daughter's agitated body language. "Gillian suffered a tough breakup with her fiancé. She came home to rest and regroup."

DC Kelly tilted her head. "That must have been some breakup?"

Gillian's fuse ran out like sand in the imagined hourglass of Deborah's life; wherever Banjo had taken her. "My fiancé abandoned me outside the church on our wedding day, before the service, okay? It was a shitty time. I spiralled into depression and tried to take my own life." Gillian noticed DC Kelly's eyes drift across the faint but still visible marks scoring her throat. "That's right, I almost hung myself. After I woke up in hospital, all this insanity started happening. I spot ghosts on occasion, too. Not everywhere, just now and again. Some I talk with. Don't ask me why I see through the eyes of this murderer's victims, but I do. There you have it. Laundry aired."

DC Kelly picked up her pen and scribbled down some more notes. "You tried to kill yourself?"

Gillian fumed. "That's right. But I didn't. And neither did Amy Yates."

DS Hargreaves' head snapped round. He'd been listening to every word while Joe and Bertram offered little in the way of actionable intelligence. "How do you know about her?"

"Because I experienced the moment your killer pushed her off the roof of that dilapidated house, live and in living - or rather dying - colour."

DC Kelly hunched over the table. "But how do you know her name? Amy Yates wasn't linked with the murders."

"In that vision, the man I described to you kept

calling her Sally. I believe it's someone he wants to punish. Instead, he's exacting vengeance on these random women. Right before she died, Amy called out: '*I'm not Sally. My name is Amy Yates.*' I shouted it myself and almost toppled off our roof while stargazing with my father."

Bertram nodded. "She's telling the truth. I caught her in the nick of time. The voice Pixie, err I mean Gillian spoke with, wasn't her own. I heard those words with my own ears. After zero news reports about her, we dug into the public coroner inquest schedules on-line."

DS Hargreaves pulled out a chair and sat down opposite the women. "Her inquest was on Wednesday. They recorded a verdict of suicide. Amy Yates had a history of depression."

Gillian shook her head, tears brimming in her ducts. "She didn't kill herself. But I'll bet her injuries were consistent with a fall from heights."

DC Kelly studied Gillian with greater intensity and less cynicism than before. "A jogger discovered her body in Old Kiln Lakes quarry at Chinnor."

Bertram scratched his chin. "I suspected the quarry, when we read the location of her death."

Gillian held her wrists together over the table. "She'd been bound."

Hargreaves and Kelly exchanged rapid-fire glances. "She wasn't when they found her," DC Kelly said. "But Amy Yates' body featured ligature marks dismissed as self-harm."

Gillian wiped one eye with her middle finger. She remembered what she'd put her own family through earlier in the year. "Please don't let her parents think Amy killed herself."

DS Hargreaves cleared his throat. "All right, Miss Crane, you have our attention. Have you endured any more of these visions?"

"Yes. That's how I know the murderer goes by the name, Banjo. He yelled: *'Don't call me Banjo,'* at a victim in the last episode I suffered. I suspect it was that missing antique dealer from Berkhamsted."

"Emma Clarkson?" DS Hargreaves asked.

"That's right. I assume you haven't found her?"

"No. Do you have any idea what state she'll be in when we do?"

Gillian took a deep breath. She pressed both palms against the conservatory table to steady herself. "He shackled her to walls inside a crumbling outbuilding or shed, then burnt her to death with a blowtorch. Slow and painful along each limb. Every inch of flesh."

DC Kelly fumbled and dropped her pen.

DS Hargreaves watched her with an emotionless emptiness. He addressed Gillian. "Could you and the gardener work with our police artist to form a sketch of this guy?"

"Yes."

"We'll run his descriptive details through our systems for potential matches with previous suspects. Does Deborah Rowling have any next of kin we should speak with?"

Gillian sucked her teeth. "No. She's an only child. Both her parents died a couple of years back."

DC Kelly rejoined the conversation. "Do you have a

photograph you could send us? We'll release a missing person report as soon as we get back to the station."

Gillian pulled out her phone. "I've got loads. What would you like?"

"A nice, clear head and shoulders shot. Nothing fancy," DS Hargreaves said. He placed a business card beside her. "My e-mail address is on there."

"What about this rundown, overgrown house Gillian keeps seeing?" Felicity asked. "Are you familiar with such a location?"

DS Hargreaves' eyes narrowed. "Not off the top of my head. A Victorian villa, you say?"

Gillian nodded while she attached a suitable photo of Deborah to an e-mail.

DC Kelly chipped in. "I'll have a word with Neighbourhood Policing. Their local knowledge is more extensive than ours. If this guy worked in your garden for some Christmas cash, I'll wager he doesn't live that far. Maybe less than ten or twelve miles. All his victims we know about originated from within a limited geographic radius."

"Good call, Frankie," DS Hargreaves replied. "My money is on a Buckinghamshire boy."

Gillian's limbs stiffened. "So that's it? You're going to circulate a report with Deborah's photo and draw a sketch of Banjo? In the meantime, he'll be killing her."

"We'll have CSI go over the room she was staying in. There may be DNA or other forensic material to help secure a conviction, later," DS Hargreaves offered. "Has anyone else been in the room today, other than you?"

Gillian stared at him. "No. Secure a conviction, later? But nothing to help save Deborah's life, right?"

DS Hargreaves sat back in his chair. "I don't know what you want me to say. If you've a specific idea where Deborah could be, I'll call in a search team. Beyond that, where do you want us to look? We have neither the personnel nor financial resources to search every forest in the county."

Gillian rested her forehead against one hand. "She's my best friend. God help me, these visions have been bad enough. I couldn't stomach experiencing her death first-hand, then carry that memory for life. That would take me right over the edge."

DC Kelly put her pocket notebook away. "We'll do everything we can; I promise you that much. Please try to get some rest. I know it's hard."

"Hard?" Gillian's eyes flashed, then softened.

DC Kelly met Felicity's gaze.

Felicity nodded her understanding at an unvocalised request to monitor Gillian.

Bertram moved towards the corridor. "Thank you for your time. I'll show you both to the door."

"Are you all right, Miss Gillian?" Joe reached down to help her up off the wooden floor in his office hut.

A police sketch artist rose from a fold-up chair, drawing pad dangling from uncomfortable hands before the sprawling woman.

With Joe's aid, Gillian re-took her seat. Blurred, motion-filled images from the perspective of someone jerking their head around, made her dizzy and sick to the stomach. Deborah's fear rippled through Gillian's body, causing her to stammer. "It's Deborah. I can feel her terror."

Joe vacillated between running to the house in search of Bertram and Felicity, or staying behind to keep watch over their daughter. From the worried look straining the sketch artist's countenance into a twisted caricature, Joe surmised the latter option was preferable.

Gillian caught her breath. "She's inside the same house. It has to be. What a filthy dump."

The sketch artist held up his drawing. "Did you see *him* there?"

"No. Deborah is alone, tied to a chair in some kind of shabby dining room with peeling wallpaper. Oh God, she's so afraid."

"How did you get on with the sketch artist, Pixie?" Bertram poured himself a glass of scotch in the living room. Felicity put down a shopping list of Christmas sundries she'd need to collect on Monday. Keeping calm and carrying on during troublesome times was her forte.

Mace whined and dragged himself away from the fender.

Bertram watched the dog sidle up to Gillian and nuzzle her ankles as she sank into the opposite sofa. "Poor Mace must miss Deborah."

Felicity noticed Gillian's zombie-like stare. "It's not

that. She's seen something." Felicity drew a deep breath. "Has he…?"

"No." Gillian stroked Mace's agitated face without looking at the concerned animal. "But I saw what she's seeing and suffered her anguish."

"Is she at that house?" Bertram put down his glass tumbler.

"Yes. Somewhere inside, towards the rear. He's bound Deborah to a chair. I didn't notice him in the room. Not yet, at any rate."

Felicity crossed to sit beside Gillian on the other sofa. "You saw through Deborah's eyes, but not at the moment of death. That's something new."

"Our bond is strong."

Bertram leaned forward. "Was there anything useful we can offer the police? Some clue or detail to help them locate Deborah's whereabouts?"

"No, Daddy." Gillian's bottom lip quivered.

Felicity caught hold of her as she broke down.

* * *

ASHBURNHAM - DECEMBER 2019.

Deborah Rowling twisted her neck as far as it would stretch on either side to build a thorough, panicked picture of her predicament and its location. A faded print of an oil painting hung askew above a dresser behind her. It depicted an autumnal woodland river and path leading to a tiny cottage. She remembered Gillian showing her photographs of a similar scene taken somewhere amidst Burnham Beeches near Farnham Common. An antique, polished oak dining table stood at an angle in one corner of the high-ceilinged room. Fresh scratch marks devoid of dust in dark wood flooring suggested it had been dragged aside to make her the centre of attention. Five matching chairs of polished oak were bundled against a wall to her right near a dresser. Plastic cable ties secured her wrists and ankles to a sixth, on which she sat. She attempted to stand, but the biting restraints prevented movement. Shafts from the last light of day withdrew through a ground floor sash window coated in grime. *It's got to be around four in the afternoon. How long have I been out? He forced me to drink something back at Retton House. Sometime after midnight, I'd guess.* Engine noises approached from the front. *It must be him. Or could it be the cavalry? Please God, let it be the cavalry.* The vehicle bumped to a halt. Its motor ceased with a rattle. Deborah jostled in her seat, hopping like a possessed jumping bean. Her chair toppled sideways as a rear door of the shabby house creaked open. Deborah's right temple struck the wooden floorboards. She blacked out.

"So you've finished playing dead and woken up, have you, Sally?" The harsh male voice simmered with suppressed aggression.

Deborah's eyelids fluttered open. She found herself sitting upright again in the middle of the wretched dining room. A salty tang of blood coated her furry tongue. Now it was dark outside and felt late. A single, undecorated and inadequate bulb cast a dim cone of yellow electric light across the space.

Four paces beyond, a huge, balding man with eyes of piercing slate leered at her from a sitting position on one of the spare chairs. He lifted a blue, tubular cardboard container with a plastic lid and shook it like a solitary maraca. "I had to buy some salt. They say salt rubbed into a cut hurts like thunder." The volume and ferocity of his tone increased. "I'm going to make you pay for trying to stab me, Sally."

Deborah recalled Gillian's retelling of how this creature addressed his victims by the name, '*Sally*.' If any faint hope lingered in her heart that some other weirdo had abducted her, it evaporated at the utterance. No doubt remained: her captor was 'Banjo,' the psychotic murderer of women and children. Despite little hope of him detecting her honesty through his madness, Deborah decided she'd nothing to lose by challenging the label. "I'm not Sally. My name is Deborah Rowling. You broke into my room at Retton House and forced me to drink something." She struggled to force the words out of an ash dry mouth.

Banjo grinned. "Sleepy juice. Did you enjoy your sleepy juice, Sally? It made you go bye byes." He feigned snoozing against an angled palm, then dropped the salt and picked up a glittering chef's knife. Its wide, freshly sharpened blade reflected Deborah's open-mouthed panic, pummelled by crashing waves of rising dread.

Deborah shrieked. "I told you: I'm not Sally. My name is Deborah."

Banjo caressed the blade's edge as though it were the erogenous zone of some worshipped lover. His voice adopted a dreamy, faraway quality. "You always were a liar, Sally. A dirty, deceptive and dishonest witch." He pinged the tip with an index finger, then sucked blood from a minuscule incision it left in the flesh. "No matter. Mum won't be here for you to run to, this time. I drowned her like you tried to drown me." Banjo rose and rushed forward. He jabbed his nose in Deborah's face and shouted. "I drowned our disgusting mother in the bathroom sink. Who will you tell now, Sally?"

Deborah's limbs shook with the uncontrolled rapidity of someone pulled from the depths of an icy lake, suffering cold shock. No words came to mind. If they had, she doubted her ability to enunciate them.

Cold steel incised Deborah's restrained right forearm with sufficient pressure to open a gouge in the flesh. Dark, crimson blood seeped upward to coat the blade. It ran down the chair arm and trickled towards its seat.

Agony, fear, and a lack of options empowered Deborah's lungs with her one hope of escaping this deranged hulk's terminal machinations. She screamed for help, straight into his ear with deafening force. Banjo dropped the blade and staggered backward, clutching his head. "You vile, fucking demon." His ears whistled.

Deborah didn't hold back. She had no clue how far this house stood from civilisation, but she would use each second her lungs still drew breath to raise an alarm. To scream until her voice grew hoarse or that kitchen blade ended her torment once and for all.

Banjo halted her desperate, continuous outburst with the back of one hand. Its impact knocked her head sideways and silenced the screams. Fresh blood and a dislodged tooth flew from her mouth while tears streaked both cheeks.

Banjo growled under his breath. "I'll cut you, Sally. I'll cut you good." He bent over to retrieve the chef's knife. "I wonder how much blood we can extract together, before you die?"

Deborah forced herself to look ahead at the straightening monster. Banjo approached, waving his blood-smeared knife. The room whirled, and a fainting darkness smothered Deborah's senses beneath its merciful cloak.

At Retton House, Gillian lurched back to consciousness in her bed. Her right arm burned with a sharp stinging sensation. Dreams of Deborah's encounter with Banjo followed her into a waking vision. The murderer's empty eyes peered out of the darkness, only to fade and be replaced with those of Gareth Morrison standing at the foot of her bed.

16

History Repeated

ASHBURNHAM - OCTOBER 1988.

"What have you given me?" Banjo clutched at his stomach and rolled over on the kitchen floor. A half-empty tumbler of orange squash he'd released during his sudden collapse, rolled over to spill its remaining contents across ageing floor tiles.

"What's the matter, Little Brother? Don't you like your orange?" Sally rested against the sink, one arm folded across her other broken one in a sling.

Banjo coughed and choked. "It burns. My stomach is on fire." He kicked and writhed, then called out, "Mum, help me."

Sally nudged a cupboard door beneath the sink until it swung back on rusted hinges. She swiped a black plastic bottle of drain cleaner, then held it aloft over Banjo's uncoordinated flurry of limbs. "I made you a special cocktail, Banjo. Now all you can do is complain? That's gratitude for you."

Banjo cried in pain.

Enid stormed downstairs. She'd been disturbed from an afternoon nap after a morning in the company of another gin bottle. "What's going on in there?" Her demanding rebuke reached the kitchen seconds before that lumbering, fiery-haired form appeared in its doorway. Her open-mouthed, Medusa-like gaze fell upon her offspring. "Sally."

"Judgement Day, Sal." Banjo rolled over, stabbing sensations evaporating from his knotted gut. "What on earth?"

Sally lay on her back beside the discarded tumbler. She convulsed into a mouth-foaming fit, eyes rolling upward into her skull.

Enid crouched by her side, then gripped the girl's shoulders to hold her steady. "Sally."

Sally's body ceased all motion.

Enid replaced the act of stilling the child's shaking form with shaking it herself. "Sally? Sally, can you hear me?" She pressed her ear against Sally's chest, then cried out. "She's not breathing." Her head lifted to where the black plastic bottle of drain cleaner now stood beside the sink. She whirled on Banjo. Contorted spasms of rage and agony flared across her face. "What have you done to your sister?" Enid's vocal pitch blew like a factory whistle. "What have you done to her?" She grabbed Banjo, then hammered his head against the kitchen floor. "You evil little monster. You've killed Sally."

On the eighth blow, Banjo blacked out.

"We're taking the lad into custody. A clinical psychologist will assess him." The detective's words followed Banjo though the rear door of a Vauxhall

Senator police car, parked beside Enid's VW Beetle. Though he'd long since come to, a certain cranial woolliness remained. Two men in overalls lugged a zipped body bag across Ashburnham's threshold, then loaded it into the rear of a van next to the police vehicle.

Banjo watched in silence. *She's holding her breath. Sally always was a liar. I hope she gets in trouble for playing dead. I'm lucky whatever she put in my orange squash didn't kill me.* He focused on his stomach, hale and hearty. It rumbled from lack of food, but otherwise gave him no trouble.

The months that followed passed in a lagging blur for Banjo. Locked in rooms; led around like a zoo animal by powerful men with uniforms and keys; then the doctors in white coats, asking him endless questions about life at Ashburnham and his relationship with Sally. The terms 'psychosis,' 'delusion' and 'confused or disturbed thoughts' accompanied their discussions about him like the obligatory pocket protectors holding their pens.

One day a judge addressed Banjo with accusations he was a monster who'd carried out '*a systematic and protracted campaign of torture*' against his older sibling, culminating in her murder. A lot of those words washed over the boy, neither heeded nor understood. Was this Sally's ultimate revenge? Had she convinced everyone in the entire world that the harm she'd inflicted on him for months, was all his fault? Even his doing? These people believed *he* was the monster. *No matter. One day I'll return home. Then Sally will pay for her crimes.*

Months stretched into years. Banjo retreated deeper inside his own head. This time the plethora of doctors became one: Anita Johnson. Banjo didn't like Anita. She reminded him too much of an older Sally. Yet she spoke with more kindness in her voice than he'd heard from anyone since his father died. He received personal education at *'The Unit,'* as the special hospital with accompanying secure detention wing was named. His body grew and aged.

One day Anita announced she was retiring at the end of the year. She'd been a clinician in the morning of her career, when Banjo came to her a quarter of a century earlier. Anita told him she was looking forward to spending more time at home and visiting family. His criminal sentence long-since served, Banjo remained at The Unit over concerns for his mental and emotional stability. Now accommodated in the minimum security wing following three years of mellower behaviour, he was allowed to sit outdoors in the nicer weather and enjoy calming mood enhancement from the sun's rays.

"Can I go home?" Banjo blurted out during his next session with the doctor.

"Would you like to?" Anita recorded their

discussion as usual. "How do you think you'd cope?"

"I want to see my mother. She must be all alone, if she's still alive. Why hasn't she ever visited? Other patients receive visits."

"Could it have something to do with your sister?" Anita cocked her head. "Do you understand what happened to Sally?"

Banjo swallowed hard. "I killed her when I was ill."

"You've come to terms with it?"

Banjo nodded. He hadn't come to terms with it at all. People told him repeatedly over the years that he'd murdered his sister. It was another of Sally's tricks. But he'd learnt that special treats and privileges followed any admission of guilt on his part over past sins. If he was going to get hold of Sally and make her suffer, he'd have to be free of The Unit first.

Anita scanned transcript summaries: typed notes from their sessions over the three years since her longest serving patient's behaviour evidenced significant improvement. "Do you know what you'd do, if you went home?"

Banjo thought for a moment. "I'd learn to drive. I'm in my late thirties and I've never driven a car."

"That's a positive desire. How about work?"

Banjo twiddled his thumbs. "I always enjoy helping in the garden whenever they let me. I'm not allowed near the sharp tools, but I love planting flowers and digging up weeds. I might look for work as a garden labourer."

Anita smiled. "You've given this some thought. Let me make you an offer."

Banjo gave her his full attention.

Anita stretched. "Write a letter to your mother, asking if she'd be willing to have you back. I warn you now, the response - if any - may not be what you're hoping. There are other options we can consider around independent living, if her answer proves negative. Those would require more significant arrangements. However, if you give me the letter, I'll post it to her along with one of my own describing your progress and our relationship over the years. Then, if all goes well, and she's amenable, I'll sign you out for a six week trial period. Does that sound fair?"

Banjo clasped his mitt-like hands together. "Would you? Please. That would help a lot. If Mum is older now, she may need me around the house."

Anita pulled out a spare pad and pen, then handed it to him. "Try not to get your hopes up. I wouldn't want to see you suffer a setback if they're dashed. Be as honest as you can in the letter to your mother. If nothing else, you may find the act of putting it all down on paper aids your wellbeing and recovery."

Banjo drummed his fingers against the pad. "I'll do my best."

It surprised Banjo when Anita Johnson informed him Enid had replied with a cautious acceptance to give her suggestion a try. Anita handed him a simple, handwritten note which read:

'*Banjo,*

Dr Johnson informs me you are better now and that you regret what happened to Sally all those years ago.

She said you've expressed an interest in gardening, learning to drive, and a desire to help around the home.

Based on her recommendation and the words you wrote, I will agree to a trial period for your return to Ashburnham. I know your father would have wanted it, were it not for the accident that claimed his life when you were still a boy. But I warn you now, my welcome will expire at the first sign of your old problems resurfacing. There is always work to do at home and you will need to live by my rules. If you are willing to accept this, I'll see you soon.

Take care,

Mum.'

Banjo folded the note. "Thank you." His mind tripped over the reference to Derek's 'accident.' *The bitch must have been sober for once when she wrote that. Or was she three sheets to the wind and didn't realise what she's agreed to? Mum is the murderer, not me. How come she isn't dead from all that booze and a solitary life of misery? She accepts my fake admission over murdering Sally, yet she must know Sally is still alive. Why is the world conspiring against me? Mother will pay and Sally will pay when I find her. But first I must play Anita's game. I must act like a good boy and be the perfect son at home, if I'm to be released from here forever. I'll adjust to life in the outside world. I'll learn to drive. Then I'll find Sally, even if she lives a hundred miles away and is married. How sweet would it feel to make her children pay too, if she has any? So many wrongs to right. I want her to account for everything she did. No matter how long it takes, I'll find a way.*

Anita stood and offered her hand across the desk. "I'll set the paperwork in motion. I couldn't ask for a brighter end to my career, Simon, thank you."

Simon's eyes flashed in recognition at the use of his actual name. Anita only did that occasionally. 'Banjo' had become such an ingrained term, mental associations with a happier past initiated by the use of 'Simon' often sent him into a depressive, downward spiral.

She must really believe I'm better, now. That's good. Not that I was ever ill. It's all a product of Sally's lies. Soon Banjo will strike up a new tune. His throat thrummed, causing Anita to frown. Banjo coughed. "I'm sorry. I'm a little emotional. It's been a long time."

Anita's brow smoothed out. "Of course. If it's all too much once the day arrives, you don't have to go. This is a trial. We can end it before it's begun, should the need arise."

"It won't. I'm ready for a new start." His grey eyes swept across a bank of filing cabinets containing personal records for all Anita's patients. "What will happen to my file once I'm released for good and you retire?"

"They'll move it downstairs to the archive block near the kitchen for a designated retention period, in case of complications."

Banjo rubbed his narrowing eyes at the word, 'complications.' "Then I'll be forgotten? My history here extinguished like a puff of smoke?"

Anita sighed. "That's very poetic. Don't worry, *I* won't forget you."

Banjo turned to leave without another spoken word. *That's what I'm worried about.*

Banjo's six week trial proved a success. The term extended to three, then six months culminating in a final full release a fortnight before Dr Anita Johnson called time on a satisfying career.

It relieved her replacement no active records were destroyed in a sudden fire that engulfed the archive block, three weeks after he began his new post. Nobody challenged a familiar face raking leaves in the garden, the afternoon the conflagration erupted. A face that hadn't appeared in those grounds for over half a year.

During the dark early evenings of the following winter, Anita Johnson's car was run off a quiet, rural road by a hit-and-run driver. A newly qualified driver - were the truth ever known. Patrons spilling out of a nearby pub noticed a wreck-damaged, battered old VW Beetle backfiring away from the scene. Nobody thought to record its registration, being unaware of the fatal road accident that had occurred a quarter of a mile down the lane.

* * *

ASHBURNHAM - DECEMBER 2019.

What the heck is wrong with him now? Deborah
Rowling tugged her secured hands in hopes the cable
ties might give. Those hopes were instantly dashed.
Banjo writhed on the floor, clutching his stomach. It
was at this moment Deborah noticed someone had
bandaged the incision in her right arm with taped rags.
*Is this devil keeping me alive so I'm conscious when he ends
the torment?* She couldn't estimate how long she'd been
out cold. Fifteen minutes? *Have I caught a break? Has
that bastard contracted acute appendicitis or something?*

Simon clambered to his feet, re-enacted memories
still fresh - though confused - of orange squash mixed
with drain cleaner in another example of Sally's
wickedness. He stared into a dark corner of the dining
room. "I'll find another Sally to pay for that one, won't
I, Mum?"

Deborah squinted hard to focus on anyone lingering
in the shadows. The corner lay empty.

Banjo picked up his container of salt and advanced
on his hostage. He grinned from ear to ear. A perverse
twanging noise emanated from his throat. "Salt may
hurt when applied to a wound, but it's also used to
purify and preserve things, Sally. I learnt that at The
Unit. That's the place they confined me when you
playacted at being poisoned. Let's see how long we can
preserve *you* for." He ripped the rags free of Deborah's

wound.

Deborah screamed in agony. Her cries intensified as a trickle of salt poured between the separated folds of flesh.

*　*　*

RETTON HOUSE - DECEMBER 2019.

"Gareth?" Gillian sat up in bed, fresh from waking with Deborah's symbiont torment in full force. Her right arm throbbed.

"You were right." The deceased boy's lifeless words matched his forlorn expression and departed state.

"What about?"

"When you said Mother and Father are dead. When you said that I'm dead."

Gillian bit her lip. "I'm sorry."

"Why am I still here, Gillian? This isn't my home anymore. Why is Avril about? She must be dead, too."

"Yes, she is. Ted Yates, one of your gardeners, strangled Avril and beat your skull in with a shovel. At least, I believe he did. I saw it in a dream."

Gareth raised a hand to the back of his shattered head, as though touching a physical object to which his soul was no longer fused. "Why did he do that?"

"He murdered Avril because she was going to expose him as the father of her unborn child. He murdered you, because you witnessed him kill her, didn't you?"

Gareth's stare darkened. Realisations of an old

memory danced behind his hollow eyes. "That's right," he gasped. "I was frightened and ran away. The last thing I remember is the smell of grass. But why aren't we in heaven?"

"Ted buried you beneath the Western Red Cedar, which he planted on our rear lawn. If I'm right, they never discovered the truth of your disappearances nor your bodies. That may be about to change. When it does, I hope you'll both find peace."

Gareth drew nearer. He may have been only a nine-year-old boy, but facing and talking with his ghost still set Gillian's teeth on edge.

"You were having a nightmare, Gillian."

"Yes. I keep seeing the last moments and experiencing the agony of women treated worse than Avril. My friend, Deborah, has been abducted by their murderer."

"The man who dragged her from the back room last night?"

"You witnessed that?"

Gareth nodded.

Gillian fidgeted. "I don't know where he's taken her. It's an old Victorian villa surrounded by woodland and not much els-"

"Ashburnham," Gareth interrupted.

"What?"

"Ashburnham. It can't be any other place. My father did some business with the owners before he marched off to war. He took me with him one day. I was only six, but I remember the house. It sits in a dark clearing. There are no other Victorian homes built in woodlands around here."

Gillian wanted to grab him and extract details, but restrained herself lest her hands pass through thin air. "Can you remember where it is? Do you know how to get there? It's important. Deborah is my best friend. That man could kill her at any moment."

Gareth pointed to the window where Gillian had watched Avril run through the garden, back in October. "Follow the grounds to the property boundary that way. There are some old earthworks near the base of a steep, wooded hill."

"I know it." Gillian recalled her uncomfortable experience of being watched while on hack, then turning her horse around at the obstructed bridleway.

"Ashburnham lies in a dip on the other side of that hill," Gareth went on.

Gillian almost tumbled out of bed. *Do I call the police? No, there isn't time. I still don't know how to approach Ashburnham from the road. Should I wake my folks or rouse the staff? Another delay with protracted explanations of what I've discovered and how. Time, time, time. Deborah might have minutes left.* She pulled on her riding clothes, then penned a hurried note and placed it in an envelope addressed to her parents.

Gareth remained at the foot of her bed as Gillian yanked the door open. "Good luck, Gillian. Be careful. I hope you save your friend."

In that moment, Gareth no longer caused Gillian disquiet. Instead, his honest wish for her success and pity-inducing mournful face broke her heart. Gillian blew him a kiss, then hurried for the staircase. At the top, near the tree's crowning star, she hesitated and held up the note. *Mum and Dad need to find this as soon as possible.* She darted to her parents' door, slid the envelope beneath it, and then ran back to the stairs.

Mace's head lifted above the edge of his basket when Gillian reached the hallway. He followed her towards the conservatory, tail wagging. A soft, playful bark accompanied hopes of an unexpected midnight walk.

Gillian pointed back along the hallway. "Go to bed, Mace. You can't come with me."

The wagging ceased. Mace sensed her turmoil. He disobeyed the command to return to his basket, stopping to watch Gillian slip outside and hurry toward the stables.

Gillian tacked Nellie in a breathless panic. The earthworks were too far to reach on foot. She couldn't drive along country lanes in the general vicinity with her car, trusting to luck she'd happen upon some concealed track into thick woodland. And all that with velvet darkness casting its veil across proceedings.

Nellie's hooves clattered on concrete. She whinnied as Gillian spurred her into a gallop from the yard across the lawn.

A rear door to the staff apartments opened. Lorcan Donnelly ran into the courtyard waving a torch beam. He caught the glint of stirrups in the moonlight as Gillian urged her mount on.

"What on earth does she think she's doing at this time of night? Sure and she's fixin' to have a nasty fall. I'd best ask Gerard to wake the Cranes."

Gillian glanced back as Nellie flashed past Old Peg. In the blink of an eye it took the cedar to be swallowed up by darkness, she fancied a woman and young boy stood at its base surrounded by a shimmering aura. Gillian set her face forward and rode Nellie with a ferocity the horse had never known.

Bertram crane reached for a bedside light and clicked it on. Furious barking and scratching at the bedroom door roused Felicity from a deep sleep beside him.

"What's going on, Bertram?"

"I don't know. Something's upset the dog. Let me check." Bertram swung out of bed and trudged across the room. "Hello, what's this?" He chuckled. "Has Santa visited us a few days early?" He crouched and picked up the envelope, then opened the door. Mace leapt up against his legs, barking louder than ever. "Easy, boy. Whatever is the matter?"

Gerard reached the landing, clothes a mess. He hurried towards the master bedroom door.

"What's going on, Gerard?" Bertram asked. "It must be serious to bring you into the main house at such an hour."

"I'm sorry, Mr Crane. Lorcan woke me. Miss Gillian has taken Nellie. She set off across the garden at a frantic rate. He's worried she'll hurt herself."

Felicity appeared in the doorway wearing a silken nightgown.

Gerard averted his eyes. "I beg your pardon, Mrs Crane."

"That's all right, Gerard. I'm glad you woke us." She

noticed the envelope in her husband's hands. "That's Gillian's writing."

Bertram tugged open the flap. "I don't see who else it could be." He unfolded the note for the couple to read Gillian's scant description of her mission and intended destination.

Felicity leaned against Bertram for support. "How can she know there's a house up there?"

"Something else she's seen, I suppose. I've never heard of it, but neither have I ventured up that hill before."

"She's been right about everything else. What if she's right about this?" Felicity asked.

"Then she's in harm's way. I'm calling the police."

"What are you going to say?" Felicity's voice strained.

"I'll give them the location and demand action."

"And if they won't listen?" Felicity tugged at his pyjama top.

"I'll phone Gary Tomlinson. He's an ACC on the chief officer team I play golf with. He'll light a fire under their backsides if I can convince him of the severity."

Felicity's jaw tightened. "How long will that take?"

A thunder of horse hooves echoed across the lawn.

Bertram looked round. "What was that?"

"Lorcan," Gerard said. "He ran to saddle your horse, Troy, Mr Crane. He's going after Miss Gillian."

Bertram reached for the phone. "God bless him. He won't know where she's headed, but I suppose he'll follow disturbed ground to find her."

Gillian slowed Nellie to a trot at the trench-like entrance to the earthworks. The bridleway obstruction remained in place, a short distance away. She dismounted upon reaching it and hitched Nellie to some thick, exposed tree roots.

"Easy, girl." She patted the horse's neck. "Catch your breath. You won't make it up that steep hill. I've got to leave you here for a spell." Gillian scrambled over the earthworks. Breath escaped her mouth in moonlit clouds from occasional pale beams poking through the dense tree canopy. By now her eyes had adjusted enough to make out the ridge far above. She slipped and stumbled towards it. Images of Banjo pouring salt into a wound on Deborah's arm flashed across the darkness. Gillian gripped her own tortured limb, feeling every sensation of the gash as though it plagued her flesh.

A pale figure appeared between two conifers near the hill's summit, causing Gillian to peer further ahead. It vanished in an instant.

Was that a teenage girl? Crap. Why don't they fit me for a straightjacket now and get this over with?

Gillian reached the top, panting for breath. She fell against one tree where she'd seen the figure. The ground beyond sloped away into a large hilltop depression and woodland clearing. She pushed herself onward. Cold steel incising Deborah's other arm caused Gillian to cry out. She slapped her forehead to dispel the accompanying visions. *I must see clearly ahead, if I'm to help her.*

A dull clank of metal accompanied a bruising sensation as her knee collided with a lump in the darkness. Gillian retrieved a small torch from her jacket pocket. She'd avoided using it until now, for fear of Banjo spotting its beam and becoming alert to her presence. From Deborah's shared experiences forcing their way into her body, it was clear the captor's attention lay elsewhere at present. Her torch illuminated a rusty, weed-choked vehicular wreck without wheels. Faded, pale blue paint still lingered on what appeared to be the remains of a long-forgotten VW Beetle. Gillian rubbed her knee, then squeezed around the car, keeping low to the ground. Her torch never rose much above long grass and bracken clogging the area.

A dark, straight outline materialised between the trees. Gillian didn't need any further visual information to recognise it. The day Amy Yates fell to her death from its roof, she'd received enough mental snapshots to forever sear it into her brain. A battered, though functional maroon Rover's paintwork reflected her torch beam, causing Gillian to extinguish it. Blood-curdling screams of terror and torment blasted from the structure beyond. *How do I stop this guy? He's huge.* Deborah hollered again. Gillian heard those cries both inside her head, and with her physical ears across the secluded glade's frosty night air. She swallowed all fear and charged the front door. From what she'd observed in her mind, Gillian knew Deborah was tied to a chair in a dining room at the back. Surprise and aggression represented her few remaining weapons, now. Those and the hope of drawing upon untapped wells of strength, opened by the love she felt for her best friend.

Ashburnham's front door flew back with a bang. Even without her mental map, the piercing screams of Deborah's vocalised agony provided clear direction. Gillian didn't stop as she passed the cellar and rounded a doorway into the dining room. Deborah's eyes, billiard balls of terror, fixed on a chef's knife raised high in Banjo's arm above her head. Gillian launched herself onto his back and the pair crashed sideways into a wall. Deborah's chair tumbled in the opposite direction, slamming her jaw against wooden floorboards. Protesting, rotted wooden joists split and shuddered beneath.

Banjo was on top of Gillian in a heartbeat. The tip of his blade flashed down towards one of her striking green eyes. Gillian grabbed his wrist and pushed with all her might against overwhelming strength. Banjo hissed and spat.

Outside in the back garden, leaves and earth surrounding the rosebush heaved and parted. Semi-skeletal hands, spattered with decomposing flesh, pushed out of the earth. A mane of fiery red hair rose from a splitting lump of stones and weeds.

Gillian brought her knee straight up into Banjo's groin. He rolled over, dropping the blade. Gillian grabbed it and dived for Deborah's overturned chair.

She sawed at the cable ties while Banjo clambered onto his knees. One tie pinged free, releasing Deborah's right foot. Gillian knew there was no way she could sever them all before their assailant struck again. She righted the chair and stood over Deborah, facing towards Banjo with the blade pointing forward. Was it a weapon or a talisman to ward off evil?

Banjo rose to his full height and smiled. He wheeled about and stomped down the hallway.

Gillian seized the moment to work on Deborah's other leg restraint. It snapped in time for Banjo to reappear in the doorway, a meat cleaver in one hand and a black plastic bottle of drain cleaner in the other.

"Time for a drink, Sally." Banjo set down the cleaver and unscrewed the bottle cap.

Deborah whimpered. Her misting eyes focused upon and recognised Gillian standing guard at her shoulder.

Gillian pointed the blade again. "Which one of us is Sally, Banjo? We can't both be her, can we?"

Banjo frowned. Confusion and fury fought for prominence across his warped visage. He stammered. "It's another of your tricks, Sally. You're a liar." He slapped a quivering palm against the side of his face. His throat thrummed.

A disembodied, faint adolescent female voice seemed to echo from Ashburnham's bones. "You're the liar. And a murderer." The sylph-like visual echo of a semi-translucent teenage girl walked through the wall. Gillian recognised her as the figure she'd seen watching from the wooded ridge during her ascent.

"Sally." Banjo backed away and put down the plastic

bottle. His harried stare flitted from Deborah, to Gillian, to the apparition of his departed sister.

Sally's outline flared with intense white light. She thrust an outstretched arm towards him, fingers splayed. Her voice slurred with a thick resonance as though backed by some angelic battle chant. "Remember."

Banjo toppled into the hallway. He clutched his head and screamed, fitting and gurgling.

Oh, how the memories flooded back, but not as he'd experienced them in days gone by. First came the time *he* lured Sally to the pond and pushed her in. Then there was the day he dug a grave for her, knocked his sister out with a rock and buried *her* alive. Banjo cried and struggled as more images swamped his brain; each a reversal. There was Sally tied with a curtain sash to a broken-backed chair in the attic, while he force fed her chocolate. She threw up and almost choked. Then the time he'd stolen Sally's favourite toy: a black wooden horse she called Tornado. After a struggle with Sally, he'd toppled out of an upstairs window while throwing the now broken model animal up onto the roof.

Banjo beat his fists against the floor. "It's not true. It's a lie." His voice heaved and cracked.

More replays of truth assaulted him. He'd written *'Sally is a cunt'* on one of the dirty kitchen windows, then set an ambush for her in the outbuilding. When she entered, he toppled shelving onto her and took pleasure in burning her arms with their deceased father's old cigarette lighter. He almost burnt the building down. When Sally broke free and ran for the house, he threw a rock which broke another kitchen window.

From somewhere beyond the staircase, the sound of dragging feet formed a growing ambient backdrop to Banjo's cries.

Two final disturbing visions surfaced. First came the moment he'd attempted to stab Sally while their mother was out, resulting in her breaking an arm while tumbling down the stairs to escape. Last of all he witnessed that fateful day he'd mixed her orange squash with drain cleaner rather than water. Sally fell to the floor in a terminal convulsion.

"Nooo," Banjo wailed.

Gillian severed Deborah's arm restraints while the fitting killer's psychodrama played out. Sally's ghost faded to nothing as the dragging noise grew louder.

"Banjo?" A hoarse woman's voice croaked. "Banjo, you've been a naughty boy."

Banjo opened his eyes. The voluminous, decaying corpse of his drowned mother stood before him, arms outstretched. Ivory white eyeballs filled her rotting skull. Strands of rank connective tissue stretched in time with a clicking of the jaw as she spoke. Her voice turned harsh. "You're going down to the cellar for your punishment, boy."

Banjo scrambled in the only direction that offered escape: back into the dining room.

Gillian brought up the chef's knife for protection, then both she and Deborah gasped at the shambling figure of Enid's corpse leering from the doorway.

"Down to the cellar, I said," she roared.

The creaking floor joists failed with a simultaneous crack. Dust and rubble flew past in a rush as the contents of the dining room and its occupants dropped into the cellar below with a deafening crash.

Gillian landed with Deborah on top. The shattered remnants of her prison chair lay all about them. Deborah coughed and rolled over. Blood seeped from the second wound Banjo had inflicted on her left arm. She clamped numb fingers around it.

Gillian coughed and fished out a pocket handkerchief. "Use this to stem the flow." Her attention wandered up through a hole that had once been the dining room floor. Far above, no talking corpse lingered in the doorway any longer. Gillian pushed aside some splintered floor timbers and attempted to sit. Ten feet away, Banjo lay pinned, face-up beneath the shattered remnants of a dresser. He gasped for air, mouth wide open as the weight compacted his lungs. The opened black plastic bottle of drain cleaner rolled down a collapsed beam to wedge against a fragment of the dresser. Its liquid contents sloshed over the rim in a chemical cascade that tumbled into Banjo's gaping orifice. His body shook with violent convulsions. He gagged, unable to halt the burning of his innards. At last his limbs slowed and the light of life extinguished from his still-open, steely grey eyes.

Gillian hugged Deborah close. "Do you think you can move?"

"I don't know." She coughed at the settling cloud of

dust. "Gillian, what happened up there? Did you see that teenage ghost and the…" Words failed Deborah to describe the living corpse who'd precipitated their collapse into the cellar.

"Yes. Let's rest while I try to figure a way out."

Some minutes later, a familiar, musical Irish voice cut through the gloom above. "Gillian? Gillian, are you there?"

"Oh, my God." Gillian took enough of a breath to project her voice. "Lorcan. Down here."

The stable manager's curly-haired noggin poked over the hole's rim. He shone a torch into the depths. "Is that Deborah with you, too? Are you both okay?"

"We're alive. Deborah needs medical attention."

"Mary and the Saints be praised. I'll ride back to… No, wait. Someone's coming."

Pulsing blue strobe lights sliced through the darkness, accompanying the engine and tyre rumbles of multiple approaching vehicles.

Gillian sat herself down on a rough section of broken patio outside the kitchen door at Ashburnham.

DS Jason Hargreaves squatted beside her. Bertram and Felicity Crane stood nearby.

Gillian's gaze wandered from the outbuilding where Emma Clarkson had been killed to an open grave with disturbed earth a few feet away. Forensic personnel photographed a decomposing, big boned woman's corpse facing up from the pit. Gillian indicated the hole. "I believe that was his mother."

DC Frances Kelly stepped out of the kitchen. "Bloomin' gruesome, leaving a grave open like that. She's been dead a few months, I'd say."

Gillian ignored the comment. She stroked a rough patch of the stonework near where she sat until her fingers halted at a dried red splotch. "DS Hargreaves?"

"You can call me Jason," Hargreaves replied.

"Jason. Can you extract DNA from dried blood?"

"It depends on the sample quality. Technically, it's possible for up to ten years. Why do you ask?"

"I'll bet if you sample that, you'll find a match with Amy Yates. It might bring her family some closure. An odd Christmas present, mind."

Jason gave a lopsided smile. "You're an extraordinary young woman. Tell you what: I'll have forensics look into it. Happy?"

"Thank you. Am I happy? I'm happy Deborah is safe and that monster won't hurt anyone else."

"Mmm. Once we get back to the station, we'll dredge up anything we can find on this place. It seems to have fallen through cracks in the grid, of late. I imagine that suited our murderer a treat. But, we'll get to the bottom of it." He stood. "The paramedics have taken your friend to Aylesbury for stitches and observation. They'll keep her in overnight. She seemed in good spirits, all things considered."

Gillian grinned. "Being lifted out of the cellar by our stable manager helped. She has a crush on him." She looked at her parents. "Where *is* Lorcan, by the way?"

"He's taking Troy and Nellie back to the house. He rode after you out of concern for your safety," Bertram replied.

"Be sure to top up his holiday bonus, Daddy. Crumbs, I'm looking forward to Christmas morning service, this year. Something fixed in my life that I can rely on."

17

Full Circle

Gillian and Deborah stepped out of St Peter & St Paul's church, Great Missenden, wrapping up against a fresh, icy Christmas morning. To their left, occasional traffic noise drifted up from a cutting made by the A413 bypass. DS Jason Hargreaves waved at the pair as he strolled up from the village across a footbridge above the road. Clouds of vapour puffed from his mouth. He hunched over, both hands stuffed deep into jacket pockets in lieu of gloves he wished he'd brought. Organ music strains of '*O Come, All Ye Faithful*,' drifted out through the stone porch.

"Good Morning, Jason. Merry Christmas," Gillian called.

"Merry Christmas to you both. I was visiting a retired officer I know, down in the village. Always do this time of year. Anyway, back at Ashburnham, I heard Gillian mention Christmas morning service, so thought I'd pop up to see you. I hope you don't mind?"

Deborah lowered her head to conceal a faint grin. "Isn't there a law against stalking?"

Jason ignored the teasing and motioned to her

stitches. "How are your arms?"

"They're healing up. Thank you."

Jason reached inside his jacket, then passed a glossy photograph to Gillian. It depicted a slender, smiling girl with blue-framed glasses and straight auburn hair. She wore a graduation gown and mortarboard.

"What's this?" Gillian asked.

Jason shifted on the spot to keep warm. "Since you saw through the eyes of Banjo's victims, I don't suppose you'd recognise their faces. That's Amy Yates. I had forensics examine that patio slab. Blood, hair and impacted bone fragments from a devastating trauma were impregnated into it. You were right, they proved a match with Amy. We took a DNA sample when circumstances surrounding her death were still in doubt. Now the coroner will amend that suicide verdict."

Gillian rubbed a thumb across the graduating girl's smiling face.

Jason went on. "I visited her family last night. Christmas Eve or not, they were glad I turned up. Much crying, of course. But I've been in this game long enough to distinguish tears of relief from other sorts."

"How come you've given me her picture?" Gillian asked.

"I wasn't specific with the Yates family. But I informed them a young woman provided us with vital evidence of murder, after insisting Amy didn't commit suicide. Her mother asked if I'd pass this on, in gratitude."

Gillian blinked back a tear.

Deborah leaned in to examine the picture. "She looks like someone we would've been friends with."

"I wish you were," Jason replied. "Her mother said she was a quiet, retiring creature. Most thought her to be a misanthrope. What is that line Dickens used? *'Secret, and self-contained, and solitary as an oyster.'* Something like that."

Deborah gawped. "YOU read Dickens?"

Jason shrugged at her incredulity. "Is that such a surprise?"

"I suppose not. You seem like more of a *'Beano'* person, that's all."

Jason snorted. "My colleague, Frankie, would appreciate that quip."

Gillian couldn't take her eyes off the picture. "Comparisons between Amy and an unrepentant Ebenezer Scrooge might not be something to circulate. They're hardly flattering. But, I understand what you're getting at. Are there any other developments?"

"Many. Banjo turned out to be one Simon Sloane. That retired officer I visited, Ned, told me of a case he worked on back in 1988. An eleven-year-old Sloane murdered his sister by giving her drain cleaner to drink."

Gillian and Deborah exchanged glances.

"He was about to do the same with us when the floor gave way," Gillian added.

Jason sighed. "Fitting - if bizarre - karma that it backfired on him in such a devastating manner. Ned reckoned Sloane was the most demented, evil child he'd ever spoken with. He'd tortured his sister, Sally, for months, but evidenced near total recall of the events as though she'd done those things to him and not the other way around."

"Gaslighting?" Deborah asked.

"That's one way of putting it, I suppose. Yes. Sloane was convicted and incarcerated in the secure wing of a medical detention facility for years."

"Did they let him out or did he escape?" Gillian asked.

"I don't know. I've only just heard the story myself. You were right about the corpse: it was his mother, Enid. She was reported missing in a boating accident off the Cornish coast, earlier this year. It turns out she drowned all right, but at home."

"No prizes for guessing who did it." Deborah shook her head.

Jason looked to his left. "Sally is buried in the churchyard here with her father. He suffered a fatal accident a few months prior to her death."

"We'll have a stroll around in a minute to find them." Gillian tucked the photograph of Amy Yates away in her pocket. "Anything else?"

"Sloane owned a rocking chair purchased from Emma Clarkson in his living room. It wasn't difficult to trace. We found teeth scattered around the back garden amidst ash from human remains. There's nothing we can do with the ash, but I'm certain when the dental records come back those teeth will match Emma's. We're attributing the murders of Enid Sloane, Tara Osmotherley, Claire and Tony Walker, Amy Yates, and Emma Clarkson to Simon Sloane."

"You could have added my name to that list, if it weren't for Gillian." Deborah hooked arms with her friend.

"Thank goodness that wasn't necessary. I'd better let you go."

"Have a good New Year, if we don't see you before. Deborah and I are off back to Hampshire, shortly after," Gillian replied.

"Thanks." He turned to go then hesitated and looked back. "Oh, Gillian?"

"Yes?"

"Should you experience any more of those visions, you've got my number. Maybe I can put you on the payroll?"

"I hope that won't be necessary. Besides, I have a business of my own to run."

Jason waved and strode off the way he'd come.

The pair found headstones for Derek and Sally after ten minutes of wandering between the graves of the churchyard's sloping hillside.

Bertram and Felicity Crane exited the church from being cornered by the vicar. They crossed the crisp, frosty sward to halt beside the two friends.

Bertram read the grave markers to himself before speaking. "Derek Sloane. Goodness, there's a name from the past."

"You knew him?" Gillian tilted her head.

"Not well. We met twice. Derek ran a small refrigeration company, much like my own. Except he preferred a boutique business with limited clientele and wasn't interested in expansion. Nothing wrong with that, of course. He suffered a fatal accident at home, before your mother and I bought Retton."

"That was his house in the woods," Gillian replied.

Bertram stared. "You're kidding?"

"It gets worse. Banjo - or Simon - was his son. He murdered his sister and mother, along with all those women and the young boy."

Bertram shook his head. "Derek was a quiet man. There were rumours his wife acted strange and wanted to live away from society. Once he died, his firm collapsed. I inherited his clients, after a fashion. That is, they came to me with their business. Someone once told me Derek's widow blamed me for their firm's failure, but that's nonsense if there's even any truth to the gossip."

"No way!" Deborah's booming, surprised voice cut through their discussion. She'd wandered up the hill a pace, to a grave nestled near a large tree surrounded by a perimeter bench. She bobbed on the spot. "You'll never guess who I've found?"

Gillian smirked. "Roald Dahl?"

Deborah's shoulders lowered. "Oh, I suppose you already knew." She reached out to touch his headstone. "I loved his books, growing up."

The four set off back towards the church and Bertram's Range Rover.

"Oh, Pixie, I meant to tell you: tree surgeons will be over the morning after Boxing Day. They were delighted - if surprised - when I requested removal of our cedar as a priority before New Year. What's this urgency all about? You've yet to explain."

Gillian gazed at the horizon. "If I'm right, you'll soon understand."

*   *   *

No small amount of relief followed when a different unit from Thames Valley Police attended Retton House the day after Boxing Day. Not that Gillian would have minded meeting DS Hargreaves again.

Tree surgeons had arrived early. They soon felled Old Peg. Joe the gardener stood, flat cap held to his chest in respect and a tear in his eye, while the majestic cedar was sawn up. Later that afternoon, while digging out its roots, the surgeons called a halt and summoned Bertram Crane to phone the authorities.

Skeletons of a woman and child were retrieved. Bones buried and concealed for more than a century.

After Deborah expressed surprise that her bathroom door hadn't re-opened that morning, Gillian came clean to everyone with the full story about Avril and Gareth.

The day before the friends were due to leave for Alresford, Gillian secured a visit to the chapel of rest where Avril and Gareth's skeletons awaited formal burial in hallowed ground. She walked into the specially lit area to find one child and one adult coffin, each open with the bones laid out inside.

Deborah tapped a dark carrier bag Gillian held

between lithe fingers. "What did you bring?"

Gillian leaned over Avril's coffin. "Something for another bride who never was." She slipped one hand into the bag and lifted her beaded, faux pearl and crystal bridal headdress clear. Its loops of fine golden leaves glittered in ceiling lamps, casting cold illumination on the browned bones.

Deborah inhaled a sharp breath. "Oh, Gillian. Not your headdress. It's so beautiful. You may want it someday."

Gillian shook her head. "I'll never wear this again, whether or not I marry. It also feels wrong to sell it." She lowered the stunning adornment onto Avril's skull. "I've spoken with the funeral parlour's owner. They'll leave it in place for the burial." Gillian backed away, eyes moving from Avril's remains to the shattered skull and smaller form of Gareth Morrison. "I would never have found you, were it not for him."

Deborah became light-headed. She rested against the back of a nearby chair. "It's all so incredible. Scary, but incredible."

Gillian lingered a moment longer, then the pair walked away.

Deborah slipped a sore arm around Gillian's shoulders. "I love you, Fairy Princess."

*   *   *

Mace barked and whined, his tail offering the occasional hesitant wag. Gillian and Deborah loading boxes and bags into two cars parked outside Retton

House meant only one thing.

"Make sure he doesn't jump inside," Felicity said with a laugh from the doorstep.

Bertram and Gerard handed Gillian her last two boxes. She secured the Qashqai's boot and made a fuss of the upset animal.

Bertram folded his arms. "You'd better keep your promise to visit one weekend in four, or he'll be inconsolable."

"I will," Gillian kissed the spaniel.

"You're welcome to join her anytime, Deborah. We'd love to have you," Felicity stepped down beside her husband.

"Thank you both for having me." Deborah shook their hands.

Bertram nodded at her arms. "May your next visit prove a little more pleasant."

Deborah grinned. "I'm all right. It was an adventure. Though, I could do without being abducted by another psychopath."

"Andrew gave the flat a fresh coat of paint," Coralie Tennyson opened the garret door and passed the key to Gillian. "We're so glad you've come back. Oh, there's a letter from a pleasant young man who stopped by the gallery while you were away. He asked if we'd give it to you, should you return. He looked familiar."

"Thank you, Coralie." Gillian walked inside, followed by Deborah.

Coralie left them in peace.

"Have you got a secret admirer?" Deborah asked.

"I don't know." Gillian opened the envelope addressed to her, sat on a kitchenette table she would never forget. Her face fell as she read.

"What?" Deborah demanded.

"It's from Larry Downes."

"Larry Downes, as in Brent's Best Man, Larry Downes?"

"Yeah. He hates Brent now."

"I'm not surprised, after what the git did to him; did to all of us. You most of all."

"He wrote to warn me Brent is back in the area."

"What? I thought he'd shacked up with some high-flying cougar in the city?"

"Larry says she dumped him, then fired his arse from the company. It seems the mere presence of Brent near her social circle was too much. The woman leveraged connections to keep him out of work. No other firm who does business with her will touch him. He's returned to Hampshire with his tail between his legs. No job. No woman. No prospects."

"Bugger." Deborah's mouth hung open. "I mean, it's nice to see the bastard get a kicking, but this means you could run into him."

Gillian re-folded the note. "Brent might have enough decency or embarrassment to leave me alone."

Deborah almost choked. "Excuse me? Did you just put the words 'decency' and 'Brent' together in the same sentence?"

Gillian inserted the paper back in its envelope. "It

was nice of Larry to give me a heads-up. Now let's forget about Brent. It's time for a new beginning."

Deborah delivered a thumbs up. "That I can get behind."

Resuming her morning constitutional along Wayfarer's Walk beside the mill, felt like being reacquainted with an old friend. Gillian wandered at a casual pace, enjoying the antics of quacking ducks on the river.

"Hello, Gillian." Those two words delivered by any other voice would have washed over her without effect. But this time they were spoken in a timbre she'd hoped never to hear again.

Brent stood in a motionless swagger with his arms crossed and shirt sleeves rolled up to the elbows in a manner he thought cool. A manner which always annoyed his onetime fiancé. Gillian had often wondered - even rehearsed - what she'd say to the man who'd caused her so much pain and anguish, were they ever to meet. Now she struggled to remember a single word.

Brent spoke again. "I owe you an apology."

Gillian flushed. "Are you kidding me?"

Brent drew nearer. "Come on, Gillian. What we had was good, once upon a time. Like a fairy-tale. What is it Deborah always calls you? Fairy Princess?"

"She's got a few names for you, too." Gillian backed away.

Brent held up his hands to chest height in surrender.

"I made a mistake, okay? Sorry. I got caught up in the buzz of London and a good promotion. Hey, I was doing it all for you."

Gillian stamped her foot. "Were you doing it all for me when you slept with your boss, then ran away with her on our wedding day? I never want to see you again, Brent."

A snide grin lifted the corners of his mouth. "I heard you tried to commit suicide over me. There must be some deep feelings buried in there."

"Yeah. Revulsion and disgust. Not to mention disbelief that I fell for your charms and bullshit."

Brent grabbed her by the shoulders. "Come on, Pixie. I'm like your father, now. I'm starting over to become a self-made man from scratch."

Gillian shoved him away and shouted. "You are nothing like my father, and only *he* calls me Pixie." She thrust a finger back along the path. "Sod off, Brent. Don't you ever touch me again."

Brent's face became inflamed. "I'll touch who and whatever I damned well please." He stormed towards her.

Some years later, Gillian still couldn't work out whence the haymaker she unleashed upon his advancing chin originated. Regardless, it laid Brent out on his back, seeing stars.

Brent sat up and shook his dazed head. Two burly male joggers powered along the path behind Gillian, out for their own morning exercise. Brent scrabbled to his feet and staggered back towards a shiny black BMW M3 parked on Ladywell Lane. He had one last journey left to make in that now unaffordable prestige lease motor: its return to the dealership.

Tyres smoked and squealed as the German executive ride skidded out of Mill Hill and roared away northward.

Minutes later, Gillian shook her head at black rubber tread marks the car had left behind. She turned onto Broad Street and walked south towards the gallery. A sudden clenching in her stomach caused her to stumble against one of many trees lining the central grass reservation.

Oh no, I thought all this had ended. What can it be now? Over-revved engine noises and the squeal of brakes echoed in her head. The street before her faded into visions of Brent's face staring wide-eyed at his reflection in a vehicle's rear-view mirror. That sudden scene ended with a dramatic impact, as quickly as it began. The M3 lost traction on an icy bend and slammed square into a solid English Oak at the roadside.

"Hey, what's wrong?" Deborah's sudden voice and a hand on her shoulder caused Gillian to straighten and snap out of her distracted state. "Are you okay?"

Gillian nodded.

Deborah frowned. "Please tell me you didn't witness another murder?"

"Nothing like that. I'm lightheaded, that's all. I haven't eaten this morning."

Deborah grinned. "There's synchronicity. I was

coming to find you for breakfast. It's Saturday morning, and the weekend is all ours." She paused. "Are you sure you're okay? For a moment I thought Brent had run into you, now he's back."

Gillian's eyes misted. "I'm certain Brent won't be running into anyone, ever again. Everything is going to be fine. I know it is."

Deborah raised an eyebrow. "That's the spirit. Come on. Where shall we eat?"

The friends wandered back through the picturesque streets of Alresford in search of a decent breakfast and happier times ahead.

A mile away, accident witnesses phoned for help to a black BMW crushed like an old beer can and wrapped around an oak tree. Once Hampshire's emergency services arrived, they'd need a mop and bucket to retrieve Brent Fawley's remains.

ABOUT THE AUTHOR

Devon De'Ath was born in the county of Kent, 'The Garden of England.' Raised a Roman Catholic in a small, ancient country market community famously documented as 'the most haunted TOWN in England,' he grew up in an atmosphere replete with spiritual, psychic, and supernatural energy. Hauntings were commonplace and you couldn't swing a cat without hitting three spectres, to the extent that he never needed question the validity of such manifestations. As to the explanations behind them?

At the age of twenty, his earnest search for spiritual truth led the young man to leave Catholicism and become heavily involved in Charismatic Evangelicalism. After serving as a part-time youth pastor while working in the corporate world, he eventually took voluntary redundancy to study at a Bible College in the USA. Missions in the Caribbean and sub-Saharan Africa followed, but a growing dissatisfaction with aspects of the theology and ministerial abuse by church leadership eventually caused him to break with organised religion and pursue a Post-Evangelical existence. One open to all manner of spiritual and human experiences his 'holy' life would never have allowed.

After church life, De'Ath served fifteen years with the police, lectured at colleges and universities, and acted as a consultant to public safety agencies both foreign and domestic.

A writer since he first learned the alphabet, Devon De'Ath has authored works in many genres under various names, from Children's literature to self-help books, through screenplays for video production and all manner of articles.